The Promenade was a wide corridor that had once been a holding bay which ran like an artery through the center of Praesidium Station. Over the years, travelers had gotten themselves comfortable and opened small shops and businesses along its length for other travelers as they made their way through the galaxy. They started with small booths with tables and chairs. Soon though, walls had been put up, their materials having been scavenged from elsewhere on the station (or from amongst its cargo). Now, it was its own economy, despite management's objections. And the action taking place down the mall, in many ways, funded its very profitable operation.

Ships came for the large processing plant hovering a few miles away, but while they were here, The Praesidium fed, housed, and amused them. Marx recognized The Promenade's scene the minute he got out of the elevator. It smelled like carnival food, Dopra Tea, and the sweet perfume of the Diluvian Hostesses.

Marx felt the cascade of memories that washed over him the second he caught the odor. He'd spent long nights in bars back when he'd come out of that first hypersleep and realized all he'd lost by leaving Earth. He'd drunk so much, in fact, that he'd almost lost his contract. Good thing he hadn't… If he had, he could have lost his ship. And if that happened, he'd have been well and truly fucked; essentially abandoned in the depths of space.

He'd pulled it together though, but it had been close

Now, he sought solace in his periodic visits to The Auxilium.

Y'know, when his loneliness got to be too much for him to take.

—from "Domiciliary"

TUXEDO JUNCTION

THOM CARNELL

TABLE OF CONTENTS

FOREWORD

"Way down south... in Birmin'ham"
Hey, there you are... welcome back! Good to see you again... I think you may have left your hat here last time. I won't forget to give it back to you when we're done here. I'm happy to see you. If this is the first one of my books you've picked up, well welcome! I appreciate you taking the time to consider reading.

The volume you hold in your hot little hands is the third short story collection I've done (the first two being *Moonlight Serenades* and *A String of Pearls*, respectively) in a sort of homage to my mother who died in 2011. Mom was something special (as all moms are) and something of a hero of mine. It was her love of all things music (particularly the music of Glenn Miller) that informed the books' titles.

The stories themselves are quite literally everything I've been working on since the *last* book. I mean, these aren't finished pieces that I've had archived or even offered to be published elsewhere. But rather, they're either entirely new tales or *radically* reworked stories from the *Carpe Noctem* days. Either way, this is my output for the last, well... year or so; literally everything in my Out Box.

Once again, I've included a short preamble before each story to illustrate a) where my head was at when it was written and b) give some insight into my intentions for the story: thematically, emotively, etc. People seemed to like it in the other books and I'm only too happy to oblige.

But I'll be honest... I love the short story format and have since forever. There's an economy of motion in them, an efficiency, which I've always found appealing. Maybe it's my martial arts background? 'Get in. Do a lot of damage. And get the f*ck out' has been my motto in their regard. But I also believe they're a great way to 'test-drive' an idea, to take them out for a spin, to see if they work, and if they have 'legs'... which I've done on a number of occasions (NFSBS2, for example).

So, think of this collection as a Jay Leno-esque warehouse full of cars that I invite you to get into one-by-one and take the wheel; open her up on the freeway. Y'know... *really* let her rip. It's okay... it's why I built them the way I did.

Careful though, some of these stories have a bite that's sure to break the surface of the skin; maybe even make you bleed. Hopefully though, they'll make you feel something or change your outlook. See, I believe that Art, if I might paraphrase Ridley Scott's BLADE RUNNER, is a test designed to provoke an emotional response. Good work does that. It transports, connects the reader directly to the writer's mind, and for one glorious instant, they are one, cohesive, imagining unit. Because when that happens, it's the closest we get to Magic. When it happens... it's better'n sex.

Next up... it looks like I'll be heading into *major* monster territory... look to things like ABBOTT AND COSTELLO MEET FRANKENSTEIN, Val Lewton's I WALKED WITH A ZOMBIE, and Martin & Lewis' SCARED STIFF for an indication of where my head is at.

After that... I think we're gonna be heading back to the Training Ground for NFSBS3 to wrap things up there. Never fear though... as there's a small chapter in this book that should hold you over until that's done, though (target: late 2020).

Anyway, that's the plan...

~Thom Carnell
Bellingham, WA
2019

THE CHILDREN'S HOUR

This is one of the Carpe Noctem pieces that I've specifically reworked for this collection. The piece was written with my daughter, Connor Shae, very much in mind. Some time has passed since this was first written. Connor's no longer a kid. She's married and works as an ambassador for Kona Bikes. As her dad, I'm really proud. If you look close, you can pretty much guess what I was reading at the time (hint: it rhymes with 'Clive Barker's uncompleted The Art series'). The story form is, again, one of my own designs called a Sijjin in which the chosen quotes fuel the narrative and act as 'palate cleansers' for the next bit of narrative. Anyway, I love this piece because it reminds me of my kid when she was young. I was working in funeral homes as a Director and Embalmer during its writing… and it kinda shows in the posture of this piece.

"Between the dark and the daylight,
When the night is beginning to lower,
Comes a pause in the day's occupations,
That is known as The Children's Hour."

—Henry Wadsworth Longfellow, "The Children's Hour"

The small, dark-haired girl quietly makes her way into the bedroom, her feet making soft, whispering sounds on the lush carpeting. Decorated in hues of deep blue and jade green, the room, with its ornate architecture and soft bedding, is a place of welcome solitude for her. Carefully stepping over the piles of her toys that she left abandoned on the expanse of the grey carpeted pastures, she wends her way from the door to the sympathetic warmth of her bed. Stuffed animals graze like forsaken steeds set loose to wander amidst alphabet blocks made from carved wood. A rubber duck and half-dressed Barbie sit alone at a tea party that no one but they have attended. They stare at one another awkwardly as they wait forever for their water to boil.

The sole window to the room is set back against one wall in a recessed seat. The trees outside are obscured by a layer of newly-formed frost on the glass. The crystalline formations hinder any view of the outside world, turning everything to blobs of color and light.

The girl snatches up her favorite doll from the foot of the bed; a hug-worn princess within whose garments are held the bitter tears of her recent loss trapped within its crinoline folds. Pulling back her length of ebony hair, she steps up to her bedside clutching the weathered doll to her chest. The doll submits silently. The child falls to her knees and takes a moment to adjust the folds of her nightdress before continuing. Pressing her palms together, she raises her head and begins her nightly prayers.

"Now I lay me down to sleep;
I pray the Lord my soul to keep;
If I should die before I wake;
I pray the Lord my soul to take."

—Children's Prayer

Her heart pours out its emotion like sweet honey that falls from her lips into God's own ear. She peeks through squinted eyes, hoping upon hope, that she will see the benevolent face of the one who holds her heart safe from the lonely Night. Her eyes gaze about with a wide wonder as she feels all of the sorrows of these past few weeks flow up from the depths of her soul. First though, she begs for forgiveness for her self-imposed sins and asks Heaven above that a compassionate eye be cast down upon those that she holds most dear: her mother, her grandmother, her dog, her doll. For even though her life has only recently become a complicated play of emotion and loss for her, she knows that, deep within her heart, her life is blessed. And, for that, she is most grateful.

"Matthew, Mark, Luke and John,
The bed be blest that I lie on.
Four angels to my bed,
Four angels round my head.
One to watch, and one to pray,
And two to bear my soul away."
—Thomas Addy, *A Candle in the Dark*

Her illusory dalliances having been confessed to the papered walls and to the child's all-seeing, but tongue-tied gods, she finishes up with a whispered "Amen," and clambers across the folds of her blankets, dragging her doll—*bumpedy-bump-de-bump*—behind her. Slipping her feet beneath the cool of the sheets, she wriggles down, burrowing deep into the pliant comfort of her berth. The downy warmth of her feather bed wraps itself around her like a cocoon and cushions her slim body tenderly, lovingly. She tugs the covers up around her chin and breathes a deep, shoulder-heaving sigh as her body's blush slowly brings the tight space between featherbed and duvet to a comfortable glow. She closes her eyes and begins her slow submersion into the infinite Ocean of Sleep.

"The day is done, and darkness
Falls from the wings of night,
As a feather is wafted downward
From an eagle in his flight."
—Henry Wadsworth Longfellow, "The Day is Done"

A single lamplight is left to burn by the side of the bed, illuminating the room in a soft, rose-colored glow. The flame flickers and invites the very shadows to dance. Darkness begins to seduce Light and their fevered antics cause the room to pitch and shift and seem to drift on air. The child lying in the warm, soft bed slowly opens her heavy-lidded eyes and looks expectantly upward toward the door. Her heart skips a beat as the shimmering image of a man—her father so newly lost—comes drifting into the room through a doorway from an ethereal netherworld.

His glimmering form stands before her, his face beaming with a love as broad as the vast realities over which he has traveled to be here with her. Her heart, so recently shattered by the events of his passing, brims once more with a love that can only be understood by daughter devoted and father dearly departed.

This spectral form, into whose arms she'd once found such solace, drifts to kneel alongside her bed. Reaching out, his translucent fingertips gently stroke the plane of her forehead. His touch is cool and deeply soothing to both her skin and her soul. She stares into deeply-benevolent eyes and all of the conundrums of the universe seem to unravel for her in his gaze.

> "I love thee with the breath,
> Smiles, tears, of all my life!—and, if God choose,
> I shall love thee better after death."
> —Elizabeth Barrett Browning, *Sonnets from the Portuguese*

Not a word is exchanged as this unlikely pair stares so deeply—so lovingly—into one another's souls and a deep and lasting understanding that transcends even Death is found there. He gives her a father's gift of his confidence and assurance; unselfish and unencumbered. Promising her that, no matter what, he will always be by her side, in this life and in the next.

Contentment blooms like a rose within her tiny breast. His voice, he vows, will forever call from across the turbulent waters of the river once christened Styx to comfort her. He places a ghostly hand upon her head and bequeaths unto her all that he has learned since his passing: the lessons of a moral—and mortal—life lived, the wisdom drawn from a fatherly heart, and, ultimately, the discipline of the unforgiving grave. For you see, she is, like all children are, extensions of her parents and of their spirit. Much like he was to his father... and his father was to his grandfather... and so on down the line since time immemorial. Creation made Process.

Certain that she now understands all that he has explained,

he bends to kiss her, his cold lips further cooling her warm brow. He offers to her the last ember of his love so that she might keep it alive within her; like a fire to be tended forever in her heart. Finally, he rises, touching the candle on the nightstand. The flame ebbs and, with a soft sputter, finally winks out. And, for an instant, the room is illuminated solely by the glow of their love for one another. And then, with the bow of a charming prince, her ghostly visitor takes his leave; his soft light dimming to the endless black of the lonesome Night.

"Now I lay me down
Now I lay me down to dream…"
                    —October Project "Now I Lay Me Down"

SAN JACINTO

I gotta admit... this one took a while. I mean, I started this piece a number of years ago, but I could never find a way to make it work. Finally, in the summer of this last year, I took another look at it. After a lot of consideration, I finally found an angle for the ending and got it done. The title obviously comes from a Peter Gabriel song. The meat of the tale though comes from a combination of things: something I once heard on a Joe Rogan podcast (of all things), my own personal experiences with hallucinogens, and some notes I took while reading John Marco Allegro's, THE SACRED MUSHROOM AND THE CROSS (a book I HIGHLY recommend, by the way). As for the cultural framework, I did my best to try and get it all right, but...

If I did happen to have messed anything up, well... mea culpa.

The late afternoon sun hung in the sky like a canary-colored flower as Jordan Sawyer trudged his way up the well-worn dirt path that led up to the highest peak of Tapinaw Mountain. Two impossibly large American Indian men strode ahead of him; leading the way. Their wide muscular backs bobbed like gulls in front of him as they walked along the trail. They'd both been at his side since he'd arrived at the Native Tribal Council chambers back in Duerte. He'd filed his paperwork, paid his fees, and, once he had the proper clearances, they'd been assigned to guide him up the mountain for his scheduled audience with the Holy Man D'Jour known only as John Smith.

Sawyer had heard a little of the old man's wisdom in an interview with a tribal elder on *60 Minutes* and had been impressed. Now, a mere week later, he was here in the middle of nowhere in an attempt to speak to him for an article Sawyer was doing for *Lore Magazine* about the resurgence of the Western World's interest in Native philosophy and culture.

John Smith was, if you believed what his followers told you, well over a hundred and ten years old and Sawyer thought it important to get his voice on tape before he finally passed. It had taken a lot of convincing and assurances (and reassurances) regarding the purity of his motives in order to finally persuade his way past his handlers and into a one-on-one with the man. Sawyer pulled his knapsack higher up his back and felt the weight of the laptop inside shift as he once again looked up into the sweltering, too-blue sky. Silently, he hoped that he'd not forgotten anything back at the motel. He nervously went over the contents of his bag once more in his head. He had his computer, his recorders, some notes, a bunch of batteries... some cash. He shrugged; figuring he was covered.

Several hawks and, a little higher up, a lone eagle circled in the air around the peak of the mountain up ahead, pin-wheeling on the warm thermal drafts in their search for the snakes and small mammals that made up their central food source. Sawyer's brain abruptly kicked up a memory of him as a kid flying kites on a warm summer's day.

One of the men ahead of him, a guy named Daniel Parker, looked back to make sure he was keeping up. Strands of his long black hair swirled around his head in the blowing wind. Sawyer winced and nodded to him. Parker smirked to himself as he returned his attention to the trail ahead. The man seemed to be amused by the way the journalist was plodding along, breathing through his open mouth, and groaning with each new peak that rose up ahead of them. "We haven't got much further to go," Parker reassured him as he winked to his partner, Jessie Nakoma. Then, they both glanced back at the out of breath journalist, grinning as Parker asked, "Hey, you ever Stairmaster?"

Nakoma slapped him on the back and they both roared with laughter that echoed back to them off the hillside. The sound though was quickly swallowed by the rushing wind.

Sawyer groaned through a pained smile as he allowed his gaze to fall back to the unforgiving monotony of the ground ahead of him. Soon, the trail began to flatten out and they came to a substantial clearing. Up ahead of them, he saw a small tarp and wood structure off the side of the trail. Plumes of thick gray smoke escaped from a flap in the top of the structure's tarpaulin covering and spiraled like candy floss into the clear sky. Nakoma, the larger of his guides, looked back at his charge and nodded as if to silently say 'We're here.' They stopped about fifteen yards off and Sawyer was grateful for the rest. Bending over at the waist, Sawyer struggled to catch his breath.

The two guides approached the lodge first; Nakoma motioning for Sawyer to remain where he was. The journalist nodded, again grateful for the opportunity to try and recover his breath. He silently reminded himself of how long he'd tried to get this interview and how much he didn't want to screw it up with some minor breach of propriety. And so, he decided to wait... and to try and breathe some oxygen into his tired muscles.

Nakoma disappeared into the structure through a gash in the cloth wall.

Parker immediately took up a sentry position to the right of the door.Sawyer looked around the clearing surrounding him as he waited. He still struggled to get his breath, but at least his heart rate was back under control. He took a minute to stare out over an expansive land that sloped off around him in all directions. The terrain fell away at such an alarming slope that it only made the view all that much more breathtaking.

In all directions, a dense forest—alive and full—made up of tall Pines, Kauri, and Juniper trees teamed with life, covering the mountainside like a thick carpet. A lush bed of pine needles lay across the ground like goose down and everywhere you looked verdant, new life sprang up from the decay of the old. Birds sang unaware in the trees while small animals went about their business in the low brush; each of them seemingly oblivious to the other's presence. It was as if every creature on the mountain instinctively knew that anyone on John Smith's land would mean them no harm. It was like a slice of what fabled Eden must have been like; untouched and unsullied by Man and his technological infringements, Sawyer thought poetically.

He mentally made a note to use that line in his article.

After about fifteen minutes, Nakoma abruptly stepped back out through the flap in the tent and approached him. As he came closer, his muscular body gave off the rich smell of burnt firewood and hemp. Sawyer noticed the soft misting of perspiration which speckled the man's forehead like rain on tan window glass; his eyes, though, were as clear as a mountain stream.

The big man motioned for Sawyer to follow him and they both approached the tent. Nakoma motioned for Sawyer to strip off his clothes before entering the tent. He said something about the structure being a sweat lodge, and it was therefore humid inside, but Sawyer wasn't really listening. His mind had already begun reflexively going over his list of questions for the interview in his head. He snapped back to reality when he was told how he would only be allowed to bring in those things that he absolutely needed.

Reluctantly, Sawyer complied with his instructions and stripped down to his boxer shorts; stacking his bag and clothes in a small pile outside of the door. In his hands, he kept only his small microcassette recorder, some extra batteries, and two blank tapes from his knapsack. He silently hoped it would be enough. Drawing one last cool breath of the late afternoon's air, he looked into the sky toward where the eagles continued their spiraling, and clicked on his recorder.

Hoping for the best, but figuring it was a little too late for that now, he ducked inside the tent to meet the legendary John Smith. It took a moment for Sawyer's eyes to become accustomed to the darkness inside the tent. But, in time, his vision had cleared enough so that he was finally able to make out some of the sparse furnishings: some urns of water, a few stacked blankets, and an old Styrofoam cooler.

An old man sat cross-legged at the edge of a large, crackling fire which had been set at the center of the space. His body's naked bulk settled upon his frame in corpulent folds. Long salt-n-pepper hair was pulled back into two long braids which exposed a cherubic sweat-soaked face. Sawyer noted that, despite its welcoming expression, it was a face that had some serious 'miles' on it. They say that we earn our faces through the way that we live our lives. If that was true, this guy must have one helluva story. But overall… the old guy just had a regal sort of countenance that was compelling. There was no way in hell that he was as old as they say he was, but he certainly looked pretty damn good for whatever the hell age he was.

Nakoma interrupted Sawyer's train of thought by tapping him on the shoulder and motioning for him to sit where he was standing. Still tired from the hike up the mountain, the journalist was happy to comply with the instruction. Once he had himself seated and more or less comfortable, Nakoma bent over and whispered something into the old man's ear. Without looking up, the old guy quietly motioned for him to leave; shooing him away like he would shoo away a bothersome fly.

Nakoma shot Sawyer a quick glance that left little of its meaning to the imagination: 'I'm just outside this door and can be back in less time than it would take for you to draw a breath.' Sawyer smiled at him and tried to look as benign as possible as he watched him disappear through the folds of the door.

The two men sat in silence in the hot tent for a long time. Sawyer noticed several rivulets of sweat as they ran down the old man's sun-hardened skin in long glistening lines of moisture. As they both sat in front of one another without speaking, he saw how the old guy's gaze never waver from the center of the small fire and the dark plumes of smoke rising from its depths. Sawyer imagined the wheels of his recorder spinning impotently as he struggled to think of a good way to break the silence and begin the interview. He finally settled on a bit of not so subtle ass-kissing.

"I want to thank you, sir, for allowing me this audience," Sawyer said.The old man sighed deeply, as if he were greatly disappointed, and slowly raised his eyes to meet Sawyer's. He adjusted himself on the ground where he sat in order to better see Sawyer, but said nothing. He just sat there and stared at him. His features remained cast in deep shadow, but his eyes burned intensely, as if an inferno raged behind them.

"You people..." John Smith said with a smirk and his deep, resonant voice cracked from lack of use, "...never comfortable with the silence that is; always rushing to fill the void with your... words." He spat on the ground. "You forget..." and he reached down absentmindedly scratch at an itch near his scrotum. "...that words have their own kind of power and *that* power is something that should never be taken for granted." He suddenly threw his hands into the air in exasperation. "And now, even *now*... words piling up behind your lips like spawning salmon and you give no thought to what it is that I'm saying..."

"I'm sorry, Mr. Smith." Sawyer stammered. "I didn't mean... "Smith sighed again as if his patience was already tried and at its end.

"You traveled so many miles to hear what I have to say, son, and still you talk on."

Sawyer opened his mouth to say something else, but when the old man looked at him and cocked an eyebrow, he smiled and closed his mouth. He wasn't exactly sure how he'd expected this interview to go back when he'd first taken the assignment, but... it certainly wasn't like this. He'd interviewed more than his share of shamanic holy men over the years back when he was working for a New Age magazine; back when that sort of thing was, well... still a thing. He'd moved on plenty since then, but he still remembered how these guys' language was always peppered with this kind of existential bullshit. Best to not take it too seriously.

Smith grinned at Sawyer's awkward silence. "Do you ever wonder, my boy, why the people you know never seem to be happy? And they've *been* unhappy since before a time they can even remember. And so, as a result, they wander through their lives without purpose..." He scratched at his nuts again and considered his own point. "Because they are unfulfilled; conflicted, and unhappy. They have convinced themselves that the way through life is a path made up of deceit and lies... and ego. And yet... their world remains empty. They consume, and yet, remain unsatisfied. Happiness... to them, and, by extension of that, to you, is but an elusive dream. A dream dreamt up by ad agencies, media, and cinema to fuel a desire that you don't really feel. More people… with more of their agendas." He sighed deeply. "How can you ever hope to have a mastery over the world, and yet, still live lives that never feel complete? I've heard these people say, 'Too much is never enough.' But do they ever ask themselves what exactly that means? Or are they happy just to consume?"

The old man sat back, looking over at the journalist inquisitively. He narrowed his eyes and looked deeper into Sawyer's gaze. Then, without looking, he picked up a small carved pipe that had been lying on the ground next to his leg.

"Well, there are those who think that mankind is…" Sawyer began hesitantly, his words coming out of his mouth in toddler's steps.

"No!" the old man interrupted. "What I want to know is… what do *you* think?"

Sawyer sat watching the old man in silence for a minute. Outside the tent, a crow called out from the trees overhead. He felt the first drop of sweat drip down the center of his back. Soon, all he could think about was the moisture he felt under his arms, between his legs, and pooling in the crack of his ass. To divert his attention, he quickly replayed in his head the last few things they'd said to one another, trying to figure out what he'd done to set them off on this line of debate.

Coming up empty, he decided to try another tack.

"Well, people want a good life. They want to be free from want, from need." Sawyer answered as he shrugged. "Doesn't everyone want to be happy?"

"Happy?" the old man guffawed and he tossed his grinning gaze skyward; like he'd just heard a small child say something especially precocious. "And so, they chase this happiness by, what? Wanting more of it; by drawing more and more *things* nearer to them?" He scoffed. "What good is a full larder if the owner of it is unable to eat all that he's collected? The food he's fought so hard for can only eventually spoil and go rotten, yes? The way to be, as you say, 'happy,' if you ask me, is to take only what you can use. Take only that which we absolutely need knowing that anything taken above that will adversely affect the overall whole. Gather the grain and harvest the fruit for each meal; hoarding nothing. To be content with what has been provided. I've heard people say, 'He who dies with the most toys wins.' What do *you* think about this statement?"

His question's sudden modern context threw him. "Well, again, I think it's important to be happy…"

"And yet, here you are, looking for insight into what it means to be human for a periodical destined to be read by people waiting in dentist's offices and hair parlors. I am not the only one who finds this fact interesting…"

"I have not come…"

Smith chuckled to himself as he began to absentmindedly twiddle the pipe between his fingers. "Look, son… we must understand that Life is a kind of circle. Modern man sees the experience as more of a straight line. And it's that difference that is the source of all of his suffering. See, a circle will always— *always*—come back unto itself. It's what makes it a circle." He made a face like his next words were to be expected. "Only to begin again. Within that circle there are two," and he held up two fingers, "whirling masses of what we'll call energy. In the East, they call them 'the Yin' and 'the Yang.' You know that. Movies… might call it a Force. But in nature, you will always find The Two; earth and sky, fire and water, light and dark, the physical and the spiritual; each component being lost without the other, each piece completing and complementing the other." He sat back and smiled, clearly pleased with himself. "Balance.

"Also…" he looked up excitedly, "Our bodies are made up of these two equal sides; two eyes, two ears, two arms, two legs. We are very much symmetrical." He raised his pipe to his lips and puffed on it to get the embers burning again. "Can you think of anything else where two things complement or equalize the other so perfectly?"

Sawyer pondered the question for a minute, wanting to get at least this point correct.

"Uh," and he paused hoping to show that he'd given his answer some thought. "A scale?"

"Ah-ha!" Smith clapped his hands wildly. "There *is* a brain in there, after all. I knew we'd find one if we gave it enough time. A scale, yes. Correct." He blew out a plume of smoke and the cloud smelled rich and aromatic and only slightly like weed. "A scale, yes... A scale that *must* have equality on both of its sides in order for it to give a balanced interpretation of a thing."

Sawyer slightly adjusted his position on the ground, stretching his legs out in front of him to shake the tingles out of them as he clandestinely checked on his tape machine. He was relieved when he saw the little wheels spinning along happily.

"Lives must remain in balance or else that is when 'ease' becomes 'disease.'" Smith continued. "Do you see? The problems that we encounter in this life, more often than not, stem from the fact that our lives have fallen out of this balance. So, these people... in an attempt to put their lives back into balance, what do they do? They look outside themselves for some much-needed ballast. They work harder so that they might accumulate more 'things.' They eat more food. They have sex with more and more people. They work themselves to death to accrue more money; look for satisfaction in *things* that are external to themselves... instead of doing the necessary thing—the *difficult* thing—and that is to look honestly inward. I believe psychologists call it The Hedonic Treadmill." He leaned back and grinned. "And that, my friend, that looking inward... is such a tough thing to do; to honestly look at your reflection in the mirror—to slay one's past—and be truthful with yourself about who—and what—you are. To say, 'I am weak' or 'I am ignoble' and to know that that is truly ok."

"Why is it okay?" Sawyer asked.

Smith smiled even broader.

"Because it is, at the very least, an honest place for us to start."

"To start what?"

"Why... the work of becoming Human, of course," Smith said laughing and his tone echoed brightly in the tent. "Someone once said, 'The keys to the universe lie within the confines of one's own soul.' But those words imply a certain amount of work—of not only finding those keys, but in *using* them— so, they naturally fall on deaf ears. Why? Because humans are inherently lazy. And so, they tend to latch onto whatever philosophy is the current trend; which is, if I'm not mistaken, exactly what brings you here to see me today."

Before Sawyer could respond, Smith plowed ahead with his next thought. Clearly, in his mind at least, the point had been made and the matter had therefore been settled. His demeanor subtly let the journalist know that, in his mind at least, the interview had officially begun.

"But our thoughts have always been as they are now. One need only peruse the world's history to see both the example and the unfortunate end result. In the past though, we who thought differently were called 'unrealistic,' 'heathens,' or 'hippies.' But, there was a lot of wisdom in what they were saying then, and there is a lot of wisdom in what they are saying now. It's only now that the 'civilized' world has come up empty in their pursuits that they come to try and find a respite from their old way of thinking."

"There are those who might say that the modern man's way is superior; hence its prevalence in the world."

The old man laughed and, once again, slowly drew from his pipe.

"Those who would say such a thing are deluded and blinded by both their egos and their own self-importance." He thought for a moment, considering the proposition a bit more, attacking the conundrum from all of its angles. Then, he pointed at Sawyer with his index finger. "And if this position you speak of is so superior, why does your world teeter on the brink of its own self-destruction on what seems to be a daily basis?"

Smith sat more erect and tossed his long braids back over his shoulder with a jerk of his head. When he had resettled himself, he continued. "I mean… think. You seem like a smart lad. Why are so many then so out of tune with the refrain of Heaven and the Earth? Your culture… your *civilization* has done little else but strip-mine all that this land has (and had) to offer. They have left little behind but a barren landscape." He stared deeply into Sawyer's eyes. "Is this the superiority of which you speak?" "Well, I don't think that's exactly fair. I mean, look at the advances we've made in science, in medicine. Ya know…" Sawyer said sarcastically, "We put a man on the moon."

The old man laughed, but not at the joke.

"Advances?" Smith scoffed. "You have harvested a tree and held a toothpick to the light saying 'Look at the marvel I have made!' Landfills, toxic waste dumps, poisonous air and water... these are your culture's legacy to Time and to the Earth."

Sawyer shifted in the dirt, suddenly annoyed by the specious attack. He'd come here to essentially write a puff piece on the guy, gin up some traffic for *Lore*'s site... and maybe even get Smith some additional press. But now, here he was the target of a tirade on cultural materialism.

In his frustration, he lashed out with the only thing he had available to him: sarcasm.

"But you aren't bitter. Nope... not at all."

The old man leaned back and roared with laughter. He gripped his pipe tightly in his hand as he fell forward onto his knuckles in a coughing fit. At one point, Nakoma poked his head into the tent to check that everything was all right. Once he saw that they were fine, he disappeared from view.

"Despite myself, son," Smith said once he'd settled down and caught his breath. "I like you. Your heart is true even while your mind remains a bit blind," he said and reached behind him for a small leather satchel. "I want to show you something; something that may well change your opinion... if not your view on things."

Sawyer stared at the old man for a moment. He noticed that, despite his advanced age, his gaze was clear and the whites of his eyes appeared to be as white as paper. The journalist smiled at him, trying to sense any subterfuge. Seeing none, he nodded his agreement.

"Okay," he replied.

Smith rummaged in his bag briefly before pulling out a worn black Velcro wallet. There was a large-nosed man stitched on the front of it with one elongated leg telling whoever bothered to look to Keep on Truckin'. The billfold was visibly old and it was clear that Smith had had it in his possession for some time; maybe even since his youth. Out from behind a state identification card, he pulled a small square of paper. He carefully unfolded it with his fingers for fear of the paper falling apart and pressed it flat against his thigh. He presented it to Sawyer like it was a piece of evidence.

Sawyer looked at what he could now see was a photograph and saw a young man—small of build, but muscular—standing in front of an old model Impala, if he was correct. The man was of average height, dressed in an ill-fitting business suit with a white button-up and a skinny tie. It took a minute for Sawyer to put it together—the cut of the jaw, the illumination in the eyes—but then... he slowly began to recognize aspects in the features that appeared familiar.

"This..." Smith said, confirming the journalist's suspicions, "was me." He sat back and smiled broadly, clearly proud of the transformation. "Age twenty-seven. I was an up-n-comer working at an insurance company, selling people protection against an unknowable future. I'd just finished college. The ink hadn't even dried on my degree yet and it had me thinking I had the world by the short hairs."

Sawyer looked genuinely surprised. Again, he wasn't sure what he'd expected from talking to this man, but... it *certainly* wasn't this.

The old man interrupted his thoughts by laughing and shaking his head.

Sawyer finally figured that he was being tricked, that he was lying. Sure, the person in the photo looked a little like the half-naked man sitting in front of him now, but nothing else in the photo made much sense. The picture was quite literally like looking at a photographic negative, in many ways.

"I know... I know," Smith said, still chuckling, as he carefully put the delicate photo back in its place behind the ID card in his wallet. "But it is indeed true."

Sawyer shook his head. "So, uh... I don't mean to be rude, but... what happened?"

Now it was Smith's turn to look surprised.

"I mean," Sawyer continued, "no offence, but... What could have happened to initiate such a drastic transformation?"

Smith chuckled and shrugged his shoulders. "Life..." and a dark shadow passed over his face. "Death. A little from Column A... a little from Column B."

Despite himself, Sawyer chuckled aloud.

"Well, it doesn't make a whole lot of sense to me."

Smith grew suddenly serious. He looked back into the fire, staring at the heart of the blaze intently. A full minute passed in silence, then he quietly said, "I... I had a wife."

The unexpected impact of Smith's statement played out across the reporter's confused face. Feeling suddenly embarrassed for intruding, Sawyer poked at the ashes at the base of the fire with his finger. "I'm sorry," was all he could manage by way of apology.

Smith stared at the fire for a bit longer before another broad smile blossomed on his lips.

"Yes, well..." he waved the morose clouds between them away. "The loss of my wife was..." He looked to the ceiling for the right word. "...transformative."

Sawyer shook his head sadly.

"I can imagine..."

"Well, the truth of the matter is..." Smith grinned. "Life is rarely forgiving; nor is it particularly free. It does exact its price... and in its own time."

Sawyer nodded knowingly. He saw the wisdom in what the old man was saying and knew it intimately. He'd lost people—family, friends, coworkers—and knew how their absence could oftentimes affect people.

"Anyway..." Smith said with another of his smiles. "Things, well... Well, things just sort of lost their appeal after that; just kind of lost their meaning. Everything I'd worked for was gone, everything that gave my Life any of its meaning... gone. So..."

Despite himself, Sawyer leaned into the amber firelight. "So?"

Smith smiled again mischievously. "So, I walked away."

Sawyer sat up as if he'd been slapped. "You... what?"

Smith paused for a heartbeat. "You heard me."

"That's it?"

Smith grinned up at him congenially as shadows from the firelight danced across his features. "Yep, I left. Abandoned their program... walked away from the *whole* thing."

Sawyer shook his head. What the hell was this old man

talking about? Mentally, he tracked back over the conversation, trying to pinpoint where it had all went wrong, where he'd lost the thread. Smith had started the interview by arguing with him. Then, he was on about materialism. And now, he was sharing hitherto unknown aspects of his past? None of this shit tracked in any of the reporter's research and he started wondering if he was now being lied to. Something else that often became a thing with these 'holy men.'

Smith shifted in his seat; somehow settling himself deeper into the ground. He took a moment to stuff his pipe again from a small pouch in his bag. As he lit it, he turned his head to readdress the reporter. Thick dragon plumes of smoke billowed from his nostrils in two wide streams. Sawyer randomly thought of the way a train blew off steam as it was pulling out of its station. The old man's broad smile emerged through the haze like a Cheshire Cat.

"It's funny..." Sawyer replied, trying to sound casual. "I didn't find any of this in my research. There was some talk about you going to seminary, getting your Ph.D., but..."

The old man chuckled again as he licked his lips. "Oh, that..." He leaned in and spoke out of the side of his mouth, like a conspirator in a French New Wave film. "That just makes for a better story, eh?" and he winked. "At least it's a far sight better than what really happened."

Smith reached for a thin, camo-painted Thermos even as he pulled a small stack of paper cups from his nearby leather bag. All the while, he kept talking. "And to be sure... I did all of those things, but first, I had a life... there was a wife, even some kids. I was never a monk, kid."

Sawyer looked up at him from watching the fire and his expression was genuinely curious. "So... what happened? What changed?"

The old man closed his eyes and he swallowed hard. He sat in meditation for the next minute or so, making his guest wait for his answer. Slowly, he began to rock from side to side and the silence seemed to expand to fill the small, hot space. The air between them grew thin and the reporter suddenly felt like he was getting a little lightheaded. It was like slipping on mental ice, if only for a moment.

Smith leaned further forward. "I was shown what I had to do to finally move on."

Sawyer laughed. He couldn't help it. It was just so ridiculous. The journalist couldn't count the number of times he'd heard that shit before: 'It's materialism...,' 'the stuff you own ends up owning you...,' and, of course, 'and only through *our* product / way of thinking can you ever achieve enlightenment...' It was a bullshit tactic that was usually only used by con men or evangelicals. He felt like slapping himself. There had been so many signs along the way... and he'd ignored them.

Sawyer eyed his recorder, watching the reels continue to spin benignly, and figured he had enough for the piece he'd come here to get. Time to bail, he thought. Get back down the mountain. Get back to the hotel, maybe write whatever the hell this was up (or begin to, at least, get it all transcribed). Then, head home in the morning. Bottom line though, he knew he had the coverage he needed; it was time to go.

But before he could begin to beg off and end the interview, Smith set the Thermos down on the ground in front of him. His manner was almost defiant as he leaned back and grinned at his guest.

"What's this?" Sawyer asked; his curiosity having been involuntarily piqued.

Smith gave him another of those broad smiles.

"This... changed *everything*. This..." and he patted the cap on the top of the bottle. "Was more transformative for me than even my wife's death..."

Sawyer eyed him suspiciously.

"Ayahuasca? Ibogaine?"

Smith waved his hand dismissively. "Child's play in comparison."

"Stronger, then?" Sawyer narrowed his gaze. "LSD? DMT? Ketamine?"

Smith stared at him blankly. "I say, 'more transformative than my wife's death' and you respond with chemical parlor tricks?"

"And I'm supposed to do what with this?" Sawyer shook

his head in disbelief. "You can't expect me to *drink* it; to take something and not know what it is? I may be an adventurer, Mr. Smith, but I'm no fool … nor am I a blushing neophyte willing to endanger my health in order to curry favor with the subject of an interview."

Smith shook his head in disappointment. "No. I have merely set something out in front of you that I have said was transformative; something that changed me for, I believe, the better. I don't believe that it's an understatement to say that it's help make me into the man I am today. And it's done the same for every single person that's taken it." Smith shrugged and waved off any further theatrics. "But, okay… if you must know, it's an herbal tea."

Sawyer's eyebrows rose at the banality of it. "A tea?"

Smith nodded. "Its ingredients can be found on the side of an extinct volcano called Monte Pissis in Argentina. I won't bore you with the details of how many years it took to pry the particulars of its manufacture away from those who discovered it." His eyes took on a faraway aspect and he laughed darkly. "Or what its price was in the end."

"And you came by it… how?"

Smith smiled knowingly even as he brushed away a fly that was crawling across his broad, sweaty belly. "We'll leave it at the fact that it was procured for me… in one of the blackest of markets." His gaze once again darkened. "And that its cost was also paid in more than mere dollars."

Sawyer once again chuckled to himself. He'd taken hallucinogens many times over the years; too many times to count. You don't write about the kinds of things he did—consciousness, morality, ethics, reality—and *not* drop a tab or two of something over the years. He was quick to discover early on that, sometimes, the best way to expand one's consciousness was by utilizing any and all available chemistry.

Dosing (or even just getting high) with an interview subject was not something that was unknown to him, and, while it wasn't exactly ethical, it could often ingratiate you with your interview subject. And sometimes you did what you had to do to get your story. He thought about it for a minute, before finally saying what the fuck?

What else did he have to do for the rest of the day? He figured that as long as he remembered to keep changing his recording tapes until the battery ran out, what could go wrong?

"And you expect me to drink it?"

"I expect that you will do what you wish to do, regardless of what I have to say on the subject, because…" the old man said smugly.

Sawyer held up a hand to stop him. "I know, I know…" and he pitched his voice to sound like Smith's, "more transformative than your wife's death."

The old man appeared quite pleased with the impression.

Sawyer sat and rubbed at the side of his jaw with the knuckle of his index finger as he weighed the proposition set before him. He knew it was absolutely crazy… and downright unprofessional, but… 'I tripped with John Smith' was something that went right to the top of the resume in his world. It was the modern-day equivalent of 'I took acid with Timothy Leary.'

Sawyer thought back to what a mentor of his had once told him back in college. He was an odd, bookish dude with Bourbon-n-Binaca breath and multiple degrees in chemistry and molecular biology. He was quoting another writer known for his excess when he said, 'ya buy the ticket, ya take the ride.' And, as he considered how he was *going* to spend the next few hours—alone in a hotel room, transcribing this bullshit—he eyed the small Thermos suspiciously.

Then, a small voice in the back of his mind suddenly tabled the age-old question, the one that has inspired (and doomed) Man since Time immemorial: 'Yeah, but… what if?'

Sawyer pondered the situation before him from every angle; well, at least all of them that he could think of in the few seconds that the two men sat staring at one another. At the very least, he mused, he'd have a great story to tell about it, right?

Smith sat there patiently waiting for his guest to come to his conclusions as he continued to smile. But, even as he did so, he proceeded to open the container and pour out a hasty splash of the brownish fluid into two of the small paper cups. When he was done, he returned everything but the two drinks to his bag.

Then, he shrugged as if deciding something for himself and picked one of them up. Without hesitation, he threw its contents down his throat in one frog-like gulp.

The old man sat quietly for a moment, still and smiling, like he was patiently waiting for something. Sawyer quickly surmised that he was waiting for the tea to kick in. When he noticed a sudden bloom abruptly redden the old man's cheeks, he figured the drug was coming and coming on fast.

The old man smiled even more broadly and rocked slowly from side to side as he whispered something that sounded like, 'Like coming home,' before slumping to the side. His breath started coming in short, fast pants and his eyes were rolled back, showing nothing but their whites.

Sawyer felt himself suddenly alone in the small tent. He could see Smith's body lying near him, still clearly alive, but… whatever presence he'd had a moment ago was now gone; evaporated into his trip like smoke. And through it all, the old man kept that same stupid grin he had on his face.

Before he could change his mind or think up any further excuses for himself, Sawyer picked up his cup and quickly moved to drink it. He paused at the last moment to stare into the thick opaque fluid. In the moment, he noticed his reflection burble to the surface of the liquid and dance across its surface. He almost backed out, but then, he decided to just go for it and tossed the foul-smelling drink into his mouth.

The dark liquid washed over the interior of his mouth and he immediately tasted cedar wood, licorice, and a strong, peppery taste that he couldn't quite identify. There was a sensation of biting on metal that made his fillings buzz annoyingly. His heart's rhythm abruptly increased and he felt the muscle beat within his chest like a trapped bird. Then, his tongue went suddenly numb and the feeling quickly spread over his body in a brisk, tingling wave.

He looked down and saw that he still held the paper cup in his fist. It had been crushed and now lay in his palm in a wet, papery wad. He dropped it and watched it take an eternity to tumble to the ground. He smiled at the slow-motion puff of dust it made when it landed. Strange geometric panels emanated from its place in the dirt in spectral, repeating patterns.

He set his hands amongst the ghostly tendrils' swimming in the air and stirred them up; absentmindedly running his fingers through the loose soil around his legs. The dirt felt both oddly pliant and half-set in his grip, like he was running his hands through a giant wad of marshmallow. It was at once weird and oddly comforting.

Sawyer heard Smith groan from his back a few feet away; his arms and legs lay splayed and akimbo. He closed his burning eyes, but was startled when he heard the sound of a man's laughter suddenly echo back to him from someplace far off behind him. He kept his eyes closed, but chuckled softly at the magic trick. His laughter seemed to echo and reverberate like they were in a large, empty hall. The sound soon dissolved away into a chaotic sonic mud.

His head grew heavier and heavier by the moment, and, after putting up a nominal fight, he finally let it float to the ground. More of the same repeating patterns danced and flickered behind his eyelids. The imagery grew so intense that it threatened to overwhelm him, but he somehow managed, through sheer force of will, to keep it together.

He heard the sound of his own voice groan as he pressed his forehead into the soft dirt. He felt his gorge rise abruptly, but he breathed deeply of the ground's rich muskiness and the nausea soon passed. Far off in his perception, his mind caught a sound—a thrum—that he finally decided was coming from deep within the earth. The tone pulsed again and again like a heartbeat. Sawyer ran his face along the dirt lovingly in response.

And then, the world beneath the ground gave way and he was suddenly falling into a cold nothingness...

The next thing Sawyer was aware of was the sensation of floating. The feeling wasn't like falling, but it wasn't exactly like swimming either. His body just felt like it was hanging in the air like a marionette. He watched amused as his feet kicked in the open space.

Yeah, he thought idly to himself as he closed his eyes, this feels just like floating.

All of a sudden, he felt a pricking sensation against the

bottom of his bare feet. A second later, the rich odor of freshly-cut grass tickled his nose, evoking memories of a summer long ago in which he spent too many days to count cutting their neighbors lawns in order to buy himself a new bike. He looked down and his eyes were met by an intense, deep green hue. The color was so vibrant that it stung his eyes. He narrowed his eyes and it became less annoying. Snickering to himself, Sawyer moved his toes amongst the pointy emerald blades.

Gravity finally intruded on his reality and he felt his full weight settle onto the pads of his feet. His spine gently compressed as it took on the heft of his body mass. When he'd settled onto his frame, he drew a deep breath and felt the oxygen immediately flood his tissues.

Slowly, he opened his eyes.

He found himself standing in an expansive, bone-white space that extended for as far as the eye could see; a polar landscape with a bright, green, grass floor. The continuous feel of the grass on his bare feet helped ground him and keep his head from spinning in the vast lightness. He didn't feel scared. There was a certain remoteness he felt from it that, for some reason, just made him chuckle.

Sawyer shot a quick glance behind him and saw Smith's body still lying on his back in the grass. He watched as the old guy's belly rose with each of his breaths. He knew that as long as he was breathing, nothing bad had happen to him and he was still alive.

A gust of wind suddenly rustled Sawyer's hair, causing the journalist to look up from the dozing old man. Above him, he saw a massive translucent bug—a millipede—with an innumerable number of clear, wriggling legs hanging like a balloon in the air. Its long body twisted and turned, performing elaborate maneuvers in the sky.

Sawyer smiled as the light struck the creature and cast phantasmagoric rainbows across the grass. There were smaller bugs and snake-like animals crawling over the beast—like pilot fish—that fed themselves on whatever morsels escaped the larger animal's maw.

The creature swam closer and Sawyer started to get a real

idea of how big it was. Longer than a school bus by far and twice as wide, the creature circled him in the air like a dirigible. It finally settled onto the grass, landing like a glider and slowly turning its face to look at him directly.

At first, the animal had a distinctly insect-like face with two large, multi-sectioned eyes and four hardened mandibles that were forever clicking in their agitation. But then, its countenance began to soften and change; becoming more human-like. Its multi-sectioned eyes started absorbing into one another like soap bubbles popping. Slowly, human eyes were formed. All the while, the thing's mandibles melted into one another, forming a proper mouth. The overall aspect started to become more feminine, and, as Sawyer's memories made their connections, he slowly began to recognize the face the insect was trying to mimic.

"Jordie?" the creature said in Sawyer's mother's rich voice. "Jordie baby, is… is that you, dear?"

Sawyer reared back as if he'd been slapped.

"M-Mom?" and his voice was suddenly choked off by his rising tide of emotion. His eyes filled with tears which he quickly wiped away with his hand. His nose ran freely with mucus and he sniffed it back.

The Millipede… or Momipede, he thought abstractedly with a chuckle, turned and its enormous body encircled Sawyer protectively. She took great caution with her massive, transparent bulk so as not to crush or endanger him in any way. Her face smiled warmly and her gaze held all of the love that he remembered so fondly. Her eyes were wet with tears, her cheeks blooming a ruddy crimson. Beneath her mass, her many legs clicked together and pawed at the ground.

"What *is* this?" he asked no one.

His mind worked to comprehend everything he was presently seeing, but then he remembered Smith's tea and he relaxed. All of this… the white space, the grass, The Momipede… it was all just the by-product of whatever drug he'd been given. He momentarily thought to call out to Smith who he knew was still laying on the ground behind him, but… the man was out of it and had given up all of his talking some time ago.

The Momipede shook her great head anxiously, interrupting his thoughts. "We have little time, Jordie... and I have so much I want to tell you."

A sudden look of anguish passed over her face and you could see the difficulty she was having expressing herself. She suddenly reached out, taking Sawyer's face in a few of her many hands and his reality slipped a gear.

"No," she gasped. "Stay with me."

For the second time in his recent memory, he felt the ground abruptly shift beneath his feet and his equilibrium pitched violently forward. He reached out for something to hold onto, but his hand landed on a thick book sitting on a pedestal instead.

"Wait..." he heard a voice very much like his own cry and the sound of it had the patina of desperation on it.

He held onto the pedestal until the spinning in his head finally ceased. Opening his eyes, he saw that the tome sitting before him was covered in dust, and its bindings looked impossibly old. Its front cover suddenly, for want of a better word, stirred. Then, a crack in the binding opened and what looked like a human eye looked up at him. As their three eyes met, Sawyer's thinking suddenly became chaotic and disorganized. Images and emotions flooded his mind in such a rapid succession that it was hard to identify them much less understand their significance. But the emotions they stirred up were full of nostalgia and the hope of youth. Like a television whose remote was stuck and constantly changing channels, the imagery played out in a head-spinning rush.

Sawyer's stomach abruptly burbled and he felt as if he had a sudden touch of motion sickness. When his legs finally failed him, he dropped to the ground into an open sitting position, his head resting heavily on his chest.

Exerting all he could of his mental energies, he grabbed onto one of the images as they whizzed past his mental screen. In it, he saw a flood of people shopping in the aisles of a large department store. His view was from overhead, like a bird or angel looking down. He watched as the people filled their arms with a variety of items from the store's packed shelves.

Like a mob, the crowd moved through each department

snatching up and carrying away their armload of goods. Sawyer was able to gather from the panicked look on their faces that their desire to pick up the next shiny thing that caught their eye was outweighed only by their dread of having to put down what was already in their arms. Like Sisyphus, they were doomed to repeat the same action over and over again.

"I never wanted any of this for you, Jordie... none of it," The Momipede's voice whispered intimately into his ear.

And he was off... pulled down what can only be described as a whirling tunnel of light. Sawyer abandoned any relation to 'level'; figuring it would no doubt assert itself later.

The next thing he knew, they were inside a small country church, its congregation flowing in and filling every available seat. A man in an impossibly clean white suit stood at the far end of the room, his hands raised toward the ceiling. His eyes were rolled back in his head, showing only their whites, while his lips mumbled silently.

Sawyer and The Momipede stood at the back of the long room and watched as the gathered congregation began singing something that sounded like a hymn as they passed around large bamboo baskets that they were filling with donations. The baskets repeatedly made their way from person to person around the room, each time making their silent request for yet another contribution. Soon, a few of the people ran out of cash, so they started dutifully removing their rings and jewelry and placing them inside. Sawyer noticed that whenever the baskets got full, the man at the head of the room would come off of the altar to take it and dump its contents into a large velvet bag that had been set on an ornately-carved wooden chair.

Sawyer noticed one woman in a tattered gray dress, her gray hair pulled tightly about her head, sitting in one of the pews. From her manner of dress, it was clear that she was not a woman of wealth. Sawyer silently watched as the basket passed her by, not once or twice, but several times. He also noted the disapproving looks of those who sat around her as she let it go by.

He watched her as she wiped away an embarrassed tear with the finger of one of her small white-gloved hands. Finally, the basket came back around and he saw her shoulders slump sadly as she stared into the hungry black nothingness of the collection basket.

Sawyer gasped when he saw the woman hesitantly raise one of her hands to her face. She struggled for a moment with something, then, with visible effort, she pulled one of her eyes from its socket. Tendrils of connective tissue were pulled taught, drawn tight enough to snap. She made a pitiful whining sound as the orb suddenly came free in her hands. She quickly regained her composure and, pushing an embroidered handkerchief to her ruined wet face, she set the last of her remaining treasures into the basket.

The woman turned toward Sawyer, blood and ichor dribbling out from under her blood-sodden handkerchief. She smiled at him, revealing that a lot of her teeth were also missing.

Sawyer assumed she'd come up short for the collection basket before.

"I'll always be with you," he heard his mother's voice whisper in his ear once again.

And, in the next second, he was back hurtling down the tunnel of light. Color illumination went past him in a dizzying display. When it all finally whirled to a stop, Sawyer found himself somewhere in the middle of a wide desert. His spinning head slowly wound down like top losing energy. He stumbled for a few steps as he tried to regain his balance.

Looking across the sand, he saw something that looked like a small spring laying directly ahead of him, its lush greenery blooming seemingly out of the coarse sand and rock. He could hear the sound of water splashing coming from somewhere far off and he was suddenly aware of how thirsty he was. Sawyer turned to look for The Momipede amidst the rolling dunes, but she was nowhere to be seen.

Realizing that he was now alone, he felt compelled to move further toward the sound of the running water. Running water meant life. Even in his present inebriated state, he knew that. Besides… he had the worst case of cotton mouth in his life.

Parting some wide fronds of vegetation, he discovered a lush oasis hidden behind a crag; like something out of a dream or a children's book. Dense vegetation covered the area in a lush emerald blanket that huddled around the abundant water source. Sawyer's mind reeled... it all seemed impossible given the amount of desiccation and ruin just a short distance away.

And yet, here it was...

Beautiful.

Sawyer again remembered the drug he'd taken and reminded himself of how he needed to keep things in perspective. None of *any* of this was real. What *was* real was that he and Smith were no doubt dozing on the sweat lodge's dirt floor. What was real was that he was trippin' balls and couldn't trust any of his senses implicitly. He made a mental note to compliment Smith on the tea. It was, quite literally, blowing his mind.

Following a vague trail in the sand, he ventured closer to the bubbling lagoon. Large stones and boulders were set around the pond that had been made by what could only have been an underground spring. Wide lily pads floated peacefully on the water's too-blue surface. Somewhere close by, a frog croaked a welcome.

Sawyer got onto his knees and bent to drink from the crystal clear water. Even before he drank, he knew the water would be everything he'd ever hoped for: cold, clean, and utterly satisfying. He drank his fill and sat back, feeling content with merely taking it all in. All around him, he saw life teaming in a stunning display of nature's raw beauty. The plants... the water... it was all so perfect; he knew it could only be a product of his hallucinations.

As he sat ruminating and watching the sunlight glimmer off of the water, he heard the sound of something moving in the brush near him. It moved slowly; almost tentatively, but whatever it was that was there, it was definitely getting closer. Sawyer assumed it was The Momipede returned, but when he turned, he saw the body of a long silver-colored viper moving like a ghost in the foliage instead. Longer than a group of men, the thing moved deliberately passed him, almost as if it didn't see him, and drank from the crisp, cool water.

Sawyer did everything he could to simultaneously remain absolutely still and to inch away from the creature, but he was having little luck. Mostly, he just sat there looking petrified. When the snake's thirst was quenched, it turned its ferocious V-shaped head to address Sawyer. The journalist noted how sunlight glimmered off each of the snake's pizza pan-sized scales as it moved. Pillars of light reflected off of its chainmail-like skin, casting a prismatic array across the sand. The snake eyed him appraisingly.

Much like The Momipede, Sawyer slowly came to see the image of his father cast within the snake's features. Between the look around its large onyx eyes to the set of his aquiline jaw, it looked nearly identical to his dad.

The snake bent its head to Sawyer in greeting.

"S-s-son," the snake purred coldly.

Despite himself, Sawyer pulled his body back, scooting himself another foot or so away. His face betrayed his alarm, but, to his credit, he was able to get a grip on himself pretty readily.

"Wow," was all Sawyer could manage though.

He'd expected this drug experience to last for a while, an hour or two, right? That's the way these things ran. But this…? It seemed like days since he'd arrived in the hot tent and drank Smith's strange concoction.

"You've s-s-seen your mother, I trus-s-st?" the snake asked and, to its credit, the serpent did its best to sound congenial.

Sawyer abruptly felt himself ripped back to a time when he was a kid and his parents were in the midst of their divorce. He'd been conscripted into service as his father's private messenger / spy for its entire duration. He'd instinctively known how wrong it was of his father to put him in that position, and the betrayal of his mother inherent in the act, but… what's a kid to do? It all happened a long time ago, back when he was like six or seven or so, but the scars from the experience still ran deep for him.

At least that's what the therapist he'd been paying had been telling him for years.

Sawyer scrambled to his feet and turned to address his father, the snake.

Dad and he had never been exactly close; not when he was a baby and definitely not as he grew older. Obsessed with his business at the law firm, Mr. Sawyer Sr. barely dealt with his son during his formative years. No fatherly talks... no bird and the bees... no baseball in the yard. Even when he'd been asked to hold him or, god forbid, feed him, the older Sawyer always remained emotionally distant and handed him off the first chance he got.

As the marriage continued to fall apart, the elder Sawyer's interest in his child was suddenly ignited. It was only after the boy figured out that he was being used as an unwitting spy to gather information for his father's divorce lawyer that he came to understand precisely from where the tinder for his father's newfound interest truly came. After that, Sawyer had no choice but to make his peace with his father's indifference. And so, he simply vowed to minimize his exposure to the man in the future when he could, and he moved on. But still... it would be a lie to say that the patriarch didn't loom large in Sawyer's personal mythology. And. despite all the therapy (and the inherent denials that came with that), his father was still an important personality for him whether Sawyer Jr. liked it or not. Sawyer couldn't remember the last time he'd seen him though. He'd tried his best to forget it. To see him here now, like this... man, it was pretty wild.

The large snake edged closer, its scales making a harsh brushing sound against the sand. The giant head came around like a ship slowly turning. When it got closer to him, a grin split the lower part of its broad face and the creature's eyes betrayed a darkly malevolent intent.

"S-s-son," the snake hissed soothingly. The creature's eyes roamed up and down Sawyer's body. He suddenly knew what a mouse felt the instant before the trap sprang shut. "*My* s-s-son..."

Despite himself, Sawyer took another involuntary small step back. He didn't like snakes to begin with, and the fact that this one was now wearing his dad's face was just a part of the deep repulsion he now instinctively felt.

"Tell me, my s-s-son, how *is-s-s* your mother?"

Sawyer felt a hydrogen bomb of anger suddenly explode within him.

Maybe it was one of the side effects of Smith's drug, maybe

it was decades of his pent-up emotion, but… the fucking *gall*.

And after *all these* years…

Sawyer stared at the ground fuming and felt much like he had as a child: incomplete, stupid, and utterly lacking. It was a place he'd vowed to never return. He set his features sternly. He wasn't a child, he thought. Not any longer. He was a grown fucking man… and he'd done a few things and people cared about him, goddam it.

Sensing a change in his demeanor, the snake sidled closer.

"Oooh… anger," The Dadsnake said, sounding a little surprised. "This is new." He paused. "Tell me, s-s-son… did you ever finis-s-sh your book, hmmm?" it asked cruelly. "You remember the one… the one you s-s-said you wanted to write; the one that you got *s-s-so many* of thos-s-se letters-s-s about?"

Sawyer closed his eyes and bit his lip angrily. How fucking dare he bring that up! The book in question was his sprawling sci-fi epic that he'd worked on for well over four years. One day, his father found a pile of rejection slips for it that he'd left out in the open during one of his fits of depression. The fact that he'd never mentioned it until now… hurt more than anything.

Incensed, Sawyer turned on him, but, just as he did so, the creature struck, burying its fangs into the meat of his shoulder. He felt the jaws immediately clamped down, crushing his arm into numbness. The pain hit him like a hammer a heartbeat after that. Initially, Sawyer thought he might pass out from the trauma, but he was able to get a grip on the shards of reality with his fingertips. And then, just as suddenly as it had happened, the jaws released him.

When he looked up, he saw The Momipede and The Dadsnake in the midst of a pitched physical battle. Rolling over and over one another, the two massive creatures were entwined in a frenzied knot, scratching and clawing at each other, driving their teeth deep into one another's flesh. Sawyer ran to the edge of the oasis to avoid being crushed by their aggressive thrashing. The battle raged until both creatures toppled into the pond, waves of water splashing over the shore.

Still fighting aggressively, the vengeful couple rose the surface and, as its head came into view, Sawyer noticed that the animal had melded into itself, the two creatures absorbed into one. The beast roared and turned toward him. Sawyer took an involuntary step back when he realized that the creature's face was his own. The animal's mass fell to the water with a great splash, then it sank to the bottom of the pond.

And then, nothing... just the sound of his own voice echoing in his brain, "It's Life, son... Es laetus?"

With a sudden electric jolt, Sawyer suddenly found himself back in the all-white space where he'd been previously. He took a moment to calm his breathing. Checking his wound, he was surprised to see that the snakebite to his shoulder had disappeared. The soft skin of his shoulder was unblemished, like there'd never been any injury. It was clear to him that the bite, the snake, even the Momipede and the oasis were all figments of his tea-inspired imagination.

The silence in the space around him suddenly felt like it was expanding and filling the room like poisonous gas. Sawyer opened his mouth to get a breath, but felt the rush of ice-cold air pour down his throat in a torrent instead. As it coursed down his throat, he had no choice but to gasp.

Then...

"Ga-huuuhh!" Sawyer coughed aloud as he sat bolt upright.

"Hey, there he is!" guffawed Parker who was now sitting to Sawyer's right.

Sawyer swung his head up and struggled to find his context. He looked around him and saw the familiar Pine, Kauri, and Juniper trees he'd seen on the hike up the mountain. Putting it all together, he realized that he wasn't walking, but being carried back down the mountain. He looked over at Parker confusedly.

"Hey, buddy... welcome back," the big Native said jovially. "You had yourself a time, didn't you?" His laughed echoed through the trees.

"Where the fuck am I?" Sawyer asked groggily.

"Here. With us. We're taking you to your ride, man."

Parker unceremoniously set Sawyer back on his feet like he was an old lawn ornament.

"You okay?" Nakoma asked as he stepped up to Sawyer

and handed him his bag. He set a tree limb of an arm over the journalist's shoulder.

Sawyer teetered on his feet, but finally gained his balance. He looked around and only saw Parker and Nakoma standing in front of him, smiling and staring at him. He returned their gazes and a new light could be seen burning behind his eyes.

"Where's Smith? I want to thank him."

Nakoma laughed. "Yeah... everybody does, but he went back to the hotel; said you were probably going to need a minute, said you'd probably feel lighter."

Sawyer looked up at him and replied, now laughing, too. "I do."

MAKING PLANS

This story is a fictionalized account of a true event. Per usual, the names have been changed in order to protect the dignity of the participants. I've not much to say about this event other than that it really did happen. We all make our choices and I'm left to respect this guy's.

The gravel crunched noisily as the red Jaguar drove into the parking lot of Gibble, Cornwall, and Johnson Funeral Home in the light of a late summer afternoon. Brian Dunaway worried for an instant about the nuggets of loose rock chipping the expensive paint on the sports car, but then thought that now, after his last meeting with his doctor, was a pointless expense of mental energy. He put the car into Park and turned the engine off. In the ensuing silence, he momentarily sat listening to the birds chirping in the trees under which he'd parked.

A cool breeze wafted in through his open window and blew a lock of his brown hair behind his sunglasses and into his eyes. He ran a finger across his forehead and pushed the strands aside. He sat for a minute while looking stone-faced at the black garment bag, a single file folder, and a brown paper grocery bag piled onto the passenger seat.

Finally, he sighed and opened the car door, stepping out onto the flat surface of the parking lot, stretching his back. After adjusting his glasses and straightening his suit coat, he pulled the newly-purchased black garment bag and file folder from the passenger seat, shut the door and began to walk across to the large Victorian building.

The grass of the lawn was neatly manicured and the bushes were closely trimmed, bringing an orderliness to the always emotionally chaotic atmosphere going on within him. The building's exterior exuded a beautiful kind of quiet elegance and propriety which helped put a more palatable face on what most people thought of as the ghoulish business taking place behind its walls. Large bay windows brooded at each corner of the building's façade. In the windows, heavy maroon drapes gave the place a sense of antiquity and punctuated the stateliness of the building.

Taking the few steps onto the porch with a hop, he steeled his nerves and walked with a certain determination until he reached the large mahogany door. He took a deep breath and exhaled slowly. Then, he reached out and rang the bell.

"Here we go," he said to no one but himself.

Joshua Cornwall had been in the family business for about three years after graduating Mortuary College. For as long as he could remember his family had been in the funeral trade; the line of Funeral Directors reached well beyond his father, grandfather, and great-grandfather, and there was little doubt that his progeny would continue on as they had. When your family's name was synonymous with death in your hometown as his was, short of doing a major relocation, changing occupations proved a difficult proposition. Besides, he actually enjoyed his work, as odd as that sounded. Yes, it could be bleak and sometimes depressing with its never-ending parade of grief and the continual rubbing of one's nose into one's own mortality, but he always felt somehow rewarded when he locked the front door and went to his upstairs apartment at the end of the day; like he'd done a good thing with his life.

Cornwall was seated behind his desk in the counseling office when he heard the front doorbell ring. He stood up, took his black jacket from its place behind his chair, and slid his arms into the sleeves as he walked toward the front of the house. By the time he reached the front of the foyer, every seam had been straightened and every rumple smoothed.

The door swung inward, revealing a man in his late twenties who stood there nervously holding a garment bag that looked as if it had never been used. His dress was casual, yet oddly cultured. His brown hair swirled in the wind of the day and Cornwall could almost see the dark eyes smoldering behind his expensive sunglasses. The man stood swaying from foot to foot in nervous agitation, his body language indicating his mood despite the outward attempt at composure.

"Good afternoon," Cornwall said in a voice calculated to calm, yet show clients that someone was in control of the situation. "May I be of assistance?"

"Morning," the man replied. He tried to hide his curiosity about the place, but, like everyone else, he couldn't help himself but to look passed Cornwall's shoulder to the interior of the building. He looked as if he expected to see the Pearly Gates themselves inside the drawing room. The man's eyes jumped back to Cornwall, but he said nothing more. Despite his best efforts, he looked like a scared little boy trying to be brave even though he was petrified beyond his own reasoning.

"May I help you?"

"Uh... yes. I've come to make funeral arrangements."

"Yes, of course... Please come inside," and Cornwall opened the door wide to allow the man inside.

"My name... My name is Brian Dunaway," the man said as he reached out and shook Cornwall's hand.

"Hello, Brian. I'm Joshua Cornwall. Please step this way." He led the gentleman through the elaborately decorated foyer down the hallway of sitting rooms to his office. "Can I get you anything? Coffee? Tea?"

"A bottle of scotch would be nice," Mr. Dunaway said under his breath.

"Excuse me," Cornwall said, turning back toward the man.

"Huh? Oh, nothing," he replied and walked toward the open door to the office.

Brian looked at Joshua Cornwall sitting behind the large wooden desk and wondered what kind of man would want to spend so much of his time in the business of death. How could a man put his hands on the dead and still eat with them at the end of the day? As Mr. Cornwall began pulling an assortment of forms and folders out of a drawer, Brian shifted uneasily in his chair. This place had already begun to give him the creeps and, as minutes ticked away, the feeling was just getting worse. He wanted to get this all over with quickly; before he had a chance to think too much about what it was that he was here to do. With every passing second, that was proving harder and harder to do.

Joshua Cornwall began shuffling papers before beginning to speak. "Let me assure you, Mr. Dunaway, I fully understand that this is a difficult time and I'll try not to keep you too long. I know you have family to attend to."

"No problem, Mr. Cornwall. I've got all the time in the world," Brian said with a smirk and silent chuckle at what was his private joke.

"To begin with, I'll need the name of the deceased."

Brian drew a stuttering breath and swallowed hard. It had always been his own personal defense mechanism to not name a thing thereby making it seem a little less real. The irony and the pain of having to now name this tragedy was not lost on him.

"The name of the deceased,"—another stuttering breath was drawn—"is Brian Dunaway."

Cornwall stared at his client with more than a little uncertainty. At first he thought that the man might be joking or some kind of prankster. Attempts at 'gallows humor' were not unknown in this business. The prank phone calls, the attempted break-ins now and then were all part and parcel of the occupation, however, one look at the conflicted expression on the face before him and all thoughts of jocularity evaporated like smoke.

"Your father?" Cornwall asked, looking up from his paper-work, hoping he was right.

"No," Dunaway answered emphatically and the corners of his mouth did a slow dip. "No. The arrangements are for me, Mr. Cornwall. In fact, the service is to be held relatively soon. It would seem that, according to my physicians, I have only a short time left. I'm told I have developed something called Glioblastoma Multiforme or Grade IV Astrocytoma."

Cornwall looked at the man as he tried to sort out the Latin.

It was pretty obvious from his expression the results of that search was all bad.

"A rather aggressive little tumor," Dunaway continued, "that will begin to grow quickly in the next few months, and eventually invade the tissue surrounding my brain." He laughed a little then, just under his breath, "I'm told to expect a lot of pain..."

"I'm sorry," was about all the funeral director could muster. It felt like a whole little given way too late.

"Yeah, well..." Dunaway said and straightened in his chair. "Life's a bitch, eh? Isn't that what they say?" The laugh that followed was hollow and seemed without heart.

"How are you doing?"

"I'm dying," he said with a smirk. "You? Look, I don't have a problem with it really. It's just how things go, right?" He stared at the floor intently as he spoke, his actions betraying his words. "I'd like it if we could just get on with this, okay?"

"Sure. I didn't mean to..."

"Of course you didn't," Dunaway interrupted. "Let's continue with this, okay?"

Dunaway breathed a sigh of relief when the last of the questions had been asked and the last bit of minutia decided upon. The man across the desk's too-calm demeanor of acceptance was beginning to get on his last nerve. Nothing seemed to affect the man. His casual attitude toward the gruesome work he performed, the all too smug look on his face, and his over-use of cologne (which still couldn't mask the chemical smell that clung to his clothing like an aromatic shroud) all added to the desire to wrap this up as quickly as possible.

Dunaway signed the necessary paperwork the second it was presented to him. He tore a previously completed check from its book, scribbled in the amount, and paid for his own funeral in full. God forbid anyone else would have to pay one red cent for his grand send off. He'd make sure of everything; each "T" had been crossed and every "I" dotted. He'd walked away from his family a long time ago and wouldn't give any of them the satisfaction of taking care of him now. His dad had been an asshole since he was a kid and his mom's silence about the fact showed exactly were her loyalties lay. His brother and sister had proven themselves to be money-grubbing, self-important weasels who would motherfuck God himself if given half a chance.

So, no… there was no love lost here.

"I've brought my suit here in this bag and, if you could keep it here for me, I would appreciate it," he said as a knot rose like a ball in his throat. He quickly cleared it, but made sure to look away.

"That'll be fine. It's not an unusual request. We've stored clothing here before and, given the situation, I don't see how it could be a problem."

Brian was struck by the man's tone and thanked him for it. He then wondered if, had things been different, he and this dealer in death would ever have been friends? He pondered what kind of interests the mortician had. What were his hobbies? He quickly pushed such thoughts away, figuring it made no difference now.

He stood up, and, without another word, walked out of the room.

Cornwall could do little else, but follow him.

At the foyer, the mortician said, "Well, good luck, Mr. Dunaway," and he opened the door.

"Thank you," was Dunaway's clipped response as he slipped his sunglasses back on. Without looking back, he walked off the porch, leaving the funeral director standing dumbfounded, and headed back toward his car.

Joshua Cornwall walked back to his desk and considered the innate sadness of Mr. Dunaway's situation. Joshua had spent his whole life with death as something of a companion and had always hoped that, when he died, things would be quick and painless. To lie in an antiseptic hospital room somewhere being cared for by a staff of people made numb by observing human suffering on a daily basis… better to go out with a bang than a whimper.

Cornwall sat down behind his desk and gathered Mr. Dunaway's forms together, sliding them into a file he marked

"Dunaway, Brian" with a black Sharpie.

Outside, he heard a pop, like a car backfiring. Cornwall glanced out the window and saw Joe the grounds caretaker drive by on his old tractor.

He placed the folder into a tray set at the corner of his desk labeled "Preneeds—Waiting to be filed" and began to prepare to wrap up for the day. It was already passed five o'clock and Joshua still had some errands to run before he would be able to go upstairs to the apartment where he lived to sit down to dinner.

He made his usual rounds of the building, locking all the doors and securing all the windows. He stopped in one last time to make sure that everything in the chapel was in order for the service scheduled early the next morning. When he was convinced that everything was right and shut tight, he returned to his office, gathered up his jacket and briefcase, and left through the door that led from the back of the building to the parking lot.

The lot was spread out before him, empty except for his beat-up old Mazda and a red Porsche which sat under the sagging willow tree standing in the center of the parking lot.

The red sports car sat idling and Joshua guessed that his new client, Mr. Dunaway, had become overwhelmed with emotion after their appointment and had, no doubt, been sitting there sorting through his thoughts. It seemed reasonable for someone who had just made plans for their own burial to be a little distraught, so he walked over to see if he could, in some small way, offer a bit of comfort.

Cornwall approached the car cautiously, not wanting to intrude or interrupt someone's private moment. He noticed that the windows were tinted, making it difficult to see inside. He could vaguely see Mr. Dunaway's form sitting behind the wheel, his head hung in understandable despair. Joshua raised his hand to knock on the glass, but paused when he saw that the front windshield had an odd spider web pattern across it. Red-tinged nuggets of safety glass spread over the hood of the car like ice and were mixed liberally with pieces of what looked like half-chewed cottage cheese.

The mortician opened the car door hesitantly and looked inside, frowning.

The car's interior smelled of burnt cordite and of deep human despair. Sitting in the driver's seat was the body of Brian Dunaway...or what was left of him, anyway. He sat slumped over the steering wheel, head bowed as if in prayer. In his right hand was a rather large handgun. The man's swollen, blood-shot eyes stared at the center of the steering wheel, as if it were the face of God. And yet, he gave no hint of what they saw. His face was covered in spent grey matter, rapidly-cooling blood having smeared a sticky trail across his lips and chin, copious amounts of crimson had poured out of his nostrils and open mouth and pooled in the lap of his suit.

There was a hastily-torn scrap of brown paper bag with meticulous handwriting in pen and pinned with a tie tack to the dead man's lapel.

It read:

> *To whoever will find this,*
> *First off, I apologize for the mess.*
> *I have decided that this is really the only way I can deal with my present situation. I could not bear the prospect of a prolonged death attached to machines that would have robbed me of whatever dignity I had left. Also, I want to leave something to those I love when I go. Medical expenses, care... all of those would deplete that to an untenable point. My funeral arrangements have been made and paid in full. The file is here with me... and also with the place where I'll undoubtedly be found. I have tried to think of everything. I can only hope that God can forgive me.*
> *Julie... I am truly sorry.*

And the note was signed in a familiar scrawl:

> *Brian Dunaway*

Joshua sighed and thought to himself about how we all deal with our impending deaths in our own ways. Funeral

Directors hoped that their deaths would be quick and easy. Most people never considered it *that* far. Here though was a man who had been dealt a raw hand and he'd decided to take an active part in its conclusion rather than as its victim. He made a choice, much like we all must, sooner or later. And that decision had to be respected, even when you didn't agree with it… or understand it.

Joshua quietly closed the car door on Brian Dunaway and his private expression of despair. He turned, and, with a shake of his head, began to walk back to the building in order to phone the authorities.

CONOCIENDO AL FANTASMA

Rather than sit and write this story as I would have any other piece of prose, I tried something different with this story; an experiment for which I'd hoped you would indulge me. Given my history of talking on mic (podcast, convention appearances, etc.), I decided to simply sit in front of a microphone and wing it. So, I fired up the ol' Blue Snowball, had myself a drink, and just went for it. While I did have a general idea of the particulars of the story, a lot of stuff came up that I definitely did not plan. Most of the flow of this is from MANY hours of watching Law & Order and a lot of crime films. The actions of El Fantasma are supposedly real. I heard an interview with a DEA agent on the radio once talking about the cartels and how vicious they could be. So... knowing that should help you sleep tonight.

A silent, darkened stage.

A single overhead light suddenly comes on and illuminates a simple metal table along with two metal chairs. A reel-to-reel tape record sits to one side on the table. A young Hispanic man is sitting, handcuffed to the table. He wears a pair of tan pants, a white 'wife-beater' t-shirt, and a Pendleton over top. There are bruises on the left side of his face and it is clear that he's been in a fight very recently.

The sound of a microphone being turned on and some high-pitched screeching erupts, there is some fumbling, but things soon settle down. After a moment, only the soft hiss from the overhead lights and air conditioner is heard

SGT. R.W. FUENTES [from off-stage]:
"Submitted into evidence: June 25th, 2014. Office of Reception: U.S. Border Patrol Station, Bisbee, AZ. Receiving Officers: Sgt. R.W. FUENTES, Sgt. Sean BRISCOE"

[FUENTES and BRISCOE enter and cross the stage. FUENTES takes a seat across from REYES, BRISCOE stands at perimeter of the circle of light. The reel-to-reel recorder is already running.

FUENTES:
"State your name and place of residence for the record, please…"

There is a long pause
.

FUENTES:
"State your name and place of residence for the record, please…"

The young man handcuffed to the table clears his throat.

REYES:
"Um… my name is… [coughs] My name is JIMMY REYES and I live at 42394 Prairie Dust Road."

FUENTES:
"Where were you born, Jimmy?"

REYES:
"Salinas."

FUENTES:
"That's in California?"

REYES:
"Yeah…"

FUENTES:

"Okay, Jimmy… Recorder's running. We need to get your story on tape."

REYES:

"And, if I tell you what you want to know… you'll protect me?"

FUENTES:

"We'll do what we can, Jimmy. But first, we need to hear what you have to say, okay? We have to see if what you have to offer us is solid."

Another long pause.

REYES:

"Okay, but can I, uh… can I have something to drink? My mouth is really dry."

The recording is stopped for a brief period—all sound onstage is silenced, but we can see the actors onstage—while a can of Coke is found. When the recording is restarted, there is an audible 'click' and all sound on stage returns. REYES is uncuffed and given the can of soda from which he greedily drinks. After his thirst is quenched, he sets the empty can onto the table in front of him.

REYES:

"Okay, well… I've been in the gang life since I was a fuckin' kid, right? I did well coming up and moved up in the ranks of *Escorpion Negra* pretty quick. I was smart, y'know? Resourceful and I was willing to do things that other people weren't, if you get me. Plus… see, I have a *good* memory for things. So, any-way, I got given jobs that a lot of other people didn't want to do; jobs they were all too squeamish for. This deal here… this was supposed to be my break."

FUENTES:
"Break?"

REYES:
"Yeah... you know, into the big money; doing more important things within the organization, and, hopefully, to become someone mi familia could be proud of, y'know?"

FUENTES:
"Tell us about what happened at the motel a few weeks ago..."

BRISCOE [from off stage]:
"The Saguaro Inn? April 10th"

REYES:
"Right... so, we go to this Saguaro Inn and it's in the middle of fuckin' nowhere, out near Bisbee. It's one of those roadside deals where it's all small bungalows that are in a long line, right? You know the kind... the ones that can be rented out by the day or the week... or sometimes even by the hour. [laughs] The motel manager was friendly and he knew our guys and what we were up to, so he gave us a room at the very end of the lot. He tol' us that as long as we left the place the way we found it, he wasn't going to be sayin' much of shit. He'd gotten *his* pay day, right? Anyway, when me and Big Jaime got there, there was nobody there... or so we thought. Jaime said he'd had done this kind of thing before and knew what was up, so he showed me how to flip the bed and get it out of the way. You know, to not get anything like blood on it. He showed me how to lay down plastic and tack it down with carpet tacks so you don't fuck up the carpeting. Things end up... the only thing left in the room was this chair that Jaime sat in the middle of the room. It was about this time that I notice that there's been this guy there this whole time; out on the balcony. He's just sitting there in a chair and there's this little table next to him with an ash tray and a couple of beers he was drinking on. And the dude is just sitting there *powering* bong rips; like one right after the other. And he'd obviously

been there for a while by the look of where he was sitting on the balcony: cigarette butts and what was left of a twelve-pack of beer littered the cement around him. But, from the time I noticed him, there was this constant cloudbank out on the balcony. It was crazy, man. Big Jaime looks at me and nods his head toward outside and he mouths the word, 'Fantasma' and he makes a shivering, scaredy-cat face. I looked back, but… all I see is this guy that's just there for no reason. I figured it was cool, because Jaime said it was cool, but… [shakes head] So, at one point, Jaime looks at his watch and says something like, 'Mala locura' under his breath. I whisper to Jaime, 'Hey, who is this fucker, anyway, foo'? What are we doing here?' Big Jaime tells me that some guy, some pedazo de mierda named Soto, decided he'd help himself to some of our guy's money, right? So, of course, he had to be made an example of… is what Jaime said. He said, 'This man… he stole from us, he stole from *El Padrino*… this man, this puto… He will say anything to get us to let him go, but he is a lyin' cocksucker and this pendejo and his people deserve to be taught a very important lesson, so that other people will think twice when they see our money and they will know to leave it alone. I'm like, 'Seriously, bro? But, like what the fuck?' Anyway, we get the place all ready, and then, the door fuckin' bursts open and two of our guys come in carrying some fuckin' guy wearing these cargo shorts and this ridiculous-looking Hawaiian shirt. He has some kinda bag over his head so we can't see his face, but we can tell that they've already fucked him up pretty good; beat this kid like a rug, claro? And now, they're bringing him here to this room… and it has fuckin' plastic on the floor? [chuckles] No, fuck that… It just felt like overkill, you feel me? But, this kid musta done something more than skim a little cream to have pissed off *all* the wrong fuckin' people. So, uh… they throw this gilipollas into this chair, see and…"

FUENTES [interrupts]:
"Did you know this man? Had you ever seen him before?"

REYES:

"Fuck no... not even when they took the hood off. They just tossed him into the chair and started duck-taping his legs and arms to it so he couldn't move. One of them grabbed a broom that was in the closet and slid it down between the back of the chair and the seat. They took more duck-tape and ran it around this poor fucker's neck and the broom, taping him there."

FUENTES:

"Why?"

REYES:

"So he couldn't move his head or look away. And, again... I'm thinking, what the hell have you gotten yourself into, Jimmy? So, then, one of the guys that was standing next to the guy in the chair, bends over, grabs him by the hood, and spitting at him. 'You are in deep, Motherfucker' as he's pulling a cell phone out of his pocket. [He picks up can of Coke and, seeing that it was empty, he sets it aside] This dude in the chair starts waking up and he's mumbling, makin' these weird sounds like he's a fuckin' cat... and he's cryin' and telling whoever will listen some shit about how he's innocent as an angel and, fuck... *no one's* fuckin' listening, man. No one. And he's confessin' his worst sins to us, man... tellin' us about his family and his kids... but we all know, it ain't doing him one damn bit of good. There isn't a person in that room that gives *one shit* about him or his fuckin' family. [chuckles] This puto was a dead man long before they ever grabbed him and brought him to that shitty motel, man. So, dude's on the phone and he's mostly just listening, right? Then, he looks at the guy in the chair and says, 'okay,' and that's it. He hangs up, puts the phone away, and everybody in the room knows... that's this guy's ass. So, dude puts his phone away and he knocks twice on the sliding glass door. Nothing happens for a minute, then the guy outside opens it. A huge cloud of smoke floods into the room from outside, and, out of the smoke, comes this guy: *El Fantasma*. And I'll tell you Jefe... when he walks in and we all see his face, I swear to God I'm looking into the face of a corpse. He has this haunted look to him and he's thin and he's pale and he had this way of looking straight into your soul. [sighs] I mean, he sees you for what you truly are and to be in that gaze was fuckin' frightening, man. [checks the Coke can for any remnants—seeing none, puts it back onto the table] So, he comes in and he taps the guy with the phone on the arm. He points at this big mirror on the wall, and then, he nods toward where a TV is bolted to a long dresser. He says, 'Obtén éso… y ponerlo allí.' And the other guy—the one that came with the guy with the phone—and Fat Jaime go grab this mirror and prop it up on the table, leaning it against the TV. *El Fantasma* motions to Big Jaime like, 'drag that cocksucker here, to the center of the room.' So, Big Jaime does just that and we all stand back."

BRISCOE [from the side of the stage]:
"I don't get it… Why'd he move the mirror?"

REYES:
"So, the whole time, this fucker would have to watch everything that was happening to him. [chuckles] Fucked up, right? Dude can't see shit now because, at this point, he has the hood on, but soon… [He shakes his head] I move over by the wall because I know… I *know*… something really fucked up is about to go down and I'm not so sure I want to get any of it on me. *El Fantasma* walks over to the guy…"

FUENTES:
"Which guy?"

REYES:
"The one taped to the fucking chair… the one with the goofy shirt. So, he leans down and he starts whispering, *whispering* something into his ear. The guy still has this hood over his face, so he can't see anything… but he can hear, and all he hears is this voice saying impossibly fucked up shit to him. The dude in the chair… [chuckles] He immediately pisses

himself. Whatever the fuck *El Fantasma* said to him… it must have terrified this guy to his very soul. At this point, Fat Jaime leans over and mouths the words to me, 'Watch what happens next, Esse;' like, 'this is something that you are going to remember for the rest of your goddam life.'"

BRISCOE [from side of stage]:
"What'd he do?"

REYES:
"El Fantasma suddenly tears the hood off and there's this white boy sitting there; this blonde-headed white boy, who, by the looks of the designer clothes he's wearing and the sun tan, comes from some money. You know the type… good skin, good teeth; some rich pendejo playin' like he's *Scarface*. Anyway, he's sitting there and his face is already all fucked up from an earlier beatin' and he's cryin' again; like I say, just confessin' the world, bro. *Fantasma* leans down and looks this fucker right in the eye and asks him just one question."

BRISCOE [after a moment's pause]:
"What'd he ask him?"

REYES:
"What do you think he asked him? He looks at him square in the eye and says, 'Where is our goddam money?' And the guy in the shirt starts talkin' and talkin' fast about, 'I don't know nottin' and 'I didn't do nottin' and 'you got the wrong guy.' All this kinda shit… *Fantasma* reaches into his pocket and he pulls out this pearl-handled straight razor. It's about six inches long and he holds it up to the light. Even at the distance I was away from him, you could see that it was sharp as fuck. So, he holds it up and he puts it right in front of the guy so there's no way he can miss it. Then, he starts sliding the back of it along the side of this puto's jaw and he starts tellin' him… Like he's lookin' at him and sayin, 'You need to start telling me where my shit is, motherfucker.'

The white kid… he keeps on with the 'I swear to God I don't have it. I didn't do nothing!' shit. *El Fantasma* leans in and I hear him say, 'You don't swear to God, Cabrone… God isn't listening to the likes of you any longer. You swear to me!' And the dude in the chair, he just starts bawlin' and screaming for help; like anyone was gonna come and save his ass out in the middle of the fuckin' desert in a motel on a highway in the middle of bum-fuck Bisbee, Arizona. Anyway, *El Fantasma* turns and says to all of us in Spanish, 'He'll tell us what we want to know… they *always* do.' Then, *El Fantasma* fuckin' grabs this guy from behind in a weird kind of headlock, like his head is a basketball or something. He grabs him by the chin and holds his head against the side of his chest. And, he just starts *cuttin'*, man… cuttin' into his forehead, from the left to the right, straight across the hairline. And he's cutting *deep*. You can hear the metal biting into the fuckin' bone. [shakes his head] And as he's cuttin' across and this cocksucker is *screamin'*, man. He's screamin' for anybody if only they would take the pain away. I mean, he's calling on God, he's callin' to Jesus, to his momma… like this fool thinks they're all listening in the other room. *El Fantasma* stops for a minute, repositions himself so he can get a better angle on the job, then he starts cutting down the side of his face. And the whole time… the *whole time*… because of him being fuckin' duct-taped to the chair, this white boy *cannot* look away. Every time—every *goddam* time—he opens his eyes, all he can see is *El Fantasma* cutting off his fucking *face*. [shakes head] Madre dios…"

REYES picks up the soda can again, and, finding it empty, sets the can aside.

REYES:
"Can I have another?"

BRISCOE steps into the light with a fresh soda and sets it in front of REYES.

FUENTES:
"Go on."

REYES
[pops can and takes a drink, setting the can aside]:
"Oh, yeah, so, anyway, *El Fantasma*... he keeps cutting, down the side of this guy's face, then along his jaw and I can't believe it! I want to turn away, but... it's *so* fucked up that I can't. You ever have that happen?"

FUENTES
"No."

REYES:
"Huh... So, uh... *El Fantasma* shifts his position again, and then, he starts cutting up the other side. It was *so* fucked up. Anyway, so now, because of the cuts he's made, it looks like this guy in the chair is wearing some kind of weird Halloween mask... but it's his *face*, man. [laughs nervously] And the blood... Shit, there's blood everywhere: all over the kid, all over *El Fantasma's* arms and chest, all over the chair, and it's pooling on the plastic around the chair's legs. The kid...? Well, he stopped screaming a long time ago. Now, he's only barely moaning. *El Fantasma* steps away from him, and he's absolutely *covered* in this white boy's blood. He goes outside and takes like four giant bong rips, and then, comes back inside without saying anything. While he's gone, we're all standing around the room like, 'what the fuck did we just watch,' right? [chuckles] Anyway, so *El Fantasma* comes back inside and he steps up behind this wrecked kid where he stands with his chest to the kid's back. And the two of them just stand there... looking at themselves in the mirror."

BRISCOE [from off-stage]:
"Sculptor and Sculpted."

REYES:
"Huh? Yeah, I guess..."

FUENTES:
"What about the kid?"

REYES:
"The kid… he's just out of it, sitting there with his head hanging down like he's prayin'. Then, he starts moaning and panting and he's still bleeding all over the place… like a stuck pig. Big Jaime suddenly nudges me, like 'watch *this.*' I look over, but I know down deep in my heart that this is definitely not gonna be something I want to see, much less remember. But, I *can't* look away now. *El Fantasma* catches the kid's eye in the mirror and says, 'The money, fucker… we want our *money!*' The kid mumbles something that no one could make out, but, whatever it is, *El Fantasma*… he doesn't like it."

FUENTES:
"What do you mean?"

REYES [nervously]:
"I mean, he doesn't like it. He just reaches over the kid's head and pushes his fingers into the cuts on each side of his jaw. Then, he slides his fingers under the skin, and starts *pulling* on it, man; fuckin' lifting it and peeling it back like the kid's face was a fuckin' orange. The kid's eyes… they go wide and he opens his mouth like he's gonna scream only… [shakes head] only no sound comes out."

There is a pause as the room considers what that amount of pain might be like.

REYES [continues]:
"So, he's pulling and there's this wet tearing sound. [sighs] I'll *never* forget it, man… Not for as long as I live. The kid? He's not really screaming anymore, but he is making these high-pitched sounds like something outta Hell, you know? Christ… [He shakes his head] Fuckin' horrific. Suddenly, the kid's face fuckin' comes off in *El Fantasma*'s hands with this gross, meaty

sound. And he's standing there holding it in his hands like it was a blood-covered dish rag. He pulls a Ziploc out of his back pocket and folds the guy's face up like it was a letter. [sniffs] Fuuuck! I look at Big Jaime like, 'what kinda shit is *this*?!' Jaime just looks at me like this was some shit that even *he* wasn't expecting. When *El Fantasma* is done, he slides the face into the plastic bag like it was a fuckin' sandwich and comes back to the kid."

FUENTE:
"Was the kid dead?"

REYES:
"He's alive, I guess, *technically*, but... he's bleeding out pretty quick and it's pretty obvious to everyone in the room, including the kid, that there's no way he's gonna make it out of this. Especially not with *El Fantasma* having his face in a bag that he clearly meant to take with him. I kept thinking, and I still think about it to this day... 'What did he need the face for?' Confirmation? A trophy? Fuck, man... those thoughts still keep me up at night. Anyway, we all kept watching as this kid slowly faded away... just retreated into his own world of pain. [He crosses himself] At that point, just as the kid was almost dead, that *El Fantasma* leans in close to the kid's ear, so's only he can hear him, and he starts whispering to him again. He spoke in such low tones that none of us could hear what he was saying, but he whispered *something* to him. As the scary motherfucker was standing up, he pulled something out of his pocket that looked like an awl."

FUENTES:
"A what?"

REYES:
"An awl."

FUENTES:
"What's that?"

REYES:
"A tool. My Tío used to do leather work—bags, belts, jackets—and he used something called an awl to punch holes in the leather. It looks like an ice pick, but sturdier. *El Fantasma*, he pulls it from behind his back, and, as he's turning away from the kid, he puts it into the kid's ear."

FUENTES:
"His ear?"

REYES:
"Yeah… and he just slides that fucker home, man. The kid… he stiffens in the chair for a second like he's being electrocuted, then he goes slack, like someone flipped a goddam switch with his name on it."

FUENTES:
[sighs audibly]

REYES:

"*Fantasma* wipes the blade off on the kid's shitty Hawaiian shirt and no one in the room is saying a fuckin' word, man. It's like we all suddenly realized that this… this was no man with us in that lonely motel room out in the middle of fucking nowhere. [laughs nervously] No, this was Death himself come to claim this poor fucker's soul and we were there only to bear witness. Everyone in the room is suddenly doing whatever they can to be invisible; just standing there in fuckin' silence, man. Tryin' to avoid his gaze."

FUENTES:
"And then…"

REYES:

"Without another word, *Fantasma* strips off his bloody clothes and he goes into the bathroom. A few seconds later, we hear the shower start running, and it's as silent as a church in that little motel room; you can believe that! The whole time he's gone, we're all standing around not saying dick. I look at this dead kid in the chair and he's just staring into the mirror, all wide-eyed and grinnin' this ridiculously wide grin."

There is a long pause where only the overhead air conditioning is heard. The actors on stage sit; each lost in their own dark thoughts.

REYES [speaks up]:

"I don't know about Big Jaime or the other guys, but... I was, and I still am, fuckin' petrified, man. I'd never seen anything like that. And still, no one in the room said dick. After a few minutes, *Fantasma* finally comes out of the bathroom and he's dressed in a whole new set of clothes. I figured he must have had them stored in the bathroom."

BRISCOE [from off stage]:

"You're a smart guy, Jimmy."

REYES [looking annoyed]:

"So, anyway, he comes out... doesn't say a goddam word to any of us and, without grabbing anything from outside, he walks out the door and that is, as they say, that."

There is another long pause as everyone considers everything they've heard.

BRISCOE [from off stage]:

"So, what happened next?"

REYES:

"Well, so, after he leaves, we all still standing there, not sayin' shit. After a while, Big Jaime decides to start on the job, I guess and starts mopping up the blood, pulling the plastic sheets off everything, wrapping this poor pendejo's now-faceless corpse in more clean plastic… that sort of thing. It took us about an hour to clean it all up. When we were done… we paid the motel guy and we left. The whole time, I kept thinking, 'This wasn't right. What happened here… it wasn't right, man.' And, I knew… I *knew* that this was some shit that I wanted no fuckin' part of. I mean, I have a *family*, man… kids."

FUENTES:
"So, was this about the time we picked you up?"

REYES:
"Pretty much, yeah… I'd barely gotten home and gotten myself cleaned up when you guys came and rousted me for this burglary thing. I only gave you this information because, well… I can't go back to prison, man. I can't. I can show you where the motel is… the one in Bisbee; I can show you where it is. And you said… you said that, if I gave you something, something you could use, you'd… you gotta keep me safe, man. I mean it's not my fault some asshole got himself clipped for taking something that wasn't his, for stealing some shit that didn't belong to hi—"

FUENTES quickly stands up, knocking his chair back. The metal chair makes a loud clatter as it falls onto its back. He turns his back on REYES.
BRISCOE suddenly steps into the light.

FUENTES [angrily]:
"Look, man… that 'asshole' was a cop, and that cop was my friend. And he… [pause] *He* had family, too. And kids. But you… you're a piece of shit that, while you may skate on this 'burglary thing,' as you call it, because of what you're giving us, you're still a piece of shit. [to BRISCOE] Get him out of my sight."

FUENTES exits stage to the sound of door shutting.

BRISCOE steps up and takes REYES by the arm. Almost as an afterthought, he reaches over and shuts off the tape machine. The overhead light on stage snaps out at the same time.

DOMICILIARY

This one was different for me as I'd never really tried Sci-Fi. It's not that I'm not a fan; it's just that it all gets a little 'hardwarey' and a smidge preachy for me. So, of course, I set about turning all of that on its proverbial head. But, me being me, yeah... I got a little sentimental with it.

The Praesidium Ore Foundry
I.F.P. Registration #G76-PL45
Planet of Origin: Diluvian
The outer rim of the Trilidulatus Galaxy
The Frontier

RJ Marx grunted as he shifted in his seat and tried to get comfortable within the close quarters of his pilot's chair. Before him, a kaleidoscopic tempest of light and color that was being projected by the command controls danced like fairies across the reflective plane of his helmet's visor.

He'd been In Deep since his ship, The Catia, left Polonius, the fuel replenishment station that was in orbit around Arturo 384. He was ready for a break. Out here, at the edge of the longest arm of the Komoda Nebula, floating in the weightless expanse of space, it was easy to become melancholic and start to miss all of the creature comforts of home with a sense of longing that was palpable. All pilots suffered from it, but, to hear them tell it, it was a prison of loneliness unique to themselves. Marx didn't think it was that bad, but then again... Pilots were, in his experience, all pretty much melodramatic divas in that respect. It wasn't Hell, but... it was certainly Hell-adjacent.

The thought of Home though…

Just the thought of it made his throat grow tight and his eyes glass over with tears that stung his eyes. He'd been gone now, what… ten years by his admittedly rough recollection? He wouldn't allow himself to think about how long it had been back home, back on Earth. He sniffed back his emotions and the sound was hollow within the confines of his helmet. A sudden hitch blossomed within the birdcage of his chest as he let his eyes drift up to the worn photo he'd kept pinned to the console since leaving.

He'd managed to scrape up enough credits to buy a Lacus Class Ore Transport called The Catia back when it seemed like *everybody* was jumpin' off-planet. He'd sold (or hocked) everything they had, worked two, sometimes three, jobs in order to be able to afford a ship that would get him to the big gold rush that space had been promised to be. They'd opened interplanetary commerce to merchants and everyone was telling him how easy the pickings were, and how vast the rewards. Hundreds left in that first wave and the few that came back told their stories of untold riches just waiting for them… out there in the vastness of space.

His plan, as stupid as it sounded now, was to go off-world, make enough to pay for his wife and their son to join him off-world. By then, his plan whispered, he would have gotten himself set up in a new place, and, once they were back together, they'd all live happily ever after.

That was the plan anyway.

After refurbing The Catia, he'd been approached by an ore transport company and had signed on impulsively. Once he had though, he was bound by the contract and nothing could change that. The only things he hadn't accounted for in his Great Plan was the time space travel took… and the ensuing collapse of Earth's environment. To be fair, there was no way he could have known that was in the cards. Hell, scientists hadn't seen it coming.

He still remembered the day when he awoke from hyper-sleep to be told that everything he knew—his wife, his kid, his *planet*—were all gone; sleep having robbed him of everything he'd worked for, everything that he held dear.

To change his train of thought, Marx checked the instruments which let him know the status of his payload. The Catia was basically a tug boat; hauling a Class C planet-sized asteroid across space so that it could be rendered for its usable resources and minerals. It wasn't an exciting job—far from it— but it was lucrative.

He glanced at the Comm and saw the Praesidium floating like a Christmas ornament against a coal-black drape.

"Praesidium escort calling G76-PL45," a tinny voice tumbled like pebbles into his earpiece.

Marx recognized the voice as an Arkadian controller he'd shared more than a few draughts with during his visits. He triggered his mic.

"Hey, Dakka..." he said, congenially. The image of the Arkadian's wide face onscreen brightened as he recognized Marx. "Back again with another load."

"What d'ya got for me, buddy?" The Arkadian asked, leaning into his camera, and snuffling up his nose.

"Vichloridium; a C-Class rock of it."

The Arkadian's image flickered on the screen. He was Calsin and sat like a puddle in a broad vinyl chair. His puffy body reminded Marx of the Tartigrades he'd learn about in high school; either that or a stacked pile of leather laundry.

"Once you're docked and through Customs, call me and I can come meet you for more Zontallah. I still tell stories about the last time you were here."

Marx laughed. "10-4, good buddy."

A confused expression blossomed in the folds of the controller's pouchy face. "Hukka?"

Marx quickly realized that the Arkadian would have no idea what he was talking about. Hell, he'd only pulled the reference reflexively from the deepest part of his memory. It was something about a radio...

"I will," Marx corrected himself.

An image of a Transfer Craft appeared on Marx's monitor. Like The Catia, the ship was a Lacus Class tow-ship that looked like a teardrop with a flattened bottom that was essentially an immensely powerful magnet that was used to grab onto the minerals held deep within the Asteroid and allowed it to be moved about in the weightlessness of space.

Flipping a few switches on the console, Marx stopped and allowed his finger to hover over a large red one. The tip of his finger sat poised like an adder above it; ready to strike.

"G76-PL45 to Praesidium Transport…"

Marx waited, staring at the mesh of the console's speaker.

"Praesidium Transport to Catia… how're things, Marx? You're coded and we're ready to take possession of your package."

Marx let his fingers rest atop the knurling of the release button.

"Release in three… two…" He jammed the red button. "One."

A weighty clunking sound rippled through the skeleton of the craft. Suddenly, the ship accelerated forward, now free from its heavy load. The Catia floated like driftwood on the swirling eddies of space. He then kicked on the ion boosters and his ship slowly slid away from the Vichloridium asteroid.

Almost immediately, the other transport backed up to the floating orb and, using its magnetics and restraining cables fired from cannons, grabbed ahold of the mass of metal ore and stone. Once attached, the ship's magnet did the rest.

"Okay, pal," the transport's pilot said over the speaker. "We have you all set across the dials and the package is now ours."

"Thanks, buddy," Marx said. He reached out and held his hand over the radio comm. "Happy to just be off the clock."

"You got it, man… I'll have your paperwork back at the office for you by the time you dock. Come 'round and pick it up as soon as you're good."

"Yup," Marx said as he punched his new coordinates into the ship's navigational computer without looking. "On my way there now."

Without waiting for the response, Marx signed off his comm and lazily redirected The Catia toward The Praesidium.

Once The Catia was docked and secure in her berth, Marx found the Arkadian Controller in his office, and checked in.

Piled like a mound of autumn leaves, he sat behind a circular desk that surrounded him like a wide metal belt. Computer monitors sat in squads across the surface of the cluttered, flat workspace. There was a carpet of snack wrappers, Florian cigar butts, and half-empty bottles of a yellow liquid that looked like piss scattered amidst the paperwork and file folders on the desktop.

"Maaarx," Dakka called out and his jowls shook like wattles. "Hello, my friend. It's been a while, no?"

Marx grinned and reached over the garbage pile Dakka called a desk to hand him his clear flight manifest and to shake hands. He watched balefully as his hand disappeared into the Arkadian's massive fist. As an afterthought, Marx wiped the imagined sweat and schmutz off of his hand onto the ass of his pants.

"It has."

Dakka's fat hands were a blur as they talked; moving paperwork, punching information into his computer's keyboard, and, all the while, smoking this turd of a Florian. Sheets of thin metal paper came off his printer like the shavings of a chef's mandolin.

"Hell, buddy…"the fat Arkadian guffawed, "You gonna have time to come out with us this trip? You're the stuff of legend around here…"

One corner of Marx's mouth rose into a wry grin.

"Not this time, I imagine. I have a short layover this time out."

"Oh?" Dakka said as he stamped the clear acetate of Marx's flight manifest.

"I have a line on an asteroid belt rich with Bornean Cobalt stuck in orbit in a very secluded part of this galaxy I once flew past. I'm planning on getting back there asap and grabbing what I can."

The Arkadian laughed over his spit-soaked stogie.

"If I had a plug for every time I heard *that* story… or a variation of that story."

Marx laughed along with him.

"We'll see," he said, taking back the manifest. "But tonight,

I'm planning to rest up, get some repairs done on my ship, and get back on my way as quickly as possible."

Dakka nodded as he finished putting his copies of the paperwork back into a different clear folder. "So... what's for supper?"

Marx stretched his back and yawned.

"Well, first... I'm going to get myself some sleep. In a *bed*."

The Arkadian laughed.

"Then," Marx continued, "I'm gonna grab a shower and get myself some decent food—something that's not wrapped in plastic. Then, if I still have time, I'm thinking I might go down to The Promenade."

The Arkadian looked up at him, slyly. Two thick plumes of acrid smoke vented from what passed for his nostrils like exhaust.

"Going to The Auxilium?"

Marx smiled and tried to look innocent.

"Maaaybe..."

The folds in the Arkadian's face all smiled together.

"You cur," he said as he clapped his big hands together joyfully.

"But first," Marx grinned, "I want to get some rest, get outta these clothes, get myself clean, and find something I can sink my teeth into.

The Arkadian laughed. "You mean dinner or at The Aux?"

They both laughed at that.

"Well, let me know if you wanna drink later."

Marx nodded as he waved over his shoulder and headed toward the door, knowing that calling Dakka was the last thing he'd do. His plans for the evening were already written in stone.

It'd been a long time... too long.

"Will do, my friend..." Marx said as he left. "I just need to wash this funk off me."

Marx checked into his room, giving his flight badge to the clerk as payment. The clerk—a D'Loidian who was a short amphib who had thick glasses and wore a bowtie like a garrote around his fat neck—scanned the small, plastic-covered card through its reader. A little green light blinked on his computer to show the charge to his account had gone through. The clerk smiled broadly and handed him his room key with a flourish.

"May we send anything along to your room, Mr. Marx?"

Marx shook his head.

"No… I just want to get a shower and get some sleep. Then, I plan to eat my way through half of whatever I find on this station."

He chuckled to show he was kidding. D'Loidians, he knew, had zero senses of humor. Nodding to the clerk, he grabbed his carry bag and headed up to his room.

Fourteen hours later, Marx woke up on his back in, what to his mind at least, was the lap of luxury. He star-fished his arms and legs, extending them across the bed like a kid. The soft linen caressed his skin as he arched his back to work the kinks out. He felt the weight of the Cagorvian duvet. Groaning aloud, he reluctantly sat up.

His cabin was small, but still seemed cavernous to his eyes. He'd been strapped into The Catia's flight chair for seemingly ever. Being out in a more open space was a welcome relief after those long weeks of being cooped up within the confines of his post.

He swung his legs out of the bed and sat up, waiting for himself to fully wake up. Since coming to space, it always took him a minute to get his bearings when he woke; where he was, what time frame it was, that sort of thing.

He looked around the room. It was a standard space station personal quarters: bed, desk, and a shower. It was a space meant to be used, cleaned, and re-rented. The only two things that didn't belong there were Marx and his bag,

In the silence of the small cabin, his stomach suddenly growled loudly. It began like a soft rumbling in his bowels, but soon rose to a full roar.

"I need to eat," he said out loud, his voice cracking from lack of use within the silence of the room. He breathed in deeply to get a rush of oxygen to his bloodstream. He abruptly smelled a sour, tangy odor coming from someplace. Only after a quick sniff test did he realize that the smell was coming from his own body. He knew he needed to change that. "But first… a shower."

He got up and walked over to the shower which had been set in one corner of the room. The thing resembled an old telephone booth he'd seen in books. Just over six feet tall and made of metal, it used recycled water that had been sterilized and pH-balanced for each visitor.

He stepped inside, closing the clear door behind him. As soon as the door lock made contact, a quick pulse of warm water blasted from a dozen nozzles, sending liquid over the entirety of his body. The water came from every direction and soaked him completely.

He pressed an octagonal green button on the wall and a thin nozzle slid out from the metal wall. He placed his hand under it and a thin stream of orange gel fell into his palms. Rivulets of soap dripped like sap through his fingers. He rubbed the viscous fluid over his body, quickly turning the orange gel into a bright yellow lather. When he was covered from head to toe in the foam, he pressed a square blue button on the wall and another series of water blasts hosed him clean. When the torrent stopped, he stood there dripping, watching the sudsy water spiral down the drain on its way to the reclamation center somewhere deep within the station.

He stepped out of the shower, picking up a small towel that had been provided to dry off. He stood for a minute in front of the mirror and surveyed the lines—both new and old—on his face in the reflected surface.

Shit… how long had he been up here? With the way space travel could mess with your sense of time and space, who really knew? He looked deeper into his own gaze and found himself momentarily drifting away on his own thoughts. It was times like these, the down times, when he got the loneliest. Alone, in deep space, and working such long hours, he could only pretend his life was normal. Then, from the depths of his reverie, a face drifted out of the mental fog: a young boy's face; a child. The little guy was looking right at him with a pained, pitiful expression.

"When's Daddy coming home?" the mirage said and its voice was like a lance to his heart.

Suddenly dizzy, he gripped the sink in front of him and

held in until the feeling passed.

"Shit," he hissed through clenched teeth, "I need to eat."

A half hour later, Marx had gotten himself into a set of clean clothes and was out the door, heading toward the elevator that would take him to The Promenade.

The Promenade was a wide corridor that had once been a holding bay which ran like an artery through the center of Praesidium Station. Over the years, travelers had gotten themselves comfortable and opened small shops and businesses along its length for other travelers as they made their way through the galaxy. They started with small booths with tables and chairs. Soon though, walls had been put up, their materials having been scavenged from elsewhere on the station (or from amongst its cargo). Now, it was its own economy, despite management's objections. And the action taking place down the mall, in many ways, funded its very profitable operation.

Ships came for the large processing plant hovering a few miles away, but while they were here, The Praesidium fed, housed, and amused them. Marx recognized The Promenade's scene the minute he got out of the elevator. It smelled like carnival food, Dopra Tea, and the sweet perfume of the Diluvian hostesses.

Marx felt the cascade of memories that washed over him the second he caught the odor. He'd spent long nights in bars back when he'd come out of that first hypersleep and realized all he'd lost by leaving Earth. He'd drunk so much, in fact, that he'd almost lost his contract. Good thing he hadn't… If he had, he could have lost his ship. And if that happened, he'd have been well and truly fucked; essentially abandoned in the depths of space.

He'd pulled it together though, but it had been close.

Now, he sought solace in his periodic visits to The Auxilium.

Y'know, when his loneliness got to be too much for him to take.

He smiled when he heard the elevator doors close behind him and the full spectacle of The Promenade spilled over his vision. There were gas-filled orbs that were suspended in the air in a vast array, but most of the light in the expansive room was provided by strings of bare lightbulbs hung from wires overhead.

The public square split off into two distinct directions. The market was, in essence, a large oval; one long street that allowed the flow of foot traffic to run down the length of the holding bay on the left and return on the right. Along the street was a garishly-lit carnival of small shops and sheds; each selling a variety of food, oddities and other momentary diversions. Every station had a place like this: a place where you could get drugs or drink or any manner of contraband. If someone needed it... someone was here to sell it to them. Management would always take their cut and look the other way.

Same as it ever was.

Marx wandered the street for a bit, but decided to head to the place he'd been thinking about for weeks: a small meat and noodle stand called *P'rof'n Tau* that he'd been brought to on his last trip to The Praesidium. The food there was so good that he'd been thinking about it ever since. On that last occasion, they'd even had *real* beef... from *Earth*. It cost a *lot*, but... man, was it ever worth it.

HE finally found the place and immediately stepped into the confined space of the shed. Marx was immediately wrapped in a swirling world of food smells he remembered: soy, Bantha Beans steaming, and some sizzling D'juanna filets. His mouth started watering almost immediately. He'd been eating little else but bug protein packs and drinking reclaimed water on this last leg Out and he was more than ready for anything that didn't taste like beetle shit and room temperature piss.

Once he was seated, he ordered so much that the waiter thought he was kidding and stopped writing his order down mid-way through. When he assured him that he was serious and *very* hungry, he continued ordering. Expecting a big tip later, the waiter scribbled feverishly and ran off to the kitchen when he was done. A short time later, Marx was sitting before an obscene pile of food and comestibles. He ate slowly, savoring each and every bite, continually ordering pitchers of Domidian Beer to keep things moist and moving. At one point, his gluttonous display drew the watchful eyes of a few folks sitting nearby.

A short time later, Marx sat back and sighed loudly; before him lay a battlefield of scattered cutlery and dinnerware. Dishes were piled on dishes in haphazard stacks, smeared in sauce and meat grease. Glasses of Kangillian wine and Satrino whiskey lay like spent artillery shells amidst the chaos. He tipped the last of the beer pooled at the bottom of his glass and drank it down.

He paid his bill once again using his flight badge. The waiter thanked him and, picking up a leftover sliver of meat, Marx returned the courtesy. His hunger now sated (and feeling just the right amount of buzzed from the hootch), Marx stepped back into the hustle and bustle of The Promenade.

All manner of traders flowed around him like salmon rushing to spawn: fat Arcturian bankers walking in groups, tall Elgolian warriors who kept to themselves by scowling at passersby from the shadows, and, of course, the seductive Oltarian dancers. All went about their business oblivious to everything—and every one—else around them.

Marx wandered the street for several hours, stopping here and there to look at some proffered trinket or bauble. All the while, he kept doing his best to avoid the ever-present pickpockets. Soon, his mind became numb to all of the lights and ballyhoo going on around him and he found himself, as he so often did when visiting here, on the steps of The Auxilium.

The Auxilium was once a section of the station that had been set aside for housing troop transport crews. It was essentially a series of suites that soldiers used as they waited for their mission's launch time. The function of the place, for better or worse, had changed over the years, imperceptibly going from barracks to den of iniquity over a very short time. At one point, the Diluvians took control and they never looked back. Diluvians were shapeshifters—metamorphs—who could, given enough time to make the transition, physically mimic just about any being in the known universe.

It didn't take a completely perverted intellect to see all of the benefits of such a thing. So much so, in fact, that the people who ran the place were fond of the slogan, "Giving Whatever the Heart Desires."

Thinking about the place and its reputation as he stared, looking up at the marquee made him feel the first blush of his excitement. Marx came to The Auxilium whenever he came to The Praesidium, Hell, if he were ever being honest, he'd have to admit to instances where he'd scheduled ore drops just so that he could visit the place.

His smile grew broader.

Space could sure be a lonely place, man.

Once inside The Auxilium, Marx waited to be seen by one of the Diluvian hostesses. Sitting alone in a small, sparsely-furnished room, he sat and waited patiently to be called.

After a relatively short time, the owner of the place, who was known around The Promenade as Mrs. Rittenhouse, came to greet him. She wore a traditional Diluvian gown that ran from its tight collar to the ground like a drape. Marx always thought of how the outfits always reminded him of the old Catholic Nun's habit: long, flowing gowns that ran from the tops of their heads to the floor. The contradiction was not lost on him.

"Good evening, Mr. Marx," Mrs. Rittenhouse said as she gently dipped the crown of her headpiece.

Marx had met with her before when she'd helped him and he liked her. She was professional... and understanding of his special requests.

"Ma'am," Marx replied and bowed his head in return.

"It's been a while..." the Diluvian madam said as she sidled behind a metal desk at the far side of the room. There was a Manerian computer set on a side table that she wheeled over to her on a wheeled cart. A delicate hand slid from the folds of her gown and Marx tried not to notice as it split into a dozen or so long, finger-like tentacles that began rapidly striking the computer's misshapen keys. The clatter was like teeth on a cold winter's day, he thought idly.

Without being asked, Marx set his flight badge onto the desktop for her to read. She smiled broadly at him and transcribed the numbers into her keyboard. She sat back regally as she waited for the computer to retrieve the file. She continued to smile at him, but said nothing. The screen abruptly flashed and she looked back for her answers.

"Ah, okay… I see. Yes," she muttered to herself as she read.

For the briefest second, Marx felt exposed and sort of violated. He knew that before her was a listing of every time he'd been here… and of what he had ordered on each occasion. It passed quickly when he realized this was true for all of their clients. And he knew a lot of folks visited here.

"Yes, all right, Mr. Marx. I believe we have your profile and have a suitable hostess available for you."

Marx smiled. "Great. It's, uh… It's been a while…"

Mrs. Rittenhouse smiled back indulgently, like a mother patronizing a child. "I'm sure it has."

She struck a few more keys on her keyboard and slid him his badge back across the table. A side door suddenly opened to his left.

"Miss P'rath will take you to your hostess."

Marx looked up to see another Diluvian hostess standing in the doorway. He turned to greet her and an Asian face with deep green eyes peered out at him from behind her habit.

Marx clumsily stood up.

"Well, thank you," he said to Mrs. Rittenhouse from over his shoulder. "I appreciate your help."

Mrs. Rittenhouse smiled up at him benevolently.

"We offer a service, Sir… a respite from the loneliness of space. It's our job here at The Auxilium to make sure every being's fantasies come true. We take great pride in the performances of our hostesses." She stood and handed a room card to the other Hostess.

"Well," Marx grinned shyly. "I've never been disappointed."

He felt a touch on his arm.

"This way, Mr. Marx," Miss P'rath said.

Not for the first time tonight, Marx dutifully followed along.

Marx walked down the long hallway, following Miss P'rath , watching her long robes sway as she moved. He knew where they were now: in the dormitory where all of the other Hostesses plied their trade. The air was thick with incense smoke and there was low-level drone music being played somewhere nearby. They passed another patron in the hallway as they walked along. They passed one another with a discrete nod, but little other acknowledgment.

Continuing on, they wound their way around a corner, and then, down another hallway.

As they passed a corridor that jutted off at a right angle to theirs, Marx looked down the hallway and saw a very angry Diluvian hostess standing in the hallway with two station security guards, The hostess was wrapped in her gown, but you could see some of her flesh was still transforming back to her normal Diluvian amphibinoid from a thick, calcified skin. It was like she'd been interrupted midway through her Change and was now too flustered to notice… and fix it.

The first cop was a big Testudian from Testudo Graeco who looked like a turtle that had lost its shell. His skin was leathery and pale; colored so green it was almost blue. The other was a Terran like Marx. Both were dressed in the station's guard uniform. They had a Lapisian in handcuffs, his thick calcified skin pressing up like sausage in the metal restraints. There had clearly been a struggle, but there was no way of knowing at a glance what it was about.

Miss P'rath finally urged Marx to continue walking.

They finally arrived at a nondescript door at the end of a long nondescript hallway. It looked like every other door in every other hallway, but tonight, he knew, it was his.

Miss P'rath turned to him and smiled warmly.

"Have a good time, Mr. Marx. If there's any problem, just pick up the phone and call. We'll make it right." She handed him the door's keycard.

"Thank you," Marx replied, but his focus had already shifted to the door and all the possibilities that lay inside. He knew they had his profile, and, therefore, he knew that they knew exactly where his interests lay, but…

Still, he was still nervous. As he always was every time he came here.

The Diluvian Hostess drifted away, unnoticed; silently leaving him to his fantasy.

Marx stared wide-eyed at the keycard. Then, he looked at its slot in the door. He pushed the card in slowly, and, closing his eyes, he slid it through the mechanism. He heard the door click open and it nearly brought him to tears. It had been so long; so very, very long.

The apartment was modestly decorated. There were some shoes of various styles and sizes piled up in a jumble in the foyer. A long woolen runner ran down the tiled hallway that ended where the hallway turned off into a room on the left. He saw framed photos hung by small brads along the wall; someone's familial rogue's gallery. Images of a small child with a woman were staggered along one wall.

Marx noticed a Jack Russell Terrier asleep on a throw rug near where the pile of shoes was. It was a wonder he didn't see it when he entered. Colored bone-white with a couple of tan splotches, the pooch looked up at him sleepily.

"Hey, pup," Marx cooed.

Marx extended his hand so that the dog could smell him. Almost immediately, the dog acted as if it recognized his scent and he jumped to his feet; rapidly wagging his tail. Now blissfully excited, he ran around in a tight little circle. He barked once, then, took off running down the hallway at a sprint. He disappeared like a ghost around the corner.

From the next room, Marx heard the sudden, surprised shout of a small boy, followed by the sound of little feet running rapidly across a wooden floor.

"Hey, Dad's home!"

AN ANGEL COMETH

Another revamped Carpe Noctem piece. I include it mostly for posterity... and to show the extent that I've changed as a writer over the years. The voice in this bears little resemblance to the way I write now, so updating it was tougher than I expected. Hopefully, it works...

"The only religious way to think of death is as part and parcel of life."

—Thomas Mann, *The Magic Mountain*

A cold wind blows across the steeples of the cathedral inside of which I kneel and pray. The clouds above, saturated beyond their capacity, suddenly burst, releasing their burden of heavy moisture into the air. The rain beats incessantly against the stained glass. The water pours down the faces of the carved stone gargoyles which line the cold gray edifice of the church. They are mute sentinels that silently watch as the melancholic procession below treads the walkway into the building. They are a parade of frail humanity who all seek absolution for the sins they clutch, like dirty little secrets, tightly to their bosoms. They come seeking forgiveness. They come seeking absolution. I watch the thundering torrent pelt the panes of stained glass, and the oppressive rhythm is one of Salvation lost. My knees, forever red and blistered, tingle with the pins-and-needles sensation of neglect as I forever kneel and pour out my immoralities in the morasses of regret to a silent and apathetic God. I cry and rend my soul for the pain in my tortured heart and I am utterly undone. My sight blurs from my salty tears as I pray for *some* kind of heavenly vision. Mine has always been a soul that craved the validation of a being greater than myself, and yet, my pleas for corroboration have always remained unanswered.

"A man can die but once. We owe God a death."
—William Shakespeare, *Henry IV*

The unexpected booming of the cathedral's front doors announces yet another reprobate's approach from the vestibule. With a rush of wind, the doors open and bang in their frames. Leaves from the trees outside swirl into the hall, carried on a wind that extinguishes a number of the candles previously lit in remembrance. I jump in my chair at the noise and draw a quick concussive breath. My heart races, my stomach light with fear. I notice a shadow move deep within the darkness of the foyer. Outside, far off in the distance, the cry of a lone crow is heard. The walls of the cathedral themselves seem to sigh and a statue of the Holy Mother suddenly begins to weep tears of blood. The soft skins of my palms follow suit, erupting into stigmata. Dark blood oozes out of my porous flesh. Horrified, but convinced I was in the midst of some kind of dream, I look toward the door and see the validation for which I had so recently longed.

"He seems so near and yet so far."
—Alfred, Lord Tennyson, *In Memoriam*

There, standing in the doorway, I see a figure clothed in a heavy dark robe; its hems caressed by the storm's insistent touch. A hood is pulled over the figure's features casting its face and expression into darkness. The thing slowly raises its head and stares in my direction. Beneath the cowl, I see that there is nothing, just the emptiness of The Eternal Void. A voice, seemingly saddened by the amassed loss in the world, whispers my name; its finality demanding a response. It's all I can do to nod my head in acknowledgement. Great leathery wings slowly spread from my visitor's back like a cat rising from a long nap. Their tattered edges flutter like sails from the cold wind still coming in from the door. The creature extends out a hand that is made entirely of bone and rotting flesh from within the folds of its robe. In that brief moment, I catch a glimpse of the whole of eternity within its sleeve. The figure beckons me closer and I move, quite against my will, toward it. My plaintive look toward the assembled statuary for any celestial assistance goes unanswered. The stone faces gaze straight ahead with their eyes fixed and dilated. None are giving absolution here today. With feet as light as those that trod on angel's wings, I take my initial steps into the aisle. Compulsorily, I take another step toward the specter before me.

"I have a rendezvous with Death."

—Alan Seeger

As I step to within mere feet of my ghostly visitor, I catch the scent of jasmine and of hollyberry as it emanates from the heavy cloth of his cloak. My skin responds by summoning a flock of gooseflesh in the sudden chill. Seemingly without choice, I tentatively reach for the proffered hand. As the skeletal grip wraps itself like a snake about my hand, I feel a frigidity that chills me to my very soul. But I am now a part of something that is beyond my mere Self. I am now nothing more than a cog in a great and mystical machine. Therefore, I am inexorably drawn into this angel's dark embrace. The neighing of a horse on the street outside catches my attention and I look over skeletal shoulders to see the thin, pale steed that waits for me and my new lover ever so patiently; like a faithful dog. I fall then into robes as black as midnight and willingly give up the very essence of what I am to this wonder of the universe. I give my newfound paramour all that I am and all that I was, as I welcome all that awaits me. Contentedly, and, without a lot of fuss, I slip into The Cosmos.

"In nature, there is less death and destruction than death and transmutation."

—Edwin Way

PLEASE LOCK CELLAR WHEN FINISHED

This, much like "Another One for the Fire," from Moonlight Serenades, is another example of me setting a writing challenge for myself: pick a single moment from a film or story and imagine it from a different character's perspective: think ROSENCRANTZ AND GUILDENSTERN ARE DEAD. I've always loved the scene this piece refers to because the character is so iconic, but also so rich. I loved this guy the first second I saw him and wanted to know more about him. Full disclosure: there are some minor plot inconsistencies in Romero's original concept (timing of SWAT's arrival, bureaucratic / social times, etc.), so... mea culpa for both me and George. I'll no doubt do more of these in the future as they're fun and help me look at scenes from different angles (which is a good thing, I assure you). By the way... the actor's name in this scene is Jese Del Dre and he was a real priest George found during filming. This was his only cinematic appearance.

A suffocating darkness lay draped over The Amplas Apartment Project like a death shroud. Shadows were dense and dark and they made even the normally happy souls huddled within the building think of the grave. The Amplas was what was known as 'government housing' and the folks that lived in these squalid apartments had already been busy battening down the hatches; settling in for the long, and usually dangerous, night ahead.

Father Thomas Morales and his sister, Isabella, lived in Apartment 4G and had done so since Morales had retired from the priesthood more than a decade ago. It wasn't long after he'd had the car accident that took his leg that they'd moved in.

He'd been driving home from visiting a sick parishioner late one night when a drunk driver had come out of nowhere and, as the patrolman had said on scene, 'T-boned' the priest's car. He didn't remember much about it other than waking up in the hospital and seeing his mangled leg.

After several surgeries and some lengthy hospital stays, the doctors finally decided that it was better for all concerned that they take the leg. A long period of rehabilitation—and much help and understanding from his sister—later and he'd been right as rain; even able to walk again; albeit with the help of his crutch. He'd used two when he first started walking again, but he finally figured out how to move with one and, as a result, it quickly became an extension to what was left of his leg. Over the ensuing years, he'd grown so adept with his crutch that his lack of a leg could barely be noticed.

His sister and he had lived at The Amplas for a number of years now in their small, sparsely-decorated apartment. Each of them had their own rooms, hers was decorated in a distinctly feminine fashion, and his was more Spartan. From the quiet vantage point of their apartment's window, they'd watched and softly clucked their tongues to themselves as a man named Martinez came and rose to prominence in the neighborhood.

He'd started by running dope and numbers in the area and had moved into The Amplas to set up shop a little over a year or so ago. Now, seen as a sort of Robin Hood / neighborhood elder, he'd garnered a reputation for helping the residents of The Amplas with loans, drugs, and protection; anything they needed… at a hefty percentage.

"Thomas?" his sister's weary voice called from the other room.

His sister, like a lot of Amplas' residents, had recently fallen ill with some kind of bug that had rendered her more or less bed-ridden for nearly a week. Her symptoms were the same high fever and sweating that had affected just about every household in the building, but it seemed to the priest to be progressing.

"Yes, Isabella?" he called as he got up from his spot by the window. He didn't really want to get up, but did so anyway. It had been a long day for him and, well… At seventy-three, he wasn't getting any younger. Despite having retired from the clergy a short time after the accident, he was still compelled to serve the people of one-oh-seven… especially now that so many had fallen ill.

"May I please have some of that juice?" she asked when he poked his head into her room, her voice weak from infection.

The priest sighed quietly, but smiled. Nodding, he moved toward the kitchen in order to comply with her request. Isabella had been such a help to him after his accident so many years ago. He'd have felt obligated to help her even without that (she *was* his sister, after all), but… it was a debt he knew he would never—could never—repay.

He opened the refrigerator door and retrieved the pitcher of grape juice he'd made from instant. The purple fluid poured from the mouth of the pitcher and into the jelly glasses he'd pulled from the cabinet in large gulps; the waves of colored liquid splashing up the sides of the glass like a turbulent sea.

From the other room, he could hear the sound of someone talking on the TV.

"People aren't willing to accept your solutions, Doctor," a man's voice proclaimed forcibly. "And I, for one, don't blame them."

Father Morales set the now-full glass aside and put the pitcher back in the fridge. He noticed a new package of vanilla cookies sitting on the counter and momentarily wondered where they'd come from. The nurse that had come by to see Isabella must have left them, he finally decided.

"I don't think she'll miss one or two…" he said to the cabinetry.

Taking the glass in his free hand, he scooped up a couple of the thin cookies, popping one into his mouth, and walked back to his sister's bedroom.

"Here you go, Bel," he said, stepping into the room while munching the last of his cookie. "It's as cold as I could get it given the state of that refrigerator. I also found a few vanilla cookies, if you want some."

It took a second for his eyes to adjust to the dim light of the bedroom. He found his way to her night stand mostly by memory. He carefully set the glass of juice and cookies next to the bottle of aspirin she'd been eating like candy over the last few days.

On the bed, he saw Isabella's thin form lying on her back. She was older than him by a few years, but still every bit as beautiful as she had been when they were kids. Her skin looked drawn and her tightly-wound, gray hair lay pressed across her head, slicked to her scalp by sick-sweat. Seeing her like she was now...

Well, it just broke his heart and made him start to suspect the worst for her.

"Can you sit up to drink, dear?" he asked.

Isabella nodded, but it was clear to him that she'd need some help getting there. It was the weirdest thing. This had all started out like flu after visiting The Marshalls in 3C, but it quickly got worse and worse. Fever, congestion, a total lack of appetite... if things didn't improve soon, he'd have no choice but to take her back to the local clinic. He made a mental note to give it until tomorrow, and if she wasn't better... he'd have no choice but to take her back on the bus to see the doctor again.

Father Morales picked up a drinking straw from a pile that he'd set on the bed stand and slid it into the glass of grape juice. The thin tube stuck out of the dark fluid like a periscope, turning around the inside rim of the glass, carried by the container's swirling internal current. Holding the straw up to her lips, he watched as Isabella sipped the dark juice, her throat convulsing visibly with each generous swallow. When she was done, she licked her lips and smiled.

Setting the glass on the nightstand, he eased her back into bed, taking time to fluff her pillow and make sure she was covered up and warm. He sat down gently next to her on the side of the bed. The sound of the bedsprings jangling seemed melancholic within the quiet room.

"Feeling any better?" he asked her gently, taking her hand in his own. He was shocked by how warm her skin felt to his touch.

She smiled, but groaned from the effort. Somehow, she sank even deeper into her pillow, closing her eyes. It was all he could get out of her for an answer and that made him feel all the worse for her.

"Well, I made some soup if you're hungry," he consoled her as he gently caressed the back of her small hand. "It's warming in a pot on the stove."

Isabella shook her head weakly from side to side and drew a breath. Another pained expression drifted over her face like a passing storm cloud.

"No," she mumbled as she drifted into sleep, "I'm just tired and want to slee' a bi..."

Father Morales continued to sit with her for a few more minutes in silence as she fell more deeply asleep. Her hand felt like a hot poker in his, the fever drawing small beads of perspiration across her skin.

He idly watched her little birdcage chest as it rose and fell with every breath. He'd never seen her have such difficulty before; not even when she'd had pneumonia as a kid. He lovingly set her hand down alongside her body and got up from the bed. The springs once again complained as they were relieved of his weight. Luckily for him, Isabella slept through it.

Just then, there was a knock on the front door of the apartment: one-two, one-two, one. The familiar knock was that of their neighbor from two doors down, Eva Jean Knoll. Eva was a divorced mother of two small boys who'd befriended the priest and his sister right after they'd moved in. The young, round-faced girl confessed to Isabella how the boys missed her parents and was kind of using them as surrogates. She'd said she hoped it was okay. Isabella assured her that it was and they were all fast friends after that.

Now, Eva Jean came over whenever she needed something... or wanted a sympathetic ear... or a break from the boys.

Father Morales went back to the living room and over to the door to open it.

From the short distance away, he caught someone on the TV saying something. It was a different voice than the last one; deeper and more resonant.

"Every dead body that is not exterminated... becomes one of them!"

It sounded crazy, but the priest almost stopped to listen, but Eva Jean rapped once again on the door.

"It gets up and kills," the deep voice continued in a monotone behind him. "The people it kills get up and kill."

Morales returned his attention to the door. He opened it a crack and saw Eva Jean's cherubic face standing there in the hall. She looked tired and more than a little flustered. Her curly brown hair was mussed, strands sticking out from her head like the quills of a porcupine, and it looked like she'd been crying.

"Father..." she began, and he opened the door a bit more in order to let her in. "Father, I... we need you."

Morales nodded and put on his sympathetic expression.

"Of course, Dear... How can I help you?"

Eva Jean closed the door behind her and sagged against it for support.

"We... oh God," the woman said distraughtly. "More people in the building have died, Father. *Many* more... They've taken them..."

The woman paused to catch her breath, like the memory of what she'd seen was too much for her to bear. She closed her eyes and tears spilled out over her cheeks.

"Easy, child," Father Morales soothed and he took her hand to calm her.

Eva Jean took a moment to try to gain control over her breathing. He watched her patiently as she closed her eyes and fought to keep from crying more. When she was finally calmer, she looked up at him, tears rising over the rims of her lower eyelids.

"They've taken them—the bodies... Martinez and his people... The dead... They've taken them all to the basement, but..." She wiped away her tears with the back of her hand. "They're asking that someone come and give them the Last Rites."

Father Morales nodded and, letting go of Eva Jean's hand, immediately grabbed his black suit coat from the back of the couch; more out of habit than anything else.

"Of course, child..." he said warmly even as he was pulling his coat on. "We'll go there right away."

Eva Jean turned and opened the door to lead the way, but Father Morales asked her to wait as he poked his head inside Isabella's bedroom.

"Bella, dear," he said softly, "I have to go… many more have passed and they need someone to give them the Last Rites."

Morales waited for her to answer, but none came. He focused his old eyes and noted the slow rise and fall of her chest beneath the blankets. He felt momentarily grateful that she was finally able to get some rest. Lord knows… she needed it. He'd pop out to help these people, and hopefully be back before she even had time to wake up.

When he returned to the living room, Eva Jean was already waiting in the hallway, pacing back and forth nervously. With a brief, backward glance into his home, Father Morales closed the door behind him and followed Eva Jean toward the stairs.

Eva Jean led Father Morales down to the basement. The tenants had been using the space for the storage of their mementos and keepsakes for years. Now, it was being used to stockpile the bodies of their dead.

The way was dark, lit solely by the building's antiquated security systems. They slowly made their way down the staircase, flight after flight, until they arrived at their destination in the basement. At the entrance of the small concrete room, Eva Jean left the priest with one of Martinez's guards, a thin guy in a leather coat named Reyes, and returned upstairs to help any of the other tenants who might be in need.

The priest entered the cold room and immediately smelled the sour tang of death. It was dark in the ten-by-ten room with only a single suspended lightbulb overhead illuminating the space. Once his eyes had a chance to adapt to the low light, he noticed some metal fencing that had been set up recently. The craftsmanship was shoddy, but it also didn't look like they had a lot of time in which to build it.

Narrowing his eyes in the gloom, Father Morales gazed through the chain-link mesh and saw the congregation of bodies that had been piled on the floor; many were people he recognized and had, in fact, led in prayer. One man was bald and had on a rumpled blue shirt. He knew his name was

Robinson and he lived on the Second Floor. There were two black men (one wore a white tee and the other had on a blue button-up) propped up against the far wall. He'd seen the two of them outside on a number of occasions, smoking and arguing sports. An Asian woman lay bound in a blanket, her bloody face exposed and leering up at the overhead light. There was one figure that had been wrapped in a heavy tarpaulin and tied with rope; bound for the grave. The body stirred beneath its covering, fingers probing for any opening. Another of them was a white woman in a multicolored shirt lying prone on the ground. There was a rosary wrapped tightly around her right wrist. Morales noticed how the beads were interlaced between her fingers. Another woman in a flowery sundress with the buttons torn down the front sat pawing at something on the ground in the far corner. Another bald white guy—his scalp violently torn away—gnawed at the stump of someone's severed foot. His mouth worked the meat of the ankle over hungrily while his eyes studied the ceiling.

The priest felt his stomach roll over and expose its vulnerabilities like a puppy. He used the act of pulling his Bible from his pocket to distract him from the imminent sensation of wanting to retch. Determined to accomplish what he'd come to do, he opened the black leather-bound book and began reading.

A short time later, Father Morales was finishing up. He turned the book's page and read the closing stanza of the text:

"Let not your heart be troubled:

Ye believe in God,

Believe also in me.

In My Father's house, there are many mansions:

If it were not so, I would have told you.

I go prepare a place for you."

Father Morales closed his Bible solemnly. "Amen."

Suddenly, a thin, black man carrying a shotgun poked his head into the room from the stairwell door.

"Father?" he called from the laundry room next door. A second later, he rounded the corner and the color in his face drained out when he got a look at the contents of the room.

Father Morales recognized the young guy as Craig Turner

from 2E. He was a student, studying for The Bar. Morales had counseled him a few years ago when the man's mother passed. And now, here he was carrying a shotgun and working for Martinez.

"Just letting you know..." Turner continued. "Cops are gathered outside: SWAT. Looks like they'll be comin' in soon... if they're not inside already. I heard gunfire on the second floor a few minutes ago, so... You should finish up here as quickly as you can, Father. Head back upstairs..." Turner looked nervously over his shoulder. "Where it's safe."

Morales nodded and felt more than ready to leave. He knew he was done here and had done everything he could to help. Besides, he was desperate to get back to check on Isabella, especially now that the police had arrived. They'd been through lockdowns before. He knew that if he wasn't back at the apartment when they finally closed the gates, it might be hours before he could get back to it. The priest looked at the piled bodies before him, and left feeling more or less satisfied he'd done all he could.

It was best for him to get back to his home.

Home to Isabella.

Father Morales nodded to Turner.

"I need to go back upstairs to be with my sister. She is alone in our apartment. She's very ill. I need to go to her."

Turner nodded. "Well, I'd get going then if I were you." He knew the priest and his sister and agreed that being with her—behind their locked door—was probably the best place for him. Hell, if things kept going like they had been, Turner thought, he might just join them.

In the ensuing silence of the next few moments, the sound of helicopters and police cars outside was unmistakable. The sound of their discordant arrival seeped through the cement and could even be heard down here in the deepest part of the building. The priest tucked his Bible back into his suit coat's inner pocket and he made his way across the room to the door that led toward the stairwell.

"You gonna be okay, Father?" Turner asked.

At the door, Father Morales turned back to him and smiled.

"The good Lord provides, son," the priest said, but his voice sounded unconvinced. "At least that's what I hear..."

Going up or down stairs was difficult for Father Morales and it had been that way since the accident, so he usually avoided them and used the elevators. But with the power to The Amplas now cut, the stairs were all he had available to him.

He slowly made his way down the short hallway, but stopped outside the door to what many of the residents referred to as the laundry room and listened. Pressing his ear to the wooden door, he was able to hear the sounds of two men talking on the other side. One of the voices was lower, deeper, than the other, but whoever that was wasn't saying much. The other was thin and reedy and was doing its best to be convincing.

Father Morales closed his eyes and listened to them talk some more, his hand hovering over the door knob like an expectant manta ray.

"Man, there's a lot of people who are runnin' out," the reedy voice said, and then it paused. "I could run." The man's voice paused again, and there were a couple of loud clicks, like someone was flicking a lighter. "I could run right tonight."

The smell of tobacco burning wafted through the closed door.

"I have a friend with a helicopter..." the man's voice continued. "He does traffic reports for G.O.N. and he's runnin' out with it. He asked me to come with him." Another pause, then, "Do you think it's right to run?"

Father Morales grew more and more frustrated as he imagined his sister lying alone and frightened in their apartment. He finally decided that he couldn't wait any longer. He was well aware of how short time was now that the police had infiltrated The Amplas. And so, without further hesitation, the priest pulled open the door and stepped into the laundry room.

THE MISSIVE

Another skeleton of a CN piece... and yes, a lot of this story is autobiographical. My Grandad was a special man... and he remains a model for me. The plot device of the letter is sorta based on an old Colin Raye song, of all things. I changed it a lot, but... credit where credit is due. I like this piece... it makes me cry.

"This is my favorite sad story."

—Rozz Williams "Flowers"

When I was young, my mother would often take my sisters and me on the long drive down dusty Highway 101 to visit my grandparents at their home in Santa Maria, CA. There, as often as not, my granddad would be sitting on his porch, waiting patiently to greet us as we drove up in our old '56 Buick.

A reed of a man, tall and lean, he always reminded me of Fred Astaire, except that my grandfather's face had a few more miles on it. He had these large hands that would appear to reach down from Heaven itself to snatch me up as I ran toward him. He'd toss me up, making me seem to pinwheel in the too-blue sky. Off I'd go, lifted into the air and into his great arms, to be squeezed tighter and tighter. I remember him softly whispering to me, "Child, I could hug on you forever."

At that time, and even now, I could think of no better way in which to spend the rest of my eternity. I would be held there, smothered in his love and drowning in his unique scent of English tea and woody pipe tobacco. As the day wore on, I would sit in his lap for hours as he'd rock us both back and forth in his old, creaking chair and tell me story after story of his coming to the U.S. from England, of working in the always dangerous coal mines of Pennsylvania, meeting my grandmother, having children, these sorts of things. His life lazily unfurled before me, for both my amusement and my edification, like a flag riding a warm summer's breeze.

He was my hero and my friend and someone who continues to be an example of what it means to be a man.

"Love, all alike, no season or clime,
Nor hours, days, months, which are the rags of time."
—John Donne

I remember one day the two of us were sitting, quietly enjoying another lazy summer's day. He sipped his tea while I attempted to drown myself in Black Cherry Kool-Aid. As he stared off into the cloudless sky, he sat back a little deeper into his chair and began telling me the story of how he and my grandmother had become "'gaged." He looked at me with those deep cerulean eyes, eyes that had seen facets of this world that I, at my age, could never imagine, and ran his long fingers through my hair as he spun magic with his words.

"Boy," he said, "I want to show you something," and he reached into the depths of his worn coat.

Out of this enchanted cloak—from which many a piece of candy, gum or dollar bill had appeared—he pulled a tattered envelope, yellowed with age and worn from what could only have been his constant re-reading of it. He told me of how he and my grandmother had been "two love struck kids," and of how they had decided, "once upon a time," to get married. One day, "a day not unlike this," he had taken her to the county fair, (a major social event in the little town they'd both called home) and, as they sat riding the Ferris Wheel for the umpteenth time, he'd professed his love for her and proposed their marriage.

He told me of how she'd cried and cried saying "yes" over and over again, kissing him until his face was covered with the smears of her bright red lipstick. He remembered that, when they'd disembarked from the ride, the two of them caught many a suspicious glance as he'd tried, in vain, to wipe her lipstick away from his cheeks. Of course, his efforts were to little avail. Now, they'd both known that her father would never agree to their nuptial plans, since my grandfather still only worked in the coal mines and couldn't afford to support my grandmother in "the style to which she'd become accustomed." But because they were young and their love was headstrong and their world was therefore alive with possibilities, they'd decided to make plans for the two of them to elope.

They agreed to meet later that night, by a willow tree where they'd shared their first kiss alongside Hilliman's Pond. It was a special place to them since it was the spot where they'd carved their initials into the great old tree with a pocketknife that my grandfather to this day kept in the lining of his magical jacket. "It was a wondrous meeting of two star-crossed lovers that rivaled anything Mr. Billy Shakespeare could have conspired to author," he'd said in his way with a bright twinkle in his eye.

> "Two souls with a single thought,
> Two hearts that beat as one."
>
> —Maria Lovell

As my grandfather continued his story, a far off look clouded his eyes and he became lost in his own vivid memories of his youth. I could tell that he was now telling this story more to savor the memory of it rather than for whatever slight benefit I might garner. I loved him and, of course, wanted to know as much about him as I could. So, there I sat, rapt and attentive, as he told his story. He went on, telling me of how, as he walked to the meeting place, his "stomach turned cartwheels from the fear and excitement" and how "the moon hung over us like a big ol' lantern."

As he had walked along, he dreamed of the grand adventures the two of them would soon be sharing, the years ahead, and of the family they would soon raise together. When he finally got to the bent old willow, there, hanging from a rusted nail, was a note penned in my grandmother's script; the very same note, which he now held in his thin, liver-spotted hand.

He carefully opened the piece of weathered paper and read

it aloud. "If you get here before I do, please wait for me here under this, our willow tree. I've just been delayed, but right as rain, I will come just as soon as I can. I long to spend eternity being held in your arms."

My grandfather's eyes glistened in the afternoon's soft light and he looked at me and smiled, hugging me close as a gentle sigh shook his angular frame. His story continued as he told me tales of their eventual wedding, her father's concern and ultimate acceptance of him as both responsible son-in-law and able provider, my mother's birth and childhood, all of the trials and tribulations that make up any man's life. I was grateful for the chance to hear about these things from him and for the opportunity for us to share a special time together on that long, languorous summer's day.

"The heart that loves is always young."

—Greek Proverb

Time passed as it so often does and, as I grew up, he grew even older. We still met together regularly for lunches or trips to the park, me using any excuse to spend time with him, and him welcoming a loving and receptive ear. I would question him endlessly, unsure of myself and confused about what I would make of my life; seeking both his advice and his approval. He would sit quietly and patiently offer me guidance and love, convincing me to trust in my instincts, to be sure of who I was, and always remain true to that. As I've said, I loved him dearly and his advice and wisdom were a wellspring for me.

Then, when I was fifteen, my mother came to my school—which, as many kids know, always heralded bad news. She pulled me out of class and, with tears filling her eyes, told me of how my grandmother had died during the previous night. She put her arms around me and told me that my grandfather had requested that I come to be by his side as soon as I was able.

The next day, my mother and I again made that long drive to his home, the trip made in mournful silence. As our car pulled into the driveway, I saw him as he sat in that old rocking chair looking older than I ever thought was possible. When I went up to him on the porch, he stood slowly and held me for a long time as he cried.

I stayed with him that night and for the many others that followed. After the arrangements for my grandmother had been made, he asked that I accompany him to my grandmother's "viewin'" at the funeral home the following day. A lump I could never seem to swallow rested in my throat and choked off any disagreement. All of the other family members were well aware of the special bond that he and I shared. So, the next day, they waited understandingly together outside while the two of us walked into the building in order for him to say his final goodbyes to his lost lady love.

"Great loves too must endure."

—Coco Chanel

We walked slowly into the side room of the mortuary where she lay in her dark wooden casket. He stopped abruptly when he first caught sight of her and gripped my hand tighter.

I squeezed back gently and whispered, "Take your time, Granddad."

His tearful smile was a grateful one.

The two of us walked softly down the ashen carpeted aisle way and we approached the casket. My grandmother lay there, looking absolutely angelic, and he stood staring at her silently for a long time. I'd never seen him cry before—he had always said it wasn't something that a man did—but cry he did as he reached out to run his finger across her pallid cheek. He withdrew his hand with a start as his finger made contact with her flesh, and he turned to look at me.

"So cold," he said and looked around the room, "you would think that they'd turn the heat up in here."

I smiled gently at him and nodded, knowing that there was no point in reminding him that she was dead and that her body's warmth had dissipated long ago. We stood for a long time, and before long, I heard my family milling about in the foyer, quietly waiting for us to finish up so that they could begin *their* grieving process. My grandfather sighed, subconsciously knowing that it was about time for him to say his final goodbyes. He slowly reached out, covered her clasp hands with his, and hung his head. It broke my heart to see this man I'd loved for so long, who'd taught me so, so much, weep like this.

With a stuttering breath, he raised his head and asked me for a moment with her alone. I smiled and again squeezed his hand, taking a half dozen or so steps back, giving him the space he requested. However, I decided to remain close enough should he need me for anything. Because of my proximity, I couldn't help but overhear him as he bent over her and spoke to my grandmother.

He laid a soft kiss on her cheek, and I heard him softly repeat the words he'd committed to memory so long ago, "Since you'll get there before I will, please wait for me beneath that, our willow tree. I've just been delayed, but right as rain, I will come just as soon as I can. I'll always love you and I'll love you forever. I long to spend eternity being held in your arms."

With shaking hands, he reached into that magic coat of his one last time and removed his beloved letter. Choking back more tears, he placed it gingerly within the folds of his wife's blouse, making sure that it rested next to her now-still heart. Then, with his engagement now set with the woman who would forever hold his heart, he stood and turned toward me. My Granddad then smiled at me, wiped the tears from his eyes, and, together, we turned to greet his heartbroken progeny.

"One word frees us of all the weight and pain of life: that word is love."

—Sophocles

THE HONEY-DO

This story came about, as a lot of stories do, in an innocent way: my wife asked me to unclog a stopped-up tub. Throw in me being tired… and having just watched THE BLOB… and voila! This is another example of how EC Comics, THE TWILIGHT ZONE, OUTER LIMITS, et al., affected me. I love a twist ending!

Morgan Parker bumped the front door to his two-bedroom condo open with is knee as he made his way into the house. He did his best to be quiet, but it was of little use. It was well after two in the morning and he was just getting home from a little overtime at his job as a 'Lacer' at the Lannister Aluminum Chair Factory just outside of Kanab in Kane County, Nevada. Kanab was small even by small town standards and, even if pressed, Parker would have been unable to tell you how he'd ended up here.

But here he was… married, for what, ten years now, and all but given up on his dreams of ever being much of anything; content just to be left alone to work his shift and to come home to try and find something resembling happiness as he and Maggie and their dog, Shiloh, sat holding hands on the couch and waiting for death.

The condo was small, but it was an obstacle course as he slowly made his way through the living room in the dark. Morgan knew Maggie would already be in bed; asleep and snoring and dead to the world. He made another mental note to try and be quiet as he set about taking his shower and heading to bed.

Walking into the kitchen, he put his metal lunchbox on

the counter; making sure to run a little tap water through his Thermos, so it wouldn't taste funny tomorrow. When everything was clean, he set the lunchbox and open Thermos into the drain rack to dry and officially called it a day.

He yawned exaggeratedly, making his usual moose-like yawning noise through his gaped mouth and he stretched his arms wide. He quickly clapped his hands over his mouth when he remembered that he was supposed to be being quiet. Then again, the way Maggie slept, he could have set off a hand grenade and she wouldn't have noticed.

He eyed the dead face of the television and debated channel surfing for a while, but he knew that would mean him falling asleep on the couch; unwashed and still in his clothes.

And that wouldn't be good...

No, first, a shower, and then bed.

He walked down the hallway and stopped to poke his head into the bedroom. In the dim moonlight, he saw Maggie's form under the coverlet, noting her chest as it rose and fell with her every breath. As he watched her, he felt familiar stirrings in his loins and wondered whether he could talk her into a late night nookie?

"Shower first," he said, sniffing himself.

Like a ninja, he grabbed a pair of shorts, some underwear and socks, and a tee shirt from the dresser and headed back out into the hallway and on toward the bath. In the dim moonlight coming in from the bathroom window, he saw that the door was open at the end of the hall. His curiosity was piqued when he noticed a small slip of paper stuck to the door. The slip of paper wafted in the gentle breeze coming in from the open window.

He flicked on the bathroom light and the room exploded into bright, fluorescent light. The small room was painted white with a faux marble countertop and a sink that sat at its center. A window and toilet lay straight ahead. A bathtub and shower was to the right, directly across from the sink. An opaque shower curtain hung like an empty sail from a rod by metal hooks.

Morgan sighed as he snatched the Post-It off the door. Maggie had taken to leaving the little notes around the house for him recently. At first, they'd been little love notes that told him how much she cared... or some naughty idea she'd come up with during the day. But then, given time, their tone turned to one that was more... instructional.

"What's the harm in me leaving you a little *Honey-Do* once in a while," she'd asked... and, of course, she was right. What *was* the harm? But over the last few months, he'd found himself growing resentful of the damn things. They were *never* good news... not for him anyway.

"Honey," this one began, "Bathtub is clogged. Can you be a dear and unclog it for me? I tried, but... it got pretty gross. I left a chopstick in the sink. See you in the morning. xoxo, Maggie."

"What?" Morgan said aloud, realizing his dream of a quick, hot shower had just gone off the rails. In that instant, he didn't much care how loud he got. "No fucking way..." He jerked the shower curtain back and groaned when he saw three to four inches of dirty, soapy water pooled at the bottom of the tub. "Ah, man..."

He set his change of clothes on the counter and eyed the still-wet, hair-covered chopstick lying in the sink. It looked like a piece of wreckage from some small ship that had been cast onto a bone-white beach. Black gunk and strands of hair coated one end of it like pitch.

"God damn it!" And his frazzled reflection concurred with the sentiment.

He thought a minute about the best way to go about this.

Looking down, he saw his uniform and decided to strip it off for fear of getting it stained with whatever the fuck was going to come out of the drain. He looked at his watch and fought to quell his rising wave of anger.

It wasn't like Maggie couldn't have...

Not like she didn't have time to...

He sighed. "God damn it..."

He finally threw his hands up in resignation; deciding to accept this karmic kick in the nuts rather than fight it. The simple fact of the matter was that Maggie was asleep and, if he wanted to take his shower (and didn't want to do it standing in a pool of this shitty, fuckin' water), he was going to have to deal with this nonsense now. He could tell her in the morning how uncool it was leaving it for him to deal with.

He shot a glance at the bathtub's reflection in the mirror and at the stagnant, soapy bathwater inside. He closed his eyes and gave himself a minute to calm down.

All night…

He'd worked all fuckin' night.

And now…

"God damn it…" he whispered.

With a resigned shrug, he pulled off his shirt and quickly got himself the rest of the way undressed. He cracked the door open and tossed his dirty work clothes out into the hallway; reminding himself to throw them in the laundry when he was done. He'd let Maggie wash and fold them… as penance for this shit.

Now that he was down to only his underwear, he picked up the chopstick in the sink by the clean end and turned, like a fencer, to address his nemesis: the clogged drain. He chuckled a little when he caught sight of himself in the mirror: half-naked, his face and lower arms covered in factory dirt, and holding a wet, hair-covered chopstick like it was some kind of lightsaber.

"That's no moon…" he chuckled.

Straddling the side of the tub, Morgan sat down, lifting his testicles so that they wouldn't come in contact with, what he knew to be, the ice-cold porcelain. Even with the protection of the cloth of his underwear, it was still cold and uncomfortable… and fuck that.

He bent over and tried to clear some of the water around the drain with his free hand. Like ink, the liquid would immediately flow in to cover exactly what he needed to see in order to assess the situation. He finally gave up and stuck the chopstick in blind at the point where he knew the drain would be beneath the water.

The chopstick trick was something Maggie had shown him when they first moved in together, having learned it from her mom. According to their theory, the broken ends of the wood acted like fingers that would grab onto whatever made up any clog; usually hair. He hadn't believed it at first, but she'd shown him and he was now a convert.

As soon as the thin piece of wood entered the drain, Morgan felt it encounter something soft and oddly pliant. He pressed against it firmly, but he soon ran out of stick. He balked at the idea of putting his hand into the dark water for fear of touching something icky in the murky depths. Expecting that there'd be *something* down in the drain, he forced the chopstick deeper into the mass. Two small air bubbles burbled up from the soapy depths in response to his prodding. The wet, rotting smell hit him like a hammer a second later.

"Ugh," he groaned and blanched. "Gross."

Using his thumb and forefinger, Morgan spun the thin plank of wood in a tight circle. He felt the frayed ends of the wood catch onto some of the hair in the clog and knew he was making headway when he felt the resistance against his rotation of the chopstick increase.

When he figured he had a good enough grip on whatever it was that was down there, he pulled with an even, gentle pressure. At first, the clog's tenacity surprised him. It was *really* holding on and he momentarily wondered if he was going to have to give up and call a real plumber for this.

Then, from somewhere deep within the bowels of the house, he heard something make a low groaning sound. The tone of it was unlike anything he'd ever heard, but its timbre increased the more effort he expended on pulling the clog out.

He initially assumed that it was just some of the pipes venting or maybe adjusting to a variance in the fluidic pressure of the house's plumbing. But then, the sound changed, and it took on a more animalistic tone; like the growl of a big dog or the snarl of a large, angry mammal. Morgan furrowed his brow, bracing his knee against the side of the tub, and yanked.

When he heard the wood suddenly sound like it was going to snap, he stopped pulling on the stick. He repositioned his grip on the stick, so that he would be applying an even pressure on either side of the wood. Then, setting himself, he began pulling once again in earnest.

Immediately, he was struck by the same fetid stench of old soap, grease, decay, and... something else. Whatever that something else was, its foul odor was so repulsive that it left a tangy taste at the back of his throat. Deep in his belly, that burrito he'd had at work from the food truck sat up like a cat and stretched its back, demanding to be noticed. Applying more pressure, he put his back into the effort and felt the clog slide slightly within the lumen of the drain.

Morgan opened one eye to check on things and was dumbfounded by what he saw. The clog was this immense knot of hair, five or six inches in length, and colored black; the same as Maggie's. Christ, he thought to himself as he struggled with it, it was a wonder she had any hair left on her goddam head given what was here.

The wad of hair and soap residue was an oily, furry mass that was as black as crude and had that rank, stomach-turning odor of a bathing suit left to molder in a plastic bag. It was a sour, wet, sumpy smell that assaulted the senses and made his stomach do cartwheels with its putrid odor.

Morgan pulled harder and a little bit more of the weird thing slid further out. As he pulled, he did his best to calm himself, but... it was all becoming a little too weird for his tastes and it was all happening so goddam fast!

He was startled when, much to his surprise, he felt the clog inexplicably pull *back*. He tried to rationalize it by thinking of 'logical' things like water pressure and fluidic gravity, but the idea that there was something on the other side of this fuckin' thing pulling back like it was a game of tug of war or something was like a spark on his nerve's tinder. A dark, irrational fear caught and it started spreading throughout the corridors of Morgan's mind like a fiery home intruder.

He shook such thoughts from his mind with the physical motion of shaking his head. He knew he was tired and his anxiety was on the rise because of that, that's all. He closed his eyes briefly as he tried to think.

When he reopened them, he set a grim expression on his face. He had his plan now and that was to clear this shit up, take his goddam shower, and head straight to bed. In the morning, he'd chalk all of this house groaning shit up to being a product of too much work and not enough food and sleep.

He eyed the mass of hair and body grease that connected the chopstick to the drain balefully. It looked like a long, black slug that had been covered in transmission fluid. Loops of sticky soap dripped from the matted hair in a viscous gel. Feeling his belly flip, he bid adieu to any ideas of 'midnight nookie.'

"Okay, fuck this..." he said and set his foot against the toilet for even more leverage.

He pulled his hardest on the chopstick and two more inches of the clog came sliding out of the water like a gigantic turd. The wood in his hand bowed and its strength—or lack thereof—started to really concern him. He paused and waited to see if it would hold, bouncing on it a time or two to test its tensile strength. Then, he pulled even harder. Miraculously, four more inches of the shit came out of the drain.

"Seriously, Maggie?" he grunted as he strained. "Like what the actual fuck?"

It was at that moment that something moved within the twisted clump of oily hair and soap. At first, Morgan thought he was hallucinating when he saw it, but... A small indent on its surface definitely twitched in the sterile fluorescent light.

Then it twitched again.

He almost let go of the chopstick when he saw what it did, but he managed to hold on despite his raging fear. Then, contrary to each and every law of nature and indoor plumbing, an aperture opened within the greasy mass, revealing an eye—almost human in its affect—that glared angrily up at him.

"What the shit?" he cried out, finally letting go of his prize.

As the clog and the stick fell from his grasp, a thin tendril of hair lashed out like a whip or an octopus' arm. It caught hold of Morgan's little finger like a free-handing climber and held on. Then, more of it flowed up his hand, moving like lava.

The grip came down like a bear trap over his hand and more tendrils reached out and grabbed hold of his wrist and forearm. Fingers of hair crawled up his arm like spiders. And, in an eye blink, his entire arm was engulfed. He felt his arm grow progressively warmer within its grasp.

The same fetid odor he'd smelled before assaulted his senses anew, only stronger than ever before. He felt his gorge rise and that burrito climbed up his throat and did its best to reintroduce itself to the back of his throat.

He fought with his free hand to pull the clotted mass from his arm, but he ended up only making things worse; a *lot* worse. More of the blob jumped to his other arm and started moving over that as well. As he struggled with it, he was momentarily reminded of a tar-covered rabbit stuck to the side of a road outside a briar patch.

Morgan strained against the clot's fatty intransigence, he never had time to consider all of the ways this situation was weird and messed up and eerie, and, well… just plain wrong. All he knew now was the blind rush of his panic as it commandeered all of his operating systems and drove his blood to redline. His only thought was to be free of this wet, smelly, disgusting thing. But, despite his frantic ministrations, whatever it was continued to pour up his neck and over his chest like a carnivorous oil slick.

Morgan groaned as he felt his strength begin to wane against his adversary. For the first time, real panic coursed through his body like electricity; adrenalin dumping like nitro fuel into his circulatory system.

Abruptly, he felt the mass grow cold and slick against his skin. He also noticed a different weird odor begin wafting from it. It was the smell of an open sewer and was rife with feces and decomposition.

He tried to get up from the tub, but his arms got stuck to his chest when he moved; cemented by the sticky glue of rot and decay. Soon, the substance was coursing over his panic-stricken jaw, reaching up like the arms of a drowning man for his face. He felt the first of the hairy fingers reach up his nostrils, probing deeper and deeper with every second.

As the clammy mass of hair and soap scum coursed over his head, he fell forward into the tub. His head struck the porcelain with a dull thud. He nearly lost consciousness, seeing stars, but managed to hold onto reality… for now.

The black goo flowed down his throat, and it suddenly became hard to breathe. He did his damnedest to draw his last breath, but had little luck. Gurgling darkly as he struggled for air, he soon grew so weak that it was hard to keep his head up.

And as the air ran out and his world went black, the clotted mass began to slowly retract, dragging Morgan Parker's body inexorably toward the bottomless maw of what lay beyond the drain.

THE MIDAS GIFT

This was an interesting alignment of ideas...First came the concept of Heidi Vidraru's predicament. Then, I remembered Riverview (yup, it's a real place) which was someplace I visited a few times covering films for Fangoria (ALIENS VS PREDATOR: REQUIEM and CASE 39 to name two). It wasn't until later that I decided to add Father Thorpe. The ending took a minute for me to figure out, but... I think it ends like it should. The question is... what happened to Heidi?

Who knows... maybe, one day, we'll see.

April 13, 2001

A cold wind blew over the open grounds of Riverview Hospital and its passing kicked up the dry brown leaves that lay like a blanket over the estate's rolling hills and ambrosial walkways. Riverview was old, established in 1876 as The Royal Hospital; it was used primarily as a mental health facility until it finally closed one frozen December day in 2015. Now, the grounds and their abandoned buildings were on the slow barely-funded slide into institutional decrepitude.

Father James Thorpe decided to leave his car in one of the far-flung parking lots rather than leave it any closer to the main building. He wanted to stretch his legs a bit before meeting up with the person he'd been asked to come and see. He'd been told by his bosses that there was something here that The Vatican very much wished to have investigated, and, hopefully, understood. There had been some wild stories being told about the only person still being kept as a patient here at the hospital and Thorpe had come to see what exactly was what.

The priest straightened his suit as he walked and subtly adjusted the leather shoulder holster beneath his suit coat. He didn't expect any trouble on this investigation, but... he kept the gun perpetually at the ready as he did the Array of Five. Both were his constant companions and he felt better for it.

Y'know... just in case.

He walked along the paved pathway, its asphalt now crumbling to rubble, that encircled the grounds; preferring to take the long way around, down along the river. He took a quick glance up toward the U-shaped structure that made up the main building of Riverview. Its face was old and it looked out over the water like a protector. There was a wide white stone edifice at the center of the U and the brown brick arms of the building spread out from its center mass like bat's wings. Wide, stone steps led up to the structure's double metal doors.

As Thorpe strolled along the tree-lined path, he decided to go over what he knew of the case he was going to review before going inside. Pulling his cell phone from his breast coat pocket, he pulled up the encrypted email he'd been sent on the case by his superiors.

Subject Name: Heidi Vidraru
Current Age: 3 months
Born: January 18th, 2001 Vancouver, B.C.
Parents:
Father: Deceased (presumed heart attack)
Mother: Deceased (died in childbirth)

According to the attached .pdf file, the girl had been born across the river in Vancouver, BC at Vancouver General. According to the reportage, the mother died post-partum with the father following her into death shortly thereafter. The child had been brought to Riverview for containment immediately after her birth; something that they started referring to as 'the incident'.

He stopped and looked out over the slowly flowing river. He already had questions... Was he to understand that both parents died one right after the other? From what? The official Causes of Death were vague, at best. Also, why would a suddenly-orphaned child need to be 'contained'... much less brought to live at a nearly closed down mental hospital?

He looked back at the building.

There was a lot more going on here than just babysitting some abandoned kid, he silently surmised.

"Father Thorpe?" a voice suddenly called out from behind him, breaking both his reverie and the chilly silence.

He turned, replacing his phone in his breast pocket, and saw a middle-aged woman in a standard-issue nurse's uniform approaching him. She was white with brown hair that was tied into a tight bun that rode her skull like a backpack. A pair of 'reader glasses' hung around her neck from a gilded string. She was already out of breath from climbing the gently rolling hill when she got to him. Thorpe saw her take notice of his clerical collar and decided to let it answer for him.

"Nurse Braddock?" he responded instead.

The woman nodded and stepped up to join him looking out over the river. She tried to catch her breath as she shook his hand.

"Thank you for coming all the way out here, Father. We're grateful for your time as well as The Church's."

Thorpe waved the comment away.

"My employers were very interested in the contents of your letter, Miss Braddock. When we dug a little deeper into it, we became even more so. It soon became pretty clear that we should come and talk. Needless to say, it's not every day that we get something like this."

She smiled at the priest's understatement.

"Yes, well… I'm sorry about that. But, as you can imagine… We've gotten pretty desperate. We're losing a good part of our funding soon and, well… there have been some pretty grim things being discussed around here as of late."

Thorpe clenched his brow.

"I apologize, Nurse Braddock, but…" he tried to explain. "The file I was sent was a little incomplete; only from the subject's initial input, I'm afraid and I'm not even exactly sure of all of the facts of *that*. All that I've received is a copy of your initial letter along with a *very* cursory file on the child. Whatever my superiors received, they no doubt decided to keep it to themselves, so as to not taint my initial impressions. If you'll just fill me in on the particulars of the case from your perspective, it would go a long way in helping me to understand what we're dealing with."

Heidi Vidraru. The child has a name. They've all *had names and it's your duty to remember each and every one of them.*

Nurse Braddock looked dismayed, but not exactly surprised by the idea that no one had taken the time to fully explain the particulars of the case to the priest. She quietly accepted the wrinkle though and quickly composed her thoughts in order to explain all of the facts of the case to him.

"Come," she said, beckoning him to walk with her down the pathway, "I'll fill you in as we head back."

Thorpe fell into step alongside her and they headed up the hill toward the hospital.

"Where to begin…" Nurse Braddock mused. "Well, first… are you familiar with people called 'travelers,' Father Thorpe?

Thorpe cocked his head. "Travelers? You mean like, nomads… Romani… what some folk derogatorily call, 'gypsies?'"

She nodded. "I mean that exactly."

"I'm familiar, but I don't see…"

The woman held her hand up, silently begging his indulgence.

"Well, the most important thing to learn at the outset is that, according to what members of the family have told us, the child's mother came from that life. Another relative we talked to after the child was born told us that the girl had fallen in love with someone who was from a different group, another clan… and the family greatly disapproved.

"It seems that the girl had been 'promised' to another family in an arranged marriage. Her falling in love with someone else caused a real problem for the family. Promises had been made. Moneys had been exchanged. Alliances formed…

"Classic *Romeo and Juliet* scenario, right?

"Anyway, it was generally felt by those close to her that she'd turned her back on her family… and on her family's traditions."

Thorpe had a little experience with these folk before, but it was back in the old country, when he was traveling through

Eastern Europe and Turkey doing some of his graduate work. They were a wily, but proud community who wouldn't have taken the daughter's betrayal lightly.

"So, the family..." Thorpe mused. "Let me guess, they reacted poorly."

The woman looked at him and raised her eyebrows at the astuteness of his question.

"Predictably, could be another way to describe it. In a word, they cursed her; both figuratively and literally. At least, again, that's what family members have said happened. 'Since she turned her back on the family over the touch of a man, may her progeny never know the loving touch of another human' was how one of them put it."

"Cursed?" Thorpe said with a derisive chuckle.

Braddock looked at him and furrowed her brows over the tops of her eyeglasses, but said nothing.

"Come on, Nurse Braddock..." Thorpe continued. "You don't expect me to believe that this family put a curse on their own daughter, do you?"

Nurse Braddock stopped walking and turned sharply to look at him.

"You can believe anything you'd like, Father. And with your reputation, I'm guessing I don't need to point out the irony inherent in all of that? You asked me for the facts in this case, and, as slim as they are, these are them."

Thorpe raised his hands in appeasement.

"Fair enough... Fair enough."

The woman began walking again, continuing to talk, not waiting for him to catch up.

"I spoke with another of the relatives at the hospital and it was pretty clear: *they*, at least, very much believed in the assertion. They—and it was one of the younger wives that I spoke with—said that the curse was very real and that we should take steps to isolate the child as quickly as possible. Isolate... if not outright kill. It's crazy... But, she said it out in the open and as plain as day." She shook her head in disbelief. "Of course, we didn't take the suggestion seriously..."

Thorpe looked over at her from the corner of his eye. "But..."

A dark shadow seemed to pass over Nurse Braddock's face and her gaze became distracted.

"But, then… the child was born."

"Was it deformed?" he asked, visibly interested in her answer.

Nurse Braddock shook her head.

"No… physically, she was perfect; beautiful… in fact. She still is to this day."

"What then…?"

"Once the child drew its first breath and we placed her on her mother's breast."

"Skin on skin contact, sure…" Thorpe interjected.

Nurse Braddock nodded gravely.

"Exactly." Her eyes drifted to a spot out over the river. "But the instant the child was placed on her mother's chest, the mother's EKG flat-lined."

"Post-partum arrhythmia?"

She shook her head.

"There was literally no reason for her to go into distress. Her vitals were all good the second before; there was no bleeding, not even shock. But the instant the child was placed upon her breast, the moment that they'd physically bonded, well…" She shook her head again. "It was like flipping a switch."

Thorpe's expression grew grave. The story made no kind of sense… a normal vaginal birth, all vitals post-partum were excellent, and then…

"And the father?"

The woman hugged herself tightly as she started walking again. She suddenly shivered as if she were shaking off a sudden chill.

"The father reacted naturally to the EKG's alarm."

Thorpe looked over at her. "By…?"

"By picking the baby up."

Thorpe looked up at the hospital, already fearing the direction the story was heading.

"And?"

The nurse stopped walking long enough to shake her head.

"He collapsed. If it wasn't for Marjorie…" She looked up at

him painfully. "She was my friend, Marjorie Clayton. I went to nursing school with her..." After a short pause, she gulped and continued along the path. "If it hadn't been for Marjorie being there, the baby would have fallen to the floor."

"And the father?"

The woman looked over at him sternly.

"Dead; dropped to the ground like he'd had his strings cut. The baby fell with him and, again... thank God, I guess, because Marjorie caught her." Her voice cut off in strangled anguish. A tear traced a trail down her cheek.

"I don't understand," Thorpe prompted her.

Once more, Nurse Braddock looked up at him stone-faced and stated matter of factly, "Marjorie died, Father. The second her hands touched the girl..." She shook her head to clear it. "It took four more people to die—including the attending doctor and a resident—before someone finally suggested that no one else touch the baby."

"Was the child in any noticeable distress?"

Braddock shook her head.

"None. In fact, she pinked right up. Her breathing was fine... started cooing right away. She was the picture of health."

By that point, the two of them had rounded the large field and were now headed back up the knoll in the direction of the hospital. The building's prominent white-painted steps led up to the main doors like a stairway made of clouds.

Nurse Braddock gently directed the priest up the stairs and across the landing. They continued on toward the entrance of the building, entering through the large set of metal doors. Their hinges squealed angrily as they were pulled open. As the two of them made their way across the tiles of the foyer, Nurse Braddock continued telling her story.

"Of course, we immediately did what we could to protect everyone, but..." She paused as she waved away the security guard (a young guy with more pimples on his face than beard stubble) that was stationed at a desk by the elevator doors. She looked back over at Thorpe. "But people continued to die."

Thorpe watched her as she hit the elevator call button.

"A virus?" he proposed.

The nurse just shook her head sadly and stepped into the elevator when the doors opened. Thorpe followed along after her dutifully.

"We tested the parent's blood and found everything to be fine. Haz Mat was called in, and, well… more people were affected."

Thorpe asked 'how many' with the raising of his eyebrows.

"Seventeen," she answered, coldly.

"*Seventeen?*" he repeated, shaking his head in disbelief. "Jesus…" and he crossed himself.

"We got lucky when one of the doctors finally figured out that the baby needed to be placed into Isolation… which we did right away."

"How?"

She smiled slyly as if proud of their initiative, "We used blankets… and robotics."

He furrowed his brow in confusion.

"We borrowed some of the robotic arms from Surgery, and we moved her that way."

He nodded. "And then, what happened?"

She looked over at him blankly.

"Well, people stopped dying… that was certainly one thing we were happy about."

Thorpe nodded his agreement. It was a smart move: isolate the problem until they could figure out what the hell, if anything, was going on. And it was clear by the number of dead people stacking up in the morgue downstairs… *something* was definitely going on. Imperceptibly, he nodded. The use of the robotic arms was inspired. It's something he might have done.

Nurse Braddock hit the button for the uppermost floor on the elevator's control panel.

"After that, we treated the child using very strict Universal Precautions; using only the mechanical hands and blankets to interact with her. We finally had to use straps to," she raised her fingers into 'air quotes,' "*marionette* her so that she could be dealt with: fed, changed, bathed… that sort of thing. It took a while, but the staff soon got a handle on it and actually developed a protocol."

Thorpe cocked another eyebrow.

"Father," the nurse said as the elevator doors slowly began to close, "please allow me to be perfectly clear here. It'll save us a lot of time moving forward." She leaned against the wall of the elevator looking tired and grateful for the support. "For reasons we don't yet know, anyone or any living thing that touches this child with, as you said, 'skin-on-skin' contact... dies. It's as simple as that."

He looked back at her incredulously. He'd seen and heard some strange things in his time working with The Vatican, but... a person who could kill with but a touch? It was pressing it. He looked over to say more, but saw Nurse Braddock standing with her back to the wall. Her head was back and her eyes were closed. For a second, he thought she might have fallen asleep. But then, the elevator bell rang signaling their floor, and her eyes sprung open.

"Coming?" Nurse Braddock asked as she strolled out of the elevator, once again, not waiting for him to catch up.

February 18, 2009...

Father Thorpe stepped out of the elevator onto Riverview Hospital's fourth floor of and immediately ran into Nurse Braddock. Not much had changed with the woman in the ensuing years since he'd first met her. Her hair was a little grayer and the lines in her face were a bit more pronounced, but... she was essentially the same woman he'd met out on the front knoll so long ago.

"Father," she said and she nodded to him in greeting in lieu of shaking hands.

Her demeanor was much as it had been on that first visit (and every visit after that): blunt, a tad authoritarian, and just this side of 'bitchy.' Thorpe had seen over the years though the effective way she'd run the facility and he knew there wasn't much that escaped the woman's watchful eye.

"I have some new data on those tests we ran the last time you were here," she continued. "Some of the hormone levels are *very* interesting."

Thorpe smiled at her as he swam into her wake.

"Listen, Annabelle..." he stopped walking so that she was forced to look at him. "I'm gonna need to spend some face time with our patient this time out. We've talked about how there might be the need for it for a while now, and yeah... It looks like today's the day. I need to get close enough to get a read on her."

Nurse Braddock nodded letting his use of her first name slide. She was well aware of what the priest was doing: buttering her up because he wanted something. Thorpe had been coming to The Unit off-and-on since the day they'd met several years ago and she'd become familiar with a few of his tactics. She'd known he would ask for this one day... and it looked like, as the priest had said, today was the day.

"Of course," she replied, biting her tongue. There was no use arguing with the man. It had been made very clear to her early on by her employers that she was to afford him every courtesy. And so, she had... and so she would.

The two of them turned a corner in the hallway and very nearly ran into a balding man in his sixties coming from the other direction. He was short and wore a blazingly white lab coat with a blue button-up shirt beneath. His eyes were clear, but there was a reddish glow to his complexion that betrayed him as a drinker.

"Oh, shit!" the older man said, raising his shoulders into a surprised shrug.

Thorpe extended a hand to steady him and to keep him from falling.

"Whoa, Doctor Sylvester..." Thorpe apologized. "Hey, I didn't mean to startle you. I didn't see you."

The doctor quickly gathered himself with a flurry of his hands.

"No... no, Jim; entirely my fault. I had my head buried in these damn funding reports." Then, under his breath, he said, "Bastards keep asking me to pull blood from a goddam stone, y'know?"

Thorpe smiled as he wondered why all administrators were seemingly cut from the same miserly cloth.

"I'm here to see Heidi again, Doc," Thorpe finally said, deciding it was time to get directly to the point. "This time though... I need to talk with her face to face."

Dr. Joshua Sylvester nodded distractedly while he fumbled with a few of the files in his hands some more.

"Of... of course..." said the older man as he joined the priest and the nurse in their walk down the hall; Thorpe and Nurse Braddock following along behind like ducklings. "She's just had her lunch and, last time I looked, she's in bed doing a bit of reading."

"She's learning at a really incredible rate," Nurse Braddock interjected. "Her reading level is *way* above average. Her understanding of science, language, and math are similarly off the charts." She paused and looked up at her two companions. "And you should see her art... her pointillism work is pretty astounding."

Thorpe smiled at her obvious admiration for the girl.

All too soon, the trio finally arrived at a set of double doors that Dr. Sylvester had to use a card key for them to enter. Inside, there was an additional set of doors and, this time, both the doctor and Nurse Braddock had to key in. Once through, the way opened up and the group followed along the corridor until they passed a combination Nurse's Station and coffee area. One more set of doors and they were soon standing inside a small observation room that looked out over what appeared to be a day care center.

The place was about the size of a studio apartment; separated from the observation room by a wall of one-way glass. The living space inside the room was divided into essentially four separate areas designed for four separate activities.

At the far left was a living room area with bookcases brimming with books, an exercise bike that looked out on a small window, a large plasma screen on a swivel (so that it might be viewed in both the living room and the bedroom), and a large, saltwater fish tank with a few Damsels swimming about. A wool-upholstered couch with blankets and pillows piled neatly at one end was set on an area rug in front of the large screen.

To the far right lay a bedroom with a large oak armoire and king-sized bed. Inked sketches had been taped to the wall around the bed. On the near left was a matted exercise floor. Toys and sports gear were piled like wreckage against the wall where the mats and the living area met. To the near right was a kitchen with a large refrigerator and an industrial microwave. A small dinette with two short chairs were set on the galley's linoleum floor.

Sylvester and Braddock went to their desks and started rifling through paperwork. Thorpe approached the glass and stared into the apartment.

The rooms appeared empty, but then, Thorpe caught sight of two small feet sticking up from the bed. Small toes wiggled at the end of each foot as they kicked up and down, appearing and disappearing amidst a turbulent duvet sea.

"There she is…" Dr. Sylvester said proudly as he came up beside Thorpe. "There on the bed."

Thorpe chuckled to himself at the thought of the kid being anywhere else. It wasn't exactly like she was going to go out for a walk. He eyed the glass in front of him critically. He'd been in cages before… and as a result, he knew how they worked.

"This is new…"

Dr. Sylvester looked the thick pane in front of him over.

"It is… and it's all thanks to you. I hope you feel that we spent your money wisely."

Thorpe waved the statement away.

"Nonsense," the priest responded. "That group wanted to invest some of its profits and I knew that you could use an influx of resources. They got their tax break… you got your funding. It was really just me putting the two of you together in a room."

"Well, however it happened," Dr. Sylvester replied with a shrug, "it helped us make the place a little more livable for us." He looked toward the bed and its gently kicking feet. "And for Heidi."

Thorpe abruptly turned to Nurse Braddock, deciding to cut to the chase and discuss the reason for his visit.

"So, as I was saying, I'd like to try something new for today…"

Nurse Braddock's eyebrows lifted as she got to her feet and joined them near the glass. She crossed her arms over her chest defensively and waited.

"I'd like to sit with her directly. No barriers. No interference."

Nurse Braddock shook her head indignantly. "I can't... I *won't* allow it."

"I'm afraid I have to agree, Jim," Dr. Sylvester interrupted. "It's just a little too dangerous. We've come to know how much we can let our guard down around Heidi..."

"...which is not at all," Nurse Braddock interjected sternly.

Dr. Sylvester touched the back of her arm in an attempt to calm her.

"Besides... you know our protocols and the reason for them," he continued, trying to head off any objections at the pass. "We've lost too many good people on this project already. The idea of anyone getting too close to her without precautions..." He shook his head. "It's simply too dangerous."

Thorpe frowned as he reached into the breast pocket of his suit coat and retrieved a letter from its depths. Reluctantly, he handed it to Sylvester and watched as both the physician and the nurse leaned together in order to silently read it over. The further into the text they got, the more their expressions hardened.

"Well, then," Nurse Braddock said resignedly, "I guess you're going inside."

"Sorry," Thorpe answered, "I hated to do that, but... it's critical that I move the project forward. I need to gain her trust... and to maybe get a read on her."

Dr. Sylvester refolded the letter dejectedly and handed it back to the priest.

"No... I completely understand." He held up his index finger in warning, though. "But if anything happens, it's on you."

Thorpe nodded his understanding as he tucked the letter back into his coat.

"I know... I know. But my instructions are to talk to her, to try and get inside her head, to find out if she holds any potential threat.

"A threat? Christ, Father... of course she's a threat," Nurse Braddock exclaimed, shaking her head in disbelief.

Thorpe nodded, but was insistent. "Even after all this time, we still have no idea how or why any of this is happening. And I don't need to tell you what zero data gets us... or her." Thorpe stared deeper into the woman's eyes. "Seven years with little to no answers... A lot of people are openly debating why, quite frankly, she's being kept as a viable resource?" He ran his fingers through his hair in frustration and licked his lips. "There has to be some *reason* for what is happening here... beyond the admittedly thin suggestion of a, what did you call it?"

"A curse," Braddock said under her breath and her voice sounded a little embarrassed.

"Right... a curse, a hex," he chuckled disbelievingly. "Look, The Church admittedly peddles in some pretty far-fetched things, but... we don't have a *single* trackable piece of data here as to the whys or wherefores of this case beyond this child's ability to kill with but a touch. We need answers, and, quite frankly, we're running out of time."

Sylvester held up his hands in surrender.

"I know... I know what people are saying, and I am quite aware of our rapidly diminishing timetable. Unfortunately, Science doesn't give a shit about timetables."

Thorpe looked over at Nurse Braddock in order to get her take on the conversation. He needed them both onboard with what he was proposing if this was ever going to work. Even a little resistance could mean more problems than he needed down the road.

"Just let me talk with her one-on-one, with no barriers, and, hell... if I die, I die. But I'll be careful..." he held up three fingers. "Scout's honor."

The doctor and the nurse reluctantly nodded their agreement.

The metal door to the apartment opened with a staticky hiss, like snakes alarming of a threatening intruder.

"Heidi?" Thorpe called out. "It's Jim Thorpe."

From the bedroom, a child's voice rang out like a bell.

"Hey, Father," he heard her say as she sprang up from the bed, the sound of her movement muffled by the distance.

She bounded around a corner, her eyes directed toward

where she knew the one-way glass was along the far wall, across the matted play area. Thorpe figured she'd become so used to directing her attention there because that flat, blank wall was, in her experience, the doctor's eyes and ears. He watched her as she happily tromped out onto the play area carrying a thin book in her hand.

"I was reading," she said to the blank plane of the wall, "It's *very* good." She held the thin volume up like it was evidence in a trial. "It's called *"Petrosinella* by Giam… Giambattista Basile." She stumbled over the foreign names valiantly.

Thorpe watched as the girl took her position at the center of the matted area; directly in front of the observation window and its cameras. She stood just over four feet tall with mid-length curly blonde hair that fell like ribbons across her shoulders. She had cold slate-gray eyes with full lips that were set in a perpetual pout. A small, turned-up nose gave her the look of a fairy. Physically, she was the perfect image of a healthy seven year old girl; good development, clear complexion. And her beauty… She was like something out of a child's picture book. Thorpe took a second and reminded himself of just how dangerous she actually was.

"It's about a girl who's locked away in a tower by an evil queen…"

Thorpe pitched his voice softly, so as not to startle her. "Like Rapunzel, right?"

She spun around, surprised by the direction and proximity of his voice. When she saw him standing a short distance away from her, she immediately retreated from him; crouching into a posture that was pure 'fight or flight.'

"Father!?!" she exclaimed and her voice sounded genuinely frightened.

It was just something that had been drilled into her thinking since the day she was born: no one was to *ever* enter her space except for Doctor Sylvester or one of the researchers; the ones with the metal arms. They'd explained the danger to her… over and over, time and time again. It wasn't hard for her to remember all the times when an accident had occurred. She'd felt horrible about it each time. But now, seeing Father Thorpe standing just a few yards away from her and knowing that there was nothing between them, she felt a dark and terrible fear rise within her.

"You *can't* be in here." She looked around the room frantically for assistance, but knew none was coming.

"Doctor Sylvester?" she called out. "Nurse Braddock? Is anybody there?"

"Heidi," Thorpe chuckled warmly. "It's okay..."

"No, you don't understand! It's *too* dangerous... Something bad could happen to you! You could *die*."

Thorpe smiled indulgently. "Why don't you let me worry about that, ok? Look, I just thought it was high time that the two of us met—face-to-face—and were able to have a talk."

He slowly ambled over toward where the kitchen was located. Approaching the child-sized dining room table, he pulled a small chair out, and, perching himself on one side of his leg, sat down.

"I thought it was rude that I hadn't come in and properly introduced myself."

The girl once again looked up to the one-way glass. She leaned forward and whispered conspiratorially, "What about Nurse Braddock and Doctor Sylvester?"

Thorpe smiled. "They're there; behind the glass... and undoubtedly convinced I've lost a bit of my mind. But I am well aware of the risks... but, given the reward of getting to know you better, I think they're acceptable ones." He looked over his shoulder at the blank wall where the cameras were. "Isn't that right, Doc?"

Doctor Sylvester's voice came tumbling out of the speakers like coins. "Yes... everything is all right, okay, Heidi?"

The girl stared at the priest suspiciously; as if she was contemplating something, some bit of minutiae that had gotten stuck in her mental teeth and she was working internally to pry it loose.

"I don't think anyone not associated with the hospital has *ever* come in here... at least not while I was still here." Then, under her breath, "...or awake."

A look of dark loneliness passed over her face like a cloud passes over the sun on a windy summer's day. Her gaze drifted off to some personal space where, it was clear, that she was still trying to work out how—and why—he might have come to be in her room. Thorpe waited patiently as she arrived at her own conclusions, in her own time, before finally continuing to speak.

"Well, again… I just thought to not come and really see you, after all this time, well… it was sort of rude. I mean, I'd like to think that we've become, y'know… friends, right?"

The little girl looked up at him and a smile slowly dawned across her cherubic features. She then looked down at the kitchen's linoleum, her cheeks reddening slightly. Finally, she quietly said, "I'm glad you did."

Thorpe smiled back at her and a moment of comfortable silence—the kind that can often occur only between friends—blossomed within the room. Thorpe's expression suddenly brightened as if he remembered something and he reached into his pocket.

"Hey, you know what? I brought you something… a gift."

Heidi's eyes lit up. She'd never been given a gift before, having only read about the practice in the books Nurse Braddock let her borrow. She became visibly excited at the idea of seeing what he had for her.

"What is it…?" she asked and her eyes were bright and clear and burning with a fierce intelligence.

The priest set a small bright yellow-colored box down onto the table and slid it toward her. The box's artwork featured a background of what looked like a cascade of lemons. A child's face had been drawn on one of the pieces of fruit, a wide grin splitting its jaundiced face.

In her excitement, she reached out for the prize.

In that moment, the tips of her fingers came just a little too close to Thorpe's; his certain death avoided purely by chance. Wide-eyed, they retracted their hands quickly, fear dancing like a flame in both of their eyes.

"Oh, God, I'm so sorry," she exclaimed, stuffing her hands under her thighs. Her face was a tapestry of fear and contrition. Her eyes filled with moisture.

That was *way* too close Thorpe chastised himself, quickly getting his initial jolt of alarm under control. He smiled and gave a little laugh in an effort to try and comfort the girl, but he still held up an index finger in reproach.

"Okay, quick agreement..." and he shot a glance toward the observation room glass. "Moving forward, we must both remain vigilant. We can't let anything like *that* ever happen again, ok?"

She looked up at him and smiled appreciatively. She'd obviously grown used to the harshness of Nurse Braddock, but... seeing the priest react so understandingly, she felt a little better about their nearly fatal transgression. But she also knew that he was right... even a small misstep like what had just happened could mean catastrophe.

Because it had happened so many times before.

Heidi scrambled out of her chair, away from the table, and suddenly ran off toward her bedroom. After a moment or two, she returned, clutching a worn cloth doll tightly to her chest. It was clear from how she handled it that the plaything was a treasured item for her. When she sat back in her seat, she set her new friend on a chair nearby. The two of them looked at the priest innocently.

"So," he said in an attempt to broach another subject, "What's your book about?"

"Oh, yeah," she said excitedly as she carefully slid the volume on the table closer to him with her finger. As she retracted her hand, Thorpe noticed that she palmed the box of Lemonheads he'd given her. She picked the box up and immediately tore into the boxes cardboard top.

Thorpe spun the book around by its spine. It was old and tattered in the way a well-loved book should be. The cover was faded and worn, but the image of a young girl looking down from a tower's lofty parapet still remained visible. Thorpe flipped the front cover open with his thumb. He peered at the book's title page and noticed an inscription written in a child-like scrawl: Annabelle Braddock, September 23, 1968.

He was surprised to see that Nurse Braddock had brought the girl the book from home. Giving the child a treasured piece of childhood memorabilia seemed incongruous for the hardened nurse he'd come to know. A moment of weakness, perhaps? Still… it showed that there was a heart beating somewhere within that cold breast of hers; that her compassion, while deeply hidden away, remained strong within her.

"Nurse Braddock gave this to you?"

Heidi nodded as she finished with the candy package top. She plucked one of the hardened yellow orbs out of the box with her fingers and held it to the light. She turned it in her hand like it was a gemstone, its surface covered in a thin, white powder.

Then, with a smile as wide as her face, she popped the canary-colored orb into her mouth. She looked up, moving the hard candy into the pocket of her cheek and sucking on it audibly.

"Ooooo… sour!" She looked at him and her face screwed itself into a wink. When the spasm passed, she continued talking through her contorted features. "She said I might find it app… applic…"

"Applicable?" Thorpe inquired.

The girl smiled and carefully reached over and took her book back with her finger. Once it was back in her hands, she began slowly leafing through its pages, her eyes darting about the text as she smacked loudly on her candy.

"I read it before, but…" she said between candy slurps. "I wanted to read it again. I think it's sad how, even though it's for her own good, she's kept in a prison," she said and her eyes glassed over once more. "Hey, these things are *really* good!"

"Yeah, I thought you'd like them. I like them, too. They're called Lemonheads… see on the box?" he replied. Then, after a moment, "I guess that's why Nurse Braddock thought you might like it…"

The child looked over at him and her expression was puzzled.

"Well," he continued, "in a way, you're a little like the girl in the story, aren't you?"

Heidi continued to look up at him questioningly.

"How so, Father?"

Thorpe allowed his gaze to casually wander the room. While it had been given the appearance of a regular home, there were still things on display that couldn't be ignored:

the electronically locked doors, the multitude of cameras that covered every square inch of the place, the thick glass on all the windows, and that giant one-way mirror. They all betrayed the space for what it really was: a cell.

Thorpe looked at the child in front of him and dimly recalled the conversation he'd had with Nurse Braddock so long ago; the one where he learned the particulars of the kid's unusual birth. Over a dozen people had died before anyone had a clue as to what they were dealing with in regard to the kid. He took another glance around the room. How many more died getting the present protocol in place? And even given all of that, they still were no closer to understanding the girl's condition. The cell… was just them being practical.

"Well, I mean, you've lived here at the hospital since you were born, right?"

"But I'm not a *prisoner*…" she replied over her lozenge.

"But… you also aren't allowed to leave.

She thought about it a while, and then said, "This is my home… It's where the people I love are. It's where people care for me." She waved her hand in dismissal. "I have everything I need here."

Thorpe nodded. "But… have you ever wondered what the world outside was like?"

Heidi looked at the back of her hands for a long time as they rested on the tabletop.

"No. Well, yeah, but… Nurse Braddock says it would be too dangerous for me out there. She said that I would be a hazard to too many people." She looked toward one of the windows at the far side of the room and her focus drifted off as she considered his point. "Out there, with my condition…" She shook her head. "And, until they can figure out what's going on… It's better for everyone that I stay here and study, right?"

Thorpe smiled as he silently considered the child's statement. He marveled at her pragmatism. It was as if she completely understood the danger her very existence posed and had, in her own way, quietly accepted its governance. This was her moving beyond her situation. He wasn't sure they were so different, he and she. He'd accepted the role Death played in his life a long time ago as well, adjusted, and never looked back.

But, then again, he wasn't a seven year old girl.

"And how do you feel about that?"

She looked at him, her brow clenched in confusion.

"Feel? About what?"

Thorpe unbuttoned his jacket and did his best to get comfortable as he teetered on the small chair. As an afterthought, he pulled his jacket closed to hide the shoulder holster and handgun. The last thing he needed was for her to see it... and misunderstand.

"Well, about... this," and he looked around the room. "About living here at Riverview."

Heidi grinned as she started quietly considering the quality of the table's veneer, running the palms of her hands across the tabletop. After coming to her conclusion, she finally looked up at him.

"It's all I've ever known, Father," she stated matter-of-factly. "And so, as a result, I don't question it."

Thorpe gave some thought as to how to put his next question.

"Do you ever get lonely?"

"What do you mean?"

"Well, do you ever wish you had other kids to play with?"

"I have my books... and the television... and my movies. And I have Doctor Sylvester and Nurse Braddock." She looked up at him beatifically and smiled. "...and I have you."

His cell phone suddenly buzzed in his coat pocket, so he got to his feet as he grinned sheepishly at the girl. He retrieved it, glanced at the screen, and then slid it back into its pocket.

"Indeed you do. And now that we've decided that, I'd like to ask you something, a favor..."

Heidi looked up at the priest, her lips still pursed by the tartness of her candy.

"I'd like to keep coming back to visit you like this again, from time to time. Would that be okay with you?"

The little girl considered the proposal for a moment. Then, she looked up at him slyly, "Will you bring me books?"

Thorpe laughed aloud. "I will. I promise… as many as you'd like."

She thought about it for another second, and then, "And more…" she picked up the box of candy and slowly read the label. "Lemonheads?"

Thorpe nodded, a grin deepening the lines in his face.

"Okay," Heidi shrugged and picked up her book and box of candy. She opened it to where she'd left off and began reading to herself.

Thorpe nodded his head, satisfied with the outcome of this first contact. "Okay, then…" He slowly turned and buttoned his jacket. "It was very nice to finally get to spend some time with you, Heidi. I look forward to the next time we can chat."

The girl nodded mechanically, but didn't look up, her curious intellect already having returned to her book and her box of candy. Kids… they were really all the same, weren't they, he thought.

Once more he forced himself to remember the substantial threat she posed.

Thorpe started walking toward the door without another word.

"Hey, Doc…" Thorpe called to the wall. "You wanna let me out?"

As he stood there waiting for the door to open, Heidi ran up to him, skidding to a stop several yards away from him. Thorpe looked back at her.

"Did we forget something?"

She shook her head, but gazed up at him with a gravely important expression on her face.

"I just wanted to… to thank you."

"Thank me?" he asked, taken aback. "For what?"

She nodded. "For being brave enough to come in here." Her face took on that same lonely expression she'd had before. "Sometimes, well… I think even Nurse Braddock is reluctant to come sometimes."

"Forget it, kid," he said jovially. "That's what friends do, right? We risk things for the ones we care about."

"And… you care about me?"

Thorpe winked at her and grinned. "With all of my heart."
A smile exploded over her face like a firework.

"Right!" she said and her tone had returned to her previous happiness. She ran back through the apartment toward her bed. A moment later, the sound of her jumping onto her bed was unmistakable.

Behind him, Thorpe heard the locks on the door release to let him out.

June 25, 2013

Nurse Braddock entered the Observation Room, her arms brimming with file folders and paperwork. A covered travel mug was clutched like a grenade in her fist. Her uniform looked rumpled, slept in, and was a fairly accurate representation of how her day had gone thus far. With reports to proof, daily H & Ps to review, and ever-constricting budgetary proposals to assess, the hours in her last few days had slipped by like the waters of a spring stream.

Now, with the blanket of night lying heavy over the isolated hospital, she came to The Observation Room for a little peace and quiet so that she could go over her paperwork, maybe even catch a few zees, without any interruptions.

As she let the door close behind her, she noticed one of the research assistants—Sam Jones, if she recalled the name correctly—sitting alone in the dark, doing a crossword puzzle on his phone. The light from the device in his hand illuminated his face in ghoulish relief.

"Evening, Ma'am," the young man said from the shadows without looking up.

"Good evening, Sam," Braddock said, her voice sounding congenial, but obviously weary. "How's our little girl doin'?"

Setting her payload of folders and coffee cup down on a tabletop, she pulled the chair out from her desk and sat down.

"She's fine… still awake, in fact."

She looked at him, her face a mixture of confusion and concern. "Still? But it's after two?"

Sam shrugged his shoulders in the gloom. Then, with a

weary sigh, he got to his feet and slowly began putting the books he had laying out on the table into his messenger bag. "Well, Father Thorpe arrived about an hour ago. They've been in there talking ever since."

Nurse Braddock frowned. The priest's visits were increasing as of late to a point that their frequency was becoming hard to ignore. And now, they seemed to include late night chat sessions as well. As the girl had grown up, she and the priest had become more and more attached, with him coming to the hospital on a monthly, if not weekly basis. To visit… and, apparently, to talk. And although Braddock reminded herself that Father Thorpe was a priest, she also reminded herself that he was also a man.

"Why's the room's audio turned down?" she asked.

Sam stuffed a small MP3 player and some headphones into his bag before looking up at her. "Thorpe requested it… said he promised her they could speak off the…" He scratched behind his ear, and then, "off the record."

Braddock walked over to the room's control panel and flipped a switch. She heard the sound of Sam's departure behind her just as the volume came online. The sound of two people quietly talking poured like molasses from the small speakers mounted on the ceiling. Reaching over, she adjusted the tone and contrast of the audio, before returning to her desk. From within the darkened apartment, the sound of Father Thorpe's low comforting tones could faintly be heard.

Father Thorpe lowered his head and rubbed at the corner of his eyes. He'd already had a tough day well before coming to visit Heidi and he needed to sleep, but… he'd promised her that he would come see her, and so… here he was.

A promise was a promise, after all.

The girl adjusted her position ever so slightly in her chair. She lounged across the seat, one leg thrown casually over one arm. Once again, the priest felt his thoughts drift back to that first day when he'd come to Riverview to investigate her. She'd grown a lot in the ensuing years. Now, long blonde hair hung like tapestry and framed an angel's face. Large blue eyes, lit by a fierce intellect, continually roamed the room, taking in and cataloging minutiae like a camera.

Off in the background, the television screen projected the image of an incredulous Tony Curtis as he confronted a silver-haired Richard Chamberlain, goading him into a sword-fight.

"Chamberlain was so good at this kind of stage fighting," Thorpe explained.

Heidi sat up in the chair to scratch her foot. "And you say the guy he's fighting is Jamie Lee Curtis, the girl from *Halloween*'s dad?" she looked dumbfounded. "Huh?"

Thorpe chuckled. "Tony Curtis had a pretty great career in his own right. *Some Like It Hot*... *The Boston Strangler*... *Spartacus*... jeez, *The Defiant Ones*! I'll bring some of his better films the next time I come." He paused as he thought it over. "Also, her mother was a terrific actress as well. *Psycho*... *The Manchurian Candidate*... heck, Welles's *Touch of Evil*! She was, and is, a great actress."

Heidi considered this, and then said with a yawn, "*The Defiant Ones* sounds like something I might like."

Thorpe lazily glanced at his watch and was surprised by how late the hour had grown. They'd talked a lot later than he'd planned. The young girl sitting near (but never too near) him sleepily wiped at the corners of her eyes with the side of her index finger.

"I'm sorry..." he suddenly said and got up in order to collect his things and leave. "I've kept you up far later than I'd intended."

The girl smiled and waved away his concerns with a twirl of her fingers.

"No... don't be silly, Father," she replied, her voice sounding fatigued despite her protestations. She yawned and rubbed the skin of her cheeks with her fingertips to try and rouse herself. "I enjoy our movie nights."

The two of them grinned at one another like kids at a sleepover.

"I know, so do I. It's just that..." he said and yawned, despite himself. "I enjoy your company... and our time together."

The smile on Heidi's face grew broader.

"You have a rare perspective on the world given your..." he sniffed, "shall we say, unique situation?"

The girl felt a soft blush abruptly bring some much-needed color to her cheeks.

"I enjoy our talks as well, Father... I mean, I talk with so few people."

Thorpe stood and he reluctantly collected his overcoat.

"Well, thank you, for once again, for indulging me and for the movie and for talking...

"Thank *you*," she said and she got to her feet to see him out. "Will I see you sometime soon?"

The priest nodded. "I'm traveling all this week, but... I'll come visit when I get back from Rome."

The girl smiled broadly and nodded.

"Ooooh, Rome! Sounds exciting."

The priest laughed. "I'm sure it will be anything but..."

"Bring me something; maybe something to read?"

Thorpe smiled and winked at her as he headed toward the door. "You know it, kid."

December 31, 2019

Dr. Samuel R. Jones was hunched over a pile of his chart notes, feverishly scribbling. Like chicken scratch, small marks became flowing lines of cursive penmanship that only he could read. Stacks of textbooks and composition books were piled haphazardly on a small table nearby. At one point, he looked up to rub at his strained eyes and to gaze through the one-way glass into Heidi Vidraru's apartment.

Jones only dimly remembered the day when he first came to Riverview, probably back when he was doing his internship, and met the remarkable young woman. He remembered Nurse Braddock and her stern warnings and iron-fisted way of doing things. He also remembered the day she retired and handed the keys to the kingdom over to him. He heard through some gossip at a medical seminar that she'd passed a year or so ago. All in all, his memories of her were as a stern, but caring and compassionate administrator.

His quiet reverie was suddenly interrupted by the opening of the Observation Room's door. The sound was a familiar one to him and Sam knew who it was before he ever looked up to see who it was.

The door swung wide to reveal an elderly man standing in the hallway; dressed in black with the small white square of a clerical collar at the base of his throat. He was wiry and thin, but had a look about him like he'd been in a war or something similarly violent. Sam had heard stories about the priest since coming to Riverview, and, to him, all of them seemed a little far-fetched and hard to believe given the frail and sickly man he now saw before him.

"Good evening, Sam," the old guy said, his voice fractured with age.

"Father," Sam replied. "You here just to see me or..."

Thorpe laughed and the sound of it soured into a small, wet-sounding coughing fit. "While I do enjoy your company, Samuel... I have a need to see your guest."

Sam nodded. He knew of the longstanding relationship the priest had with the medical oddity that they had stored in the apartment next door. Even after all these years, even with all of their advanced medical equipment and knowledge, academia was still at a loss to explain the girl or her macabre condition. All anyone knew was... to touch or be touched by the young woman in the next room meant to die instantly.

"I was gonna go meet the pizza guy at the front desk. Anyway, you know the way into the apartment. I won't bother you."

Thorpe bowed his head in acknowledgement. "I appreciate that."

"Cool," Sam commented as he walked out of the Observation Room.

Then, the door shut and the only sound in the room was the labored breathing of the priest.

Thorpe entered the familiar apartment hesitantly, like a burglar, and called out to let Heidi know that he was there. In the years since their first meeting, he'd watched the child grow from a scientific anomaly into an impressive young adult: smart, creative, and, despite her situation, surprisingly funny. She had evolved, year by year, visit by visit, into a beautifully imaginative young woman.

"Hey, Father! I'm happy that you're here. Happy New Year!" he heard her sing-song voice long before he caught sight of her doing something in the kitchen. She was over by the large microwave that was set on the counter. "I was just making some popcorn to watch a movie before ringing in the New Year. Care to *join* me?" Her voice rose an octave to entice him. "Two thousand eight…" Prachya Pinkaew directing… JeeJa Yanin in her first feature role…"

The priest nodded knowingly as he moved deeper into the living room. "*Chocolate* … aka *Chocolate Fighter* aka *Zen—The Warrior Within*. Excellent flick… I'm surprised you'd not seen it."

Over the years, one of the things they discovered about one another was their mutual love of cinema. It was the seed of that common passion that had blossomed into what Heidi called 'their thing.'

"Well, I loved the *Ong-Baks* and *Tom Yum Goong* and wanted to see more of Pinkaew's work; those *ridiculous* tracking shots, man…"

Thorpe smiled to himself with pride and wandered over to where the couch and television were. Not long ago, he'd introduced Asian cinema into their mutual viewing schedule and she'd taken to it like a duck to water. It made him happy to see that initial spark of her interest catch fire and bloom into a real passion. It was further gratifying to see that passion motivate her to branch out into Japanese, Hong Kong, and South Korean films from there. As a result, too many nights had been spent between them talking together into the night and diving deep into the fevered visions of men like Johnny To, Ringo Lam, Tsui Hark, and the great John Woo.

"I also finished that book you gave me. I'll give it to you when you leave," Heidi explained, her voice ricocheting off the kitchen linoleum from the other room. "As you know, I *loved* Yoshikawa's Musashi biography…"

"Aaaand?" he asked, his eyebrow cocked in amusement. He

sat down at his usual spot at the end of the couch with a low groan, rubbing under his arm and wincing.

"I was happy to see that *Taiko* lived up to that brilliance. I thought it was just fantastic!"

She suddenly came bouncing into the room, long blonde hair cascading over her shoulders, carrying two still-steaming bowls of popcorn in her hands. The rich smell of butter hung heavy in the air. He smiled at her warmly and his eyes followed her as she made her way to the couch. Her body moved across the room like a leaf on the wind. She took her seat at the other end of the sofa from him. Both discreetly checked to make sure they were a reasonable (i.e., safe) distance from one another.

She set the two bowls down on a low table that sat in front of the sofa. The two friends talked briefly about their respective days, some reading they'd been doing in a kind of two-person book club, and generally getting settled for the promised movie.

Soon though, their conversation petered out and it was left to them to simply sit together in quiet comfortable silence. Heidi finally got up from her seat and went over to turn the television on. She picked up a Blu-ray that was sitting next to the monitor and held it up for his silent inspection before removing the disc and inserting it into the player. Snatching up the remote, she hit 'Play' on the way back to her seat, aiming the invisible beam casually over her shoulder like a phaser.

Thorpe smiled to himself as he watched her take her seat on the couch, marveling to himself at how quickly time passed. Her motions were concise and fluid, he thought idly, not a lot of wasted movement. She had indeed grown into a remarkable woman, he thought with a distinct sense of paternal pride.

Even with the whole 'touch of death' thing...

Just as she was sitting down, she suddenly stopped and looked at him questioningly. It was clear to her from his demeanor and the expression that was playing out on his face that there was something on his mind; something other than Asian gangster cinema. So, as the opening credits of the film started, Heidi abruptly hit pause on the remote and looked over at Thorpe. Her brow was furrowed and she clearly had something on her mind.

"Okay, Father… what's up with you? You look lousy; like somebody shot your dog or something."

Thorpe gazed at the strong young woman sitting before him and, once again, thought back to the child he'd met in this room so long ago. *So much* had happened; to the both of them. They'd been friends for nearly two decades now and their conversations had always had a gentle flow to them: him patiently guiding her and watching her grow, her forever asking questions about the world outside her small safe space.

He'd come to visit her as much as he could, but, admittedly, it was not as often as he might have liked. His work… always seemed to intrude. But this was an important relationship in the priest's life. One he'd protected over the years. God knew… he didn't have a lot of them. In many ways, this lethal little girl was the only friend he had. And as he looked at her, he silently mused how the same undoubtedly went for her… although for vastly different reasons.

"I've never been able to hide anything from you, have I?" he laughed and his laughter soon turned into a coughing fit. When it subsided, he continued. "Heidi, I need to talk to you about something… need to tell you something …"

He paused and his eyes silently implored her to give him the space to tell it. He momentarily pressed his finger against his throat and winced as if in pain.

Heidi looked over at him. The serious tone of his voice and his obvious discomfort was finally starting to concern her. As she gazed into his eyes, she marveled at the passage of time as well. He'd been a vibrant—and, if she were being honest, a little frightening—man when she'd first met him as a child; a far cry from the frail geriatric now sitting across the couch from her. She blinked at him with concern in her eyes in the half-light.

"What is it, Father?" She smiled at him and the room somehow felt a little bit warmer. "How can I, of *all* people, do anything for you?"

He stared back at her for a moment, beaming. Despite himself, he felt the first of his tears spill over the rim of his eyelids and roll freely down his cheek. Silently, he hated himself for each and every one. The only thing that made it worse was when he noticed the same happen in her eyes as well.

"Father... you're *scaring* me," Heidi pleaded. She drew her legs up and hugged herself tighter.

Thorpe tried to smile for her through his silent grief, but couldn't.

"I... I'm sorry. I don't mean to scare you," he said as he brushed away his tears with the back of his hand. "It's just that... I've never wanted this day to come, but... I knew it would. I've grown old, Heidi. My body... it's not what it once was. My spirit still rages against that good night, but..." He chuckled darkly and gently shook his head. "All those years of wear and tear, well..."

The young woman grinned at him despite herself. Then, she wiped her own tears away with a sniff.

"But Father..." she chastised him, shaking her head in denial. "In all the time I've known you, I mean... You've never even been so much as sick with the flu. I..."

He held up a hand to stop her. This pushback was something he'd expected and had, in fact, planned for. It didn't make it any easier though... He just needed to weather this initial storm of her uncertainty before proceeding with his explanation.

"Please..." he implored as his voice strangled itself on the rope of its own tortured emotion. "This is hard enough as it is."

Heidi shifted in her seat, wrapping her arms even tighter around her knees. It was as if she were using her body as a protective shield against whatever it was that he had to say. It was something she did, he'd noticed in the past, whenever she got nervous or afraid.

"I'm sorry," she whispered sheepishly.

"No," Thorpe implored, "it's I who am sorry, kid. It's just that I... I..." His face hardened as he attempted to gain control over the flurry of emotions. He steeled his nerves and, once he had a grip on himself, he looked at her gravely.

"Father," she asked before he could speak, her voice now sounding genuinely frightened. "What is it?"

He stared into her big eyes and tried to smile as he knew he was about to do the one thing he'd said he'd never do: break her heart.

"Heidi, I'm dying."

The young woman reared back like she'd been struck. She looked around for something to do with herself, more to keep her hands busy than anything else. Finding nothing, she picked up the remote control and fiddled with it nervously. She thought a minute, trying to find exactly the words that she wanted to say. When she'd found them, she smiled up at him and tried to hide her fear by being flippant.

"Aren't we all, Father? I mean, isn't it the nature of Life; to live and to eventually die? Trust me… I know *all* about it; especially the latter." She chuckled to herself, but kept her eyes locked on the image frozen on the plasma screen.

Thorpe nodded and had to admit that she was right. The kid had seen more death in her few years than most doctors… or even soldiers, for that matter. He looked around the apartment and idly thought of how, even with the upgraded security, a lot of people had died over the years keeping this woman alive.

"No, kid… I'm afraid it's different this time; a little more imminent."

Heidi thought it over for a second in silence; like it was a puzzle that she needed to solve.

"Is it… Is it because you've been coming here… to visit me all these years? Was there some kind of residual effect we hadn't considered?"

Thorpe shook his head mournfully, noting how instinctively she took ownership of her situation.

"No… this is something a lot simpler: Non-Hodgkin's Lymphoma. They say four to six months… if they did their math right. I'm told by some very knowledgeable people that I may or may not have been exposed to a lot of strange substances over the years." He chuckled darkly, but still shook his head in his own disbelief. "Let's just say that, for a priest, I've led a less than pious life."

Heidi nodded, but her brow remained furrowed by her considerations. Thorpe noticed more of her tears as they rose up in her eyes like flood water. He sighed softly; somehow feeling worse than he had before when he saw her lower lip sticking out like a bookshelf.

"Heidi..." he began, but any argument he might have mounted immediately lost all of its energy; spiraling into nothingness.

The girl looked at him and shook her head vigorously as the reality of what he was saying slowly became more and more real.

"No... No... No. I need you here," her voice rose with panic. "I need you... to help me."

"To help you?" the priest asked and he closed his eyes, bracing himself for the intensity of her answer.

The dam within her had finally burst and the tears were flowing freely down her cheeks as she wailed and pressed the palms of her hands to the side of her face. It took everything within him—as both a man and as a man of the cloth—to not reach out to comfort her.

"To not be alone; so god *damn* alone! You..." She glared up at him. "You're the only one, Father... the *only* one who comes here... who knows what it's like. You can't leave me! You can't leave me alone. You just can't."

Her tears flowed for some time, even after her words failed her, before they finally slowed to a stop. She sat quietly after that, although her frame remained bent and wracked from the exhaustion of her weeping.

"I'm sorry," was about all Thorpe could muster, so he repeated it like a mantra.

It was only after a few more moments of suffocating silence that the girl finally spoke, looking back up at him with a wry grin, her eyes still glassy from her tears.

"Non-Hodgkin's, eh? Painful."

Thorpe smiled to himself. He'd also expected her to lash out at him like this at some point, at least once, with something cruel; and man, she did not disappoint. Then again, if he were being fair, he didn't exactly blame her. Anyone in her position—born into a world where she would never fit in, constantly and consistently treated as a threat, and denied anything that even remotely resembled human kindness—would feel the same level of isolation, abandonment, and well... betrayal. It didn't take any of the sting out of the words she'd said, but, at least, he understood the place from which they'd come.

"Yes... so I've heard."

Heidi sighed loudly, her breath quivering. "I didn't mean that... it was cruel." She sat up, composed herself, and wiped her face dry. "Unnecessarily so."

Thorpe waved the apology away, preferring to move onto something more constructive. "I've seen to it that the program here at Riverview will remain funded until the time of your passing," Thorpe said, staring at the floor. "If something were to ever happen, I have people in place to take you someplace safe." He held up his hand. "You'll know them by this ring."

"Thank you." They sat staring at the motionless image on the screen for a minute. Then, she turned and looked at him gravely. "I could... I could spare you that pain."

Thorpe snickered morbidly. "That... is not something I'm completely comfortable with. While the sentiment is appreciated, I am, after all, still a man of God."

The young woman chuckled and the sound was constricted and thin. "Father, to be fair... While you and God are in the same general business, from what I can tell, the two of you are definitely not in the same line of work. Not after some of the stories I've heard."

Thorpe nodded and looked embarrassed. He rubbed his nose with the side of his index finger. "Probably true..."

Heidi smiled, but her attention soon drifted off into her own thoughts. "I don't think I've ever asked you, Father..." She abruptly turned to address her friend, "You've said that you've seen many die..."

"Yes."

"Have *you* ever killed?"

They sat together staring deeply into one another's eyes as he weighed the advantages and disadvantages of being truthful.

"Yes," he finally said and his voice was barely a whisper.

Heidi shifted in her seat again, trying to better see his face.

"And yet... you remain, as you say, a man of God?"

"Yes."

"Isn't that gonna make getting past Saint Peter a bit of a problem?"

Thorpe smiled and shrugged. "Perhaps... but one hopes their overall life will be judged by The Father rather than by any individual acts."

Heidi grinned wryly. "Yeah, but, Father... killing? Isn't that one of your guy's Top Ten?"

Thorpe looked at her sideways, narrowing his eyes, but said nothing. "I believe so, yes."

"Like I'm anyone to talk, eh?" She giggled to herself as she spun the remote in her hands like it was a Rubik's Cube. After a moment, she said quietly, "You know that you're special to me, Father."

Thorpe smiled and he fought back a new wave of tears. "As you are to me, kid." He shook his head to clear it. "Look... we still have a bit of time. *I* still have some time. Four months can be a long time, after all. We needn't figure it all out tonight, right? I just thought I should tell you.

"And now, I'd like us, if only for tonight, to forget about it all and..." He paused and nodded his head toward the screen. "Just watch a movie with my friend."

Heidi smiled warmly. "So, movie time."

Thorpe winked through the last of his tears and returned the smile. "Movie time."

Heidi raised the remote and pressed the 'Play' button on it to restart the film. The image on the screen stumbled to life and the two of them sat back to watch the film together.

Thorpe let the images on the screen wash over him and he was grateful for the respite from his maudlin train of thought. As the story began to unfold, without really thinking (and more out of habit than anything else), he reached out and picked up his bowl. He plucked a handful of popcorn and ate it.

When she heard his munching, Heidi did the same.

The film's story, a rollicking revenge saga about a young autistic girl who just happened to be a martial arts savant, unspooled before them and, for a few minutes, things were how they'd always been. Or at least, they were like they were before they'd had their talk. And, for the moment, they were back to just being two friends having a bowl of 'corn and watching a movie... and it was enough.

When he'd finished eating his snack, he set his bowl on the table and sat back. Without really thinking too much about it, he let his hand drop onto the seat of the couch between them; the white skin of his palm pointing upward toward the ceiling.

For a flash, their eyes met, much like they had that first day at the kitchen table when he'd come into the apartment, and an electrically-charged moment hung in the air between them like an accusation. Then, like an idle thought, it passed.

When Heidi finished the contents of her bowl, she set it aside and sat back in her seat, getting comfortable. And for just a few more precious moments, the two of them simply relaxed and basked in the glow of their friendship, each setting aside any previous concerns—no matter how grave—for their mutual love of cinema.

When the film was finally over, Heidi got up and immediately put on another: a classic King Hu production from 1966 called *Come Drink with Me* starring the great Cheng Pei-pei as a young adventurer named Golden Swallow. It was as if the girl was suddenly aware of how brief their time was together, and, as a result, she didn't want to waste any more of that time with tears and protestations of grief. There would be time enough for that later.

At about the midway point in the film, she heard the first of Father Thorpe's snores and she smiled to herself when she saw that he had gone to sleep. He'd done it more and more over the years. Especially as he grew more aged.

By the time the film had ended and Golden Swallow and her band of female warriors were victorious, Heidi had joined him.

January 1, 2020
(the following day)

Dr. Samuel R. Jones arrived for his usual shift at six o'clock as had been his practice for a few years now. He found Riverview as noiseless as an ossuary when he arrived and it took him nearly an hour before he finally discovered Heidi asleep on the couch.

Finding her here wasn't unusual. The girl often fell asleep

on the couch while watching TV. What surprised him was to find Father Thorpe lying next to her. At first, he thought that he too had simply fallen asleep. But it was only after he'd physically tried to wake him that he discovered that he was dead.

What happened wasn't too difficult to figure out. It was pretty clear from the positioning of their bodies that the two of them had been sitting and watching something on TV... and, they'd both fallen asleep. Then, at some point during the night, one of them reached over and took the other one's hand... It was that simple. And that one small act of endearment sealed the priest's fate.

They were still holding hands when Dr. Jones woke the girl.

Her reaction to the priest's death when she woke up was to fall into near catatonia and Dr. Jones left her crying in her room when he left to call his superiors.

The official Cause of Death for Father Thorpe was a Myocardial Infarction with a secondary of Non-Hodgkin's Lymphoma. His death was determined to be from 'natural causes,' despite the circumstances of his body's discovery.

By week's end, all traces of Heidi Vidraru had disappeared from the archives of Riverview Hospital. Some say that the subject of the controversial study was terminated and that all of the research that had been gathered was destroyed. Others say that it was an experiment that was conducted as a part of a secret government program that bred super soldiers for the military and that the woman was moved to another secure location where she works as a contract killer. Still others... say that the girl was taken by friends of the priest and currently lives on a ranch in Montana.

The truth, as usual, lies somewhere in the spaces in between.

DOGWATCH

This little bit of unpleasantness is based on fact. That's not to say that I've personally done any of the things talked about in this story, but… I did go to mortuary school and I have a wife who watches a lot of Food Network, so draw your own conclusions.

The night had already been a long one for Det. Cliff Durbin and Det. George Ross and it didn't look like the bullshit was going to let up any time soon. The hour had already grown late and they'd been at it since six when their phones went off with the news of a break in the case they were all working. They'd been at their respective dinners, but had been forced to leave before their meals arrived.

They were looking into a series of murders that was starting to lead them toward the infamous Mexican cartels, but… It was still too early to tell where it would all lead, but, if the stuff they'd found turned out to be legit, it would provide them with a window into how these guys operated.

The Interrogation Room they'd taken over was small, even by Interrogation Room standards. They'd brought in one of them old, big-tube televisions and a seemingly prehistoric VCR. Next to the TV lay a pile of six or seven worn VHS tapes. A few of them had labels; their inscriptions written in Sharpie with a hasty hand. Others had been left blank.

A stable of empty Styrofoam cups were stacked at the edge of the table where they were sitting. Gum wrappers were piled like hay bales in an otherwise empty ashtray. Both policemen had given up smoking, but shared a common passion for Nicorette gum. The room was painted that flat, toneless gray that was fashionable in institutions back when Ozzie was first dating Harriet. The metal industrial table and chairs completed the scene.

The tapes were the product of a warranted search of one, Gladys Eloise Fuhrman's home. Mrs. Fuhrman was the mother—and presumed accomplice—of wanted torturer and serial killer, James Hughford Fuhrman. Fuhrman was suspected by authorities of hunting, capturing, and murdering a half dozen women in the area and the police were keen to have a word with him.

If they could just find him.

The hope was that these videotapes might offer some clue as to where he was and why he did the awful things he was accused of. So far, they'd only seen a bushel of '70s 'big bush' porn, some early UFC bootlegs, and a female fight tape called "Brawlin' Broads'" or some shit. The few tapes that remained were the ones that were unlabeled and covered in dust.

Ross pulled the last tape they'd looked at out of the VCR and set it aside in the 'viewed' pile. It, much like the others, was useless; just eight hours (with commercials) of some old episodes of USA's "Up All Night" with some squinty-eyed comedian as host. He picked up the next cassette and slid it into the machine and hit Play.

And so it went… Hours bled into hours and the night soon gave way to the first light of dawn. Finally, they were down to the last two tapes and they decided to take a break to order pizza. As they waited for the pie to arrive, they watch the next to last tape which was another bootleg: the 2001 World Series and WrestleMania X-Seven with Stone Cold Steve Austin and The Rock.

As the tape finished up with some old music videos, the pizza arrived and, as they settled in to eat, Durbin picked up the last tape and put it into the player. "This is probably utter bullshit…" he mumbled over a mouthful of food, "just like the rest."

Ross nodded and continued to eat. As he swallowed a bite, he said, "Yeah, well… LT said that we watch 'em all, so…we watch 'em all." He raised his half-eaten slice of pizza in a toast.

"At least, we have munchies."

Durbin hit Play and the tape sputtered to life. At first, Ross thought something was wrong with it. The image was bleached out and grainy. The camera kept moving around drunkenly, before finally settling down.

The scene was of an empty white room. The sound was hollow and every noise echoed against the tile. Everything, from the floor to the counters to the ceiling, appeared to be covered in white porcelain or linoleum. It all looked decidedly medical; like they were shooting in a hospital or clinic.

Suddenly, a man stepped into frame. He was Hispanic, of medium height, and had dark hair that stuck out from beneath his surgical cap like hay. He was wearing scrubs that were several sizes too big for him and wore a thin surgical mask over the lower half of his face. The mask both protected him from germs as well as also hiding his identity. The skin that was visible around the mask was tanned and patinated in sweat.

He stared out from the television screen blankly, but then, his gaze was drawn off-camera by someone or something. He abruptly pulled himself erect, his back straightening stiffly. Clearing his throat, he began speaking in a low, basso voice.

"I'm told that we're recording, so..." He adjusted the hem of his shirt nervously before continuing. "Welcome to this instructional video on Field Dressing the Simiiformes Hominidae. This will be a step-by-step guide on how to reduce this animal's form from the full figure into serviceable cuts of meat.

"Before getting to the task at hand, it must be mentioned that the complete rendering of any animal—especially one this large—requires a large amount of uninterrupted time, a good deal of effort, and enough space in which to work."

Some kind of graphic printed on cheap poster board was moved into frame behind him and the man onscreen took a minute to readjust himself.

"What the fuck is this?" Durbin asked, over a mouthful of pizza.

Ross narrowed his eyes as he did what he could to sort through what he was seeing. He dug deep into his memory to retrieve what he could of his high school Latin for the name, but came up empty. "I don't know... shut up, okay?" he said, and his voice trailed off to nothing as he shook his head in consternation.

The man on the TV screen continued speaking. "If one does not wish to go through the ordeal of processing and storing the bulk of their entire animal, an easy alternative is as follows."

He pointed to the chart and the camera suddenly cut to a close-up of the chart. It was clear that the graphic was of some kind of animal—four-limbed lying on its back with small dotted lines which delineated different portions of its anatomy.

"Simply saw through both legs at the points directly below the groin, along the inguinal line," he continued as he pointed to another part of the graphic, "and again, a few inches above the knee. Once the animal is skinned, these portions may then be cut into round steaks in the client's preferred thickness, cut into fillets, deboned for a roast, or what have you; which means that the meat for several meals is readily obtained without the need for addressing the complexities of the entire form."

The man in white stepped away from his chart and the camera reset.

"Referred to throughout culinary history as 'long pig' and 'hairless goat,' the animal in question is not generally thought of as a staple in, well... most people's diets. Observing the anatomy and skeleton, one can see that the animal is neither built nor bred for its meat, and, as such, will not provide nearly as much flesh as, say, Sus scrofa domesticus or Bos taurus. The large central pelvis and broad shoulder blades also interfere with achieving perfect cuts. But, there are advantages to this however, especially when the typical specimen will weigh between one hundred and two hundred pounds. At that weight, it can be readily manipulated by one person given sufficient leverage and preparation."

"Waaait a second..." Ross said under his breath, his tone sounding concerned. But before he could continue with the thought, the man on the television screen continued speaking.

"The meat of each animal will be of varying quality; it being subject to an enormous range of diseases, infections, chemical imbalances, and a life-long array of bad habits, all typically increasing with age, location, and level of affluence. Also, as the animal ages, its meat loses a lot of its tenderness, elasticity, and pliability; making it tough and chewy."

The man actually used air quotes with his rubber-gloved hands on the last word.

"As a result you will want to select a youthful but physically fit carcass in relative good health." He smiled beneath his mask. "Remember, a certain amount of fat is desirable as 'marbling' can add a flavorful quality to the meat.

"You'll need a large interior space in which to work, with as many large flat surfaces as possible. An overhead winch will be helpful when it comes time to hang the carcass, so make sure you either have one or can gain access to one. You won't regret it.

"Large tubs for waste are an absolute necessity. And, of course, you'll need a reliable water source. You'll be able to do the work with a few simple tools," and the camera cut to a cloth-lined metal tray in which an array of metal instruments gleamed in the half-light, "like a few sharp, clean, long-bladed knives, a cleaver, and a hacksaw."

Durbin leaned forward when he saw someone enter the shot behind the guy onscreen. "Is that what I think it is…?"

Ross looked over at what he was looking at and saw another person—a *different* person also clad in surgical scrubs—wheeling in a long surgical gurney. There was a body of *something* on it, but its bulk was covered by a white hospital sheet. The table was wheeled in and the assistant locked each of the four wheels with the tip of his shoe before leaving. The main guy re-centered himself and continued speaking to the camera.

"How you acquire your meat is up to you. For best results and health though, freshness is imperative. When possible make sure the animal is not given any food for 48 hours to minimize toxins, but allow it plenty of water to flush the tissues. Under ideal conditions, your carcass will be freshly deceased or stunned into unconsciousness by a blow to the center of the forehead or at the back of the skull where the spine meets the skull. Use a mallet or small hammer. Sharp unexpected blows work best. Word of warning: the use of any drugs will distort the flavor of the meat."

"Jesus," Durbin said as he snatched up the telephone on the desk. "Hit pause for a second."

Ross reached over and did as he had been instructed. The image of the man onscreen froze, his finger pointed upward, like he'd just gotten a swell idea.

"Yeah, LT?" Durbin suddenly said, talking into the phone. "I need you to come down here right now." He paused as he listened. "No, now. You're *really* gonna want to see this. Okay." He hung up. "LT coming down. Go ahead. We can run it for him when he gets here."

Ross hit 'Play' again and the onscreen image of the man in scrubs leapt to life. The camera shifted and showed an overhead shot of the table. The corpse beneath was long and multi-limbed, but what it exactly was remained a mystery.

That mystery was soon solved when the man pulled the sheet back with an understated flourish to reveal the body of a young, fairly well-developed man, maybe nineteen or twenty years old. His body was well-defined, but still sort of soft looking, like he'd once maintained an exercise regimen, but it wasn't a passion or anything any longer.

"The first thing you'll want to do is lay the cadaver supine," he continued. "You can raise the carcass up in order to work with it more freely, but you'll want to secure the feet first with a simple loop of rope tied around the feet."

He quickly tied a length of rope around both of the dead man's ankles.

"Then, attach the line to a crossbar or overhead beam via the overhead winch. You can also cut just behind the Achilles tendon and insert a butcher's hook into each ankle for additional hanging support."

He completed each instruction dutifully for the camera and the camera dutifully documented every move and action.

"The legs should be spread apart so that the feet are outside the shoulders. Be careful… the arms will want to hang. Don't worry… we'll get to them in a moment. This open position of the legs provides access to the pelvis, as well as the rest of the trunk. It is suggested to work with the feet slightly above the level of your head. This will go a long way in protecting your back."

Without a word, he started pulling the body up and off of the table using the rope and overhead winch. When he was done, the dead man's body hung upside-down by its feet.

"Is this guy fuckin' serious?" Durbin asked.

His tone had gone grave, but it was clear that he already knew the answer. As the man spoke, he continued following his own instructions; complying with every word he said.

And through it all, the camera's unblinking eye caught it all.

"Place one of the containers beneath the animal's head. You can remove any hair with an electric razor." He picked up a particularly nasty looking knife. "Then, with a long-bladed knife, start at one corner of the jaw and make a deep 'ear-to-ear' cut through the neck and larynx to the opposite side.

"This will sever the internal and external carotid arteries (as well as the jugulars) and musculature of the throat. If the animal is not quite yet dead, this will immediately kill it. But mostly, severing these vessels will allow for the body's blood to drain into the receptacle of your choice.

"After the initial rush of blood (which will undoubtedly come out in a gush) slows, the stream will become more manageable. Drainage can be assisted by soaping and massaging the extremities inward to the center of the trunk; 'milking the tissue.'

"A mature specimen will contain as much as six liters of blood. Have that volume of receptacle available. You don't want to run out of storage space midway through the procedure." He stopped and looked up at the camera. "Also, remember that blood is a pigment and a little goes a long way. For instance, one ounce can, believe it or not, paint an entire room. Be aware of this as you work."

Ross jumped in his chair at the sound of Durbin unceremoniously dropping his slice onto his paper plate. He looked over at the seasoned veteran and noticed that he looked a little green around the gills.

"I'm gonna be sick..." Durbin groaned as he pushed the

greasy plate away from him.

"Once the bleeding slows," the man on the television continued, "you may start preparing for decapitation. Continue the cut around the entirety of the neck, from the jawline to the back of the skull. When all of the muscle and ligaments have been separated, the head can be removed by slicing through the vertebral discs; up at the Foramen Magnum, where the spinal cord meets the skull. The head can then be removed with a quick, sharp twist.

"It's best to utilize this method for dividing the other bones or joints in the body, in that the meat should generally be cut first with a knife, and the exposed bone then separated between the joints with a heavy knife or cleaver.

"I'll leave the merits of keeping the skull as a trophy to you or your client. Know though, that thorough cleaning is difficult due to the enclosed brain mass, which is hard to get to without opening the skull. Don't be too concerned as the brain is not particularly good to eat and may expose the consumer to Creutzfeldt-Jakob or 'Mad Cow Disease.'

"If you do decide to keep it, removing the tongue and eyes, skinning the head, and placing it outside in a wire cage amidst scavengers is advised. The cage will allow foragers to cleanse the flesh from the bones, while preventing it from being carried off by anything larger, such as dogs and birds. After a sufficient period of time, once it looks sufficiently cleaned, you may boil it in a diluted bleach solution to sterilize it and to macerate and wash away any of the remaining tissue."

The door to the interrogation room suddenly opened and the squad's lieutenant came in. The man was tall, blonde, and looked like he might have played varsity football back in high school.

"Okay, so…" the man said, getting right down to business. "What do you think is so important that I need to come down to hold your hands?"

Durbin brought the LT up to speed. The lieutenant grabbed a slice of pizza and munched on it as they replayed the tape. Once they had gotten to where they were before, they sat back and watched the rest of it unfold.

The man on the television screen was, by now, covered

in blood. His arms were solid red up to the elbows and there was a lot of blood splattered across his chest. As he worked, he continued talking.

"After disposing of the head, hose the rest of the body down. This will remove any dirt, substrate, or bodily fluids from the meat. There is no real market for this animal's hide, so removing the skin in a single piece should not be a concern. The skin is in fact a single organ, and, by removing it, you not only expose the muscular configuration, but you also get rid of all body hair and the tiny glands just beneath the skin that produce sweat and oil.

"A short-bladed knife should be used to avoid slicing too deeply into muscle and viscera. Remember that the skin is composed of two layers: an outer thinner derma with a slightly thicker layer below it. When skinning, score the surface first, cutting lightly to ascertain depth. Remove the skin by lifting it up and peeling it back with one hand, like an orange. While doing so, bring the knife in as flat as possible and cut away any and all connective tissue."

"Christ," LT said with a moan. Despite himself, he couldn't take his eyes off the screen.

"Remove all outer components of the external genitals. It's important to leave the anus untouched at this point, and a circle of skin around the sphincter should be left behind. Also, there's no need to skin the hands and feet as these are not worth the effort; unless you plan to dry the meat or use them in a soup.

"The skin can be disposed of by making it into fried rinds. Boil the strips and peel away the outer derma layer, then cut it into smaller pieces and deep fry them in boiling oil until puffy and crisp. Dust with garlic salt, paprika and cayenne pepper."

Durbin shook his head and looked disgusted. "He's thought of everything."

LT ran his hands over his face. "We need to have Forensics go over this tape once we're done here. I want to know everything we can about this thing by morning, okay?"

Durbin nodded and they all returned their attention to the man onscreen.

"The next step is evisceration of the carcass." He turned to better access the dead man's chest. "To begin, make a downward incision from the solar plexus, around the pubis, continuing down almost to the anus. Be very careful not to perforate into the intestines, as this will contaminate the meat with bacteria. If this does occur, wash thoroughly with lots of water. A good way to protect against this when inside the abdominal wall is to use the knife with the blade facing toward you. Remember... go slow."

Ross reached over and shut the tape player off. His face was flushed and he looked like that pizza had turned on him. "I'm sorry, guys..." he said and even his voice sounded a little green. "I need a minute."

"Yeah, me too..." LT added. He looked over at Durbin. "Is this for real?"

Durbin nodded solemnly. "Apparently so." He looked at Ross. "You okay, champ?"

Ross nodded. "It's not going to get any better, is it?"

Durbin laughed and hit Play.

"Make an incision around the anus and tie it off with twine. This will also prevent the body from voiding any contaminated material left in the bowel and ruining the meat. Cut through the center of the pubic bone with a heavy saw. The lower body is now open, and you can begin to remove the organs (large and small intestines, kidneys, liver, stomach); cutting them away from the body."

For the next few minutes, the man onscreen worked in silence, completing each task methodically and sequentially.

"Moving on to the upper torso..." he said as he washed the blood from his hands in a sink on the counter. When he was done, he returned to his work. "Cut through the muscular membrane that divides the thoracic and abdominal cavities. This is called the diaphragm and it's how you get air into your lungs.

"Next, remove the sternum by separating it from the ribs on each side, and detaching it from the collar bone with a saw. Lift the sternum off and that will expose the organs of the upper chest. Cut through the larynx, trachea, and sternocleidomastoid muscle on the sides of the neck. Remove the heart, lungs, liver, etc. Once all of the inner organs have been removed, trim away any remaining connective tissue from the interior of the carcass, and wash it out thoroughly.

"Actual butchering of the carcass can now begin. Carve into the armpit, around the deltoid muscle, straight to the shoulder, and remove the humerus and the forearm from the collar bone and shoulder blade. Remove the hand an inch or so above the wrist. The meat here consists of the biceps and triceps, as the muscle groups are larger here. That said, there is still plenty of meat around the radial and ulna, the two bones of the forearm. Cut into and pull apart the elbow joint. The two halves of the arm are now ready for carving. Remember… these cuts should always be properly cooked before eating."

Ross got up suddenly and walked out of the room.

LT followed him a minute later.

"Okay, so…" the blood-covered man on the television said as he clapped his hands together. "The main body is now ready to be halved. Some will prefer to saw through the spine from buttocks to neck which will leave the muscle fiber encasing the vertebrae at the end of the ribs. Others won't. It's purely a matter of taste.

"Word of caution though… The meat here is tightly wrapped around the bone which makes it kind of hard to get to. Frankly, this meat is tough and more suited (if used at all) to be boiled for stock or soup, so I suggest leaving it. Therefore, My recommendation is to remove the backbone by cutting down either side from the tailbone on through."

"Look how calmly he's acting," Durbin said to no one but the empty chairs. "No matter what he does…" He shook his head. "How many times do you gotta do something like this before you get this comfortable doing it?"

"The halves may now be taken down from the restraints and placed on one of your flat surfaces. Go ahead and slice along the side between rib cage and pelvis.

"Now is the time for you to begin thinking about how you would like to serve the finished meat, as this will determine the style of cuts you will be making. Remember, your cuts will be greatly affected by the muscular configuration of your carcass, so you may need to improvise in this regard."

The camera shifted to a closer angle.

"First, remove the feet about three inches from the ankle. The bones are very thick where the leg connects to the foot, so take your time. You'll want to divide the side of meat into two principal sections: the ribs and shoulder, and the half-pelvis and leg. In between is the 'flank' and belly, which can be used for specialty-cut fillets or steaks.

"Use the back-strap for bacon strips if you wish to cut it thinly. Thin, wide strips may also be rolled, and served as a roast. Trim away any excess fat along the edge of the ribs, keeping some as 'marbling' for added flavor. Remember... fat equals flavor.

"You can now trim away the neck, or leave it connected to the shoulder. The next step is to remove the shoulder blade and the collar bone. Some refer to this area as 'the shoulder girdle' and is made up of the trapezius, deltoids, and the sternocleidomastoid muscles. The best and easiest way we've found is to just cut along the outline of the shoulder blade, along the trapezius, removing the meat on top and then dislocating and separating the large bone. To remove the collar bone, make an incision along its length and then cut and pry it away from the manubrium.

"Depending upon your cadaver's development, you may decide that you want it as a 'brisket.' You can remove it before cutting off the ribs. In the female, the breast is made up mostly of glands for lactation and fatty tissue, and they should be discarded." He clapped his hands again. "On to the ribcage, eh?"

Durbin had had enough. He pretty much knew that the tape would be entered into evidence and gone over, quite literally, like The Zapruder Film. The cop had been on the force for over twenty years and he'd never seen anything like this. He doubted anyone had.

He got up from his seat and walked out of the room, leaving the player running.

Onscreen, the man in the bloody scrubs continued with his macabre work, playing to an empty room.

"The ribs are really the choice cut of this portion of the carcass. A perennial favorite for barbecuing, you can divide the rack into sections of several ribs each and cook them as is or divide the strip in half for shorter ribs. This is where most of the meat is."

The camera racked in for a close-up of the cadaver's legs.

"The lower quadrant," the man continued. "Humans being upright animals, this muscle mass—the legs and rump—is the largest muscle group in the body. Its mass is so large that you can do just about anything with it, but we recommend cutting along the muscle groups which, if you know your anatomy, won't be difficult.

"Refer to your medical charts and, again, go slow. The typical protocol is to remove the leg at the bottom of the buttock, then carve away the bony mass around the knee. Start roughly two to three inches in either direction, on either side of the knee.

"You may now remove the calf muscles—the gastrocnemius and the soleus—from the lower leg. Cut the Calcaneal tendon and remove the meat.

"The upper leg is now ready to be addressed; specifically making round steaks. The rump can be carved from the pelvis in a vaguely triangular piece. Again, check your anatomy charts. The legs attach at the hip at a forward point on the body, so there may be some interference as you carve along the curve of the pelvis (along the Illiac Crest). What remaining meat there is will be on the lower belly, in front of the pelvis.

"And that's basically it. An average home freezer provides plenty of storage space, or you can contract to have the meat smoked. Waste trimmings can be disposed of in a number of ways: burial, ground into animal feed, and pureed to flush, being but a few.

"Bones will become dry and brittle after being baked in an oven and can be pulverized and used as mulch for your garden."

The man stood awkwardly for a moment, his scrubs splashed in blood. Next to him was a pile of perfectly butchered meat, steaks, roasts, and the like. He suddenly reacted as if someone had motioned for him to wrap it all up. His eyes lit up in recognition and he looked into the camera.

"So, this uh… this concludes this lesson. Uh… be careful out there."

The tape continued playing to the empty room until it reached its end. The television abruptly went to snow and white noise filled the room.

A few minutes later, the tape player stopped and shut itself off.

TORCH

*This is another Carpe Noctem piece. I returned to it because, well…
it gave me an excuse to listen to all of the music again. As anyone who
has read my other work can attest, I love jazz and I adore jazz culture
and this allowed me to indulge that. Thematically though, this piece
is about loss, love, grief, and how we carry pieces of people we've lost
with us after they've gone. Tying the two of these together was what
made writing this so much fun.*

> "I get along without you very well
> Of course I do
> Except when soft rains fall
> And drip from leaves, then I recall
> The thrill of being sheltered in your arms."
> —Hoagy Carmichael,
> "I Get Along Without You Very Well"

A cold breeze blows across the expanse of manicured lawn
as I kneel before what has become your earthen bed. The turf
has gone yellow now, like a child's tousled hair, and it partially
obscures the laser-etched granite where your name has been
engraved with a generic simplicity. How often are the markers
for a life extinguished able to hold the perfection of the person
which they commemorate? The smell of flowers slowly turning
beneath the unforgiving rays of the sun curls around me like a
kitten craving affection. As I kneel here, I absentmindedly begin
to tug away the shafts of grass one blade at a time, unexpectedly
dislodging bits of memory with every pull: the night we met
(snap), our first kiss (snap), the first time we made love (snap),

the look on your face when I asked you to be mine forever (SNAP). All of the images torn from the fabric of our shared lives flutter to the ground like remnants of a tattered cloth. Ours was a love forged by our hope, bound in our mutual desire, and consecrated in the fires of our mutual passions. And now, as the days and months without you slip by, I fret over the possibility that one day I might forget the subtle lines and curves of your beautiful face. My heart splinters like sea-sodden wood with every reminder of who you once were as they recede down the cold corridor of memory, becoming more indistinct with every reverberation.

> "There's somebody I'm longin' to see
> I hope that she turns out to be
> Someone who'll watch over me."
> —George Gershwin & Ira Gershwin,
> "Someone to Watch Over Me"

I run my fingertips over your inscription like a blind supplicant who is desperately seeking a glimpse of some immaculate truth. As usual, enlightenment proves elusive. My mind then slips back to the last time I saw you. You'll never know how many times I cursed myself for letting you leave that rainy night. You dismissed my worries regarding the inclement weather saying that you were all right to drive. I can still remember your iridescent smile cutting through the rain like a light warning ships at sea of the terrible dangers that lay ahead of them. I remember how I stood, awestruck by your beauty, held rapt by the glow of your love. I *almost* told you to come back inside and stay the night with me; very nearly begged you to follow me to bed and allow me to kiss the rain from your hair. But I knew how you could be once you set your mind to something. And so, you got behind the wheel of your car and gave me the last of your smiles to keep with me forever. I remember how your eyes shimmered at me with reassurance through the beads of water that peppered the windshield. A lump suddenly arose in my throat as big as a fist as I watched as you drove away. I remember marking the palpable feeling of dread I felt as I watched your taillights grow smaller and dimmer with distance. I've replayed those final moments—*our* final last moments—over and over again in my memory, hoping to command, by the sheer force of my will, a different outcome to the events that ultimately transpired.

"So kick me I won't feel a thing
My senses have been run
And there's nothing left of the used to be
But the weeping that's just begun."
—Nicholas Holmes, "Blue of Blue"

I remember the phone ringing with such urgency that I almost didn't answer it. No good news ever came from a call made that late in the night. It was as if bad news knew to come under the cover of night, like some furtive thief, to steal away your dreams. It was like catastrophe instinctively knew the exact time to best strike at the soul in order to do the most damage. I reached for the receiver and listened in the darkness as the unthinkable became a mind-numbing reality. The subdued voice on the other end of the phone set the scene of a rain-slicked road, a curve freshly graveled, and your car rolling over and over and over again. The soft voice poured its regret into my ear like Claudius's own poison and spoke of emergency measures taken, deliverances denied, and our collective dreams destroyed. Numbly, I hung up the phone and looked at my bed where, just a few short hours ago, you had lay. I realize with a heart-rending certainty that the impression you made there, the warmth of your body left in the folds of bedding, will all soon be pressed out of its fabric; the first of the traces of you that would be gone forever. No, it seems that the only keepsake I will be left to remind me of you will be the weight of my grief, hung like a millstone around my neck, there only to pull me like an anchor ever deeper into the blackness of my despair. I stood by the phone for some time. I couldn't think of what else to do. So, I eventually went back to bed. I remember lying there, staring at the empty canvas of the ceiling, for some time. Having no other ideas, I silently hugged your pillow, smelling the scent of your hair, savoring the pungency of your perfume, and I cried until my eyes could cry no more.

> "My heart is sad and lonely
> I sigh for you
> For you dear only
> Why haven't I seen it
> I'm all for you body and soul."
> —Heyman / Sour / Eyton / Green, "Body and Soul"

The saltiest of my tears still drain from my eyes, unbidden, whenever I pause long enough to sift through the wreckage of our love. And it happens far more frequently than I'd like to admit. But when it does, I often feel like the sole survivor of some impossible plane crash walking stunned and zombie-like through the carnage of my life. Left to forever wander and wonder why I alone was spared. Was it that my life was too perfect with you in it, so God felt the need to impart a lesson in humility? Maybe. Did Fate feel that I had no understanding of the word gratitude and so decided to give me a lesson I would never—could never—forget? Possibly. I curse myself either way for ever taking for granted the time we had together. How precious were those frivolous moments lying in your arms! How golden were the days when I would listen to you as you sang along with the radio in the kitchen? If I had only known how finite our time was to be, I would have done so many things differently. But now, as the remainder of my life stretches out before me like a desolate wasteland, and the prospect of your absence makes itself more fully known, my heart rests shattered like so much brittle glass here upon your grave. I rest my forehead against the dark stone of your marker and my brow is momentarily soothed by the cool of the stone. It's almost as if I can feel your delicate hand caressing my fevered forehead, telling me that as long as I hold you in my heart, you will be with me always... And if you *are* always with me, then everything *will* be okay.

"Save every moment, save every hour
Gone are the golden days we knew
Someone is lonely, in love with the other
And I'm still in love with you."
                    —Gino Vannelli, "Sally
                    (She Says the Sweetest Things)"

CONCRETE ANGELS

This is a piece I did EARLY on in my writing career... even before Carpe Noctem. *The text is super muscly and is rooted in things like 'tough guy fiction' and films like DIRTY HARRY. I decided to take it back out for a spin for this collection to see if I could improve on it and had a delightful ride. Not sure if we'll ever see Det. Secord again, but... never say never, eh?*

The parking lot outside the Quik-N-Save Market on Jackson Boulevard in Middleton, Delaware was in a state of chaos when John Secord, a detective for the Middleton P.D., pulled his dark green Suburban to a stop near one of the parking lot poles. Half a dozen patrol cars sat in a sloppy semi-circle around the front of the convenience store, their doors open, with patrolmen kneeling behind, guns drawn. Emotions were running high and every one of them played out in a dozen different shades across the faces of the men gathered there. Despite their consternation, all of their gazes remained locked onto the front of the store.

There, standing nervously, weaving back and forth like drunken revelers at an all-night dance marathon, were two people: one male standing front to back with a much younger female. The man dragged the girl around with him everywhere he looked, careful to keep his human shield directly in front of him.

This whole scene added up immediately for Secord and he didn't like the sum of it one damn bit. It had already been a long night for the cop and the scene he saw before him didn't look like it was gonna get resolved any time soon.

With a weary sigh, Secord casually stepped out from his

vehicle, drew his weapon, and secreted it along the side of his right leg. He walked silently through the line of cars and patrolmen without ever once taking his eyes off his newly acquired target. Without hesitation, he strolled into the open area between the phalanx of cops and cars and the front of the store.

"Get away from me!" the kid screamed as he held a small .22 caliber pistol to the girl's shaking head.

The girl was young, attractive, and, by the frantic look in her eyes, pretty fuckin' scared. Her long blonde hair hung in sweaty strands in front of her face and Secord could see her petrified blue eyes peering out; like some terrified neighbor peeking through vertical blinds. She strained to pull her head as far as her neck would allow away from the gun barrel pressed painfully to her temple. Thin cords bulged out from the soft flesh of her throat. Her every feature was stretched to a Dali-esque mask by her fear. Secord was shocked she hadn't passed out.

The kid continued holding her tightly, protecting himself from any sharpshooter's crosshairs with the bulk of her trembling body. The panic musk coming off of his body made her feel greasy and dirty.

"Help me..." she whispered softly.

"Shut the fuck up, Bitch!" the kid screamed into her ear. As punctuation or punishment, he pressed the gun's barrel painfully against her temple.

The girl could do little else but wince fearfully.

Secord, a large Swedish bear of a man, judged the boy to be in his late teens—clearly a junkie—with sweat-slicked hair and *angry* red skin; out for some fast cash. He had probably been hopped up on one thing or another and had miscalculated the swiftness of the initial police unit's response time. And by the time he figured it out, it was too late. Whatever buzz he had abandoned him a long time ago. And now, there was only adrenaline coursing through his bloodstream like electricity.

As he approached, Secord made note of the pearls of perspiration beading on the kid's tense, oily brow from over the sight of the his now raised-and-aimed Smith and Wesson. The pistol was not exactly "standard issue;" not at .40 caliber and capable of delivering rounds that kicked like a mule, but on the streets you learned to improvise. It was a heavy and damn unsightly weapon, but it would stop a rhino at full charge and could punch a hole the size of your fist through a human's chest... if you ever needed one punched.

The weapon was, to be sure, the motto of the Round Table in action: "Adapt, adopt, and improve."

"Listen, go ahead and kill her," Secord said as he ran the stubby set of fingers on his free hand through his flat top.

The girl's expression fell and it damn near broke his heart. In the moment, he wished he was someplace—anyplace—else: watching a ball game, maybe having a quiet drink... But he somehow knew that was not going to be in the cards any time soon tonight. Not with the way this punk was acting.

"But know one thing, pal, you off her and there's not a damn thing standing between you and me." He pulled the heavy hammer back on the bazooka he called a handgun. "Now, the way I see it, you only have two choices," he continued as calm as if he were ordering a pizza. "Give it up and let her go or cash it in."

"Keep the fuck back!!!" the boy screeched, his voice rose into its upper registers as the finger resting on the .22's trigger clenched incrementally tighter.

Secord knew he was running out of time, so he inched imperceptibly closer. He'd never been good at subtlety, not at six foot six and two hundred and fifty pounds, but this clown was getting desperate and that alone made him think that some drastic action was needed on his part. It was only now beginning to dawn on the kid that his position was hopeless and there was no way for him to back himself out of this jam safely.

Secord knew that if he didn't drop him soon, he'd have another mess like the one he'd had at the Civic Center six months ago. He'd waited too long on that one as well; went too much by the book. There were still stains on the marble floor down there to remind him of his lapse in judgment... should he ever *need* a reminder. It was the memory of that day and the lives that were lost that drove him forward now.

"I can give you my personal guarantee that nothing will

happen to you, man, if you just let her go. Hell, I'll escort you outta here myself and even do my best to get you a 'Get Outta Jail Free' card." Secord smiled his warmest smile and took another small step forward.

The tall Swede relaxed, biding his time now that he had come to within twenty yards of his target. Now that the shot wasn't questionable any longer, he only waited to see enough of the kid's skull for a placement. "Just let the girl go and it'll *all* be ok."

"Get the fuck back, God damn it!!" the kid screamed and leaned out away from the blonde to get a look at Secord; just a little, just enough. "I said, get ba—"

THOOOOOM!!!

The .40 cal. roared and the right side of the kid's skull exploded in a fireworks pop of blood and bone. The three hundred grain slug tore through the kid's head like a cannonball through a paper kite. His right eye blew out intact, hit the ground, and rolled to a stop a dozen feet from Secord; an offering for forgiveness arriving a little too late.

The young girl, her ears ringing, dropped to the ground the second she felt the hold on her tense and release. She scrambled to the left, her face and hair slick with her abductor's spent bone and gray matter. She spit a substance she didn't want to identify from her mouth, found her voice, and started screaming.

In the scant milliseconds it took for the slide on the Smith and Wesson to recoil and chamber another round, Secord took the time to stare at the still-standing kid and wonder what the hell was keeping him on his feet. Half of his brain was splattered across the parking lot like the aftermath of a smoker's early morning spittin' contest and still he stood. Oh, well, Secord thought, time for that drink and he squeezed the trigger and let a bullet wipe away what was left of the kid's dumbfounded expression.

"Sit down!" Secord ordered as he lowered the still-smoking gun.

The kid was slapped flat like a shooting gallery target. A last bit of skull and hair sailed through the air like a Frisbee in a high wind. The wet divot hit the convenience store window with a sickening 'thwap,' and then, slid down to the concrete, leaving a glistening smear in its wake.

Secord approached the kid's body as it lay on the concrete. As blood poured from his shattered head onto the pavement, an image of a child making snow angels flashed before the detective's mind's eye. A crimson halo grew to complete the image. Secord shook his head sadly as he holstered his still warm weapon.

He walked over to the cowering girl curled up on the ground, his shadow from the street lamps covering her like a cloak. She looked up at him with eyes no one that young should ever have. The dam broke and she descended into hysterics.

After a few minutes, she settled down and he tried to get her to talk.

"You gonna be OK?" Secord said in a quiet, measured tone.

"I-I think so," her voice came out squeaking between jags of heavy sobbing.

"If that's your answer… you are," he said as he extended his massive hand and quietly beckoned her to take it, "Let's get you home, ok?"

The frightened girl looked up at him and slowly reached out her hand to him. She took his hand and allowed the Swede's strength to lift her to her feet.

"What's your name, little girl?"

"Mary… Mary Walker," she responded and emotion twisted her voice like putty.

"Well, Mary, I think we've both had enough excitement for one night," he said as he took his coat off and wrapped it around her shoulders.

She accepted his kindness and even leaned against him, allowing him to wipe away some of the sticky material which still coated the side of her face.

"Say, Mary," he said looking up at the moon, "I know this is gonna sound odd given the situation, but… I could really use a drink and I hear there's a Yankee's game on. Care to join me?"

The girl looked up at the Swede, but then, looked at the chaotic scene around her.

Despite herself, she cracked a wry smile. "Yeah… okay."

NEVER MY LOVE

This is the last piece written for this collection. I had the entire book locked down, reviewed by Beta Readers, and ready to go. But then, my brain kicked in and the story pretty much leapt onto the page; complete and fully formed. The title comes from a song by a group called The Association, a 1960's era folk rock band that had a string of hits like "Cherish" and "Windy." I'm hopeful that this tale sticks its landing in a satisfying way. You let me know if it does, okay?

Paula Randall was startled when the front door of the apartment burst open. She laughed and shook her head at her own jumpiness as she wheeled herself across the small, haphazardly-kept living room toward the door. Piles of laundry that had been left to be folded lay across the seat of the recliner sitting in front of the TV. There was a large space left open next to the vinyl-clad chair for her and her wheelchair. Her and her boyfriend, Gordon Winfield, spent a lot of time there, watching their shows, embroiling themselves in the lives of others, and living adventures they'd never encounter in real life.

Gordon came stomping onto the linoleum foyer from outside, flurries of snow followed him in the door like vapor. He was dressed for the Iditarod, bound head to toe in either wool, fur, or rubber. In his hands were several bags of groceries, the fruits of his polar excursion. His eyes behind his glasses lit up over his ski mask the moment he saw her sitting near the kitchen and waiting for him.

"He', Bab'," he mumbled through the scarf he had drawn around the lower half of his face. He set the plastic bags on the small dinette table in the space they called The Dining Room, but it was really just an open area that was flanked on all sides by the kitchen, foyer, and living room. "Col' ou'." He stood a second and shook as much of the snow and ice as he could from his shoulders. Clumps of white powder fell to the carpet and instantly melted.

Paula tried to smile, but her sense of concern finally won out.

"I was so afraid," she said in an anxious tone. "You're *so* late…"

Gordon tugged the scarf and ski mask from his face.

"I'm so sorry, honey… I tried to hurry, but…" he groaned and looked back at the front door for corroboration. "The snow…"

Paula shrugged and it looked like the small gesture stole the last of her energy.

"I know," she pouted. "I was just scared."

Not really thinking or caring about the melting snow covering his jacket, Gordon rushed over to her and knelt down beside her. He put his arms around her gently and hugged the air around her. He was well aware of the fact that Paula was sensitive to touch and that she hadn't been able to walk since she was eight or so. She'd told him many times all about how difficult it had been for her as a kid.

Paula and Gordon met during one of her visits to her doctor. Gordon worked in Billing at the clinic and they'd met and been able to talk during one of her many visits. She sensed in him a sympathetic ear and someone who'd listen—really listen—to her when she talked. And she'd been right. All too soon, they both leaned into the relationship and fell completely in love. And the rest, as they say, was history.

"Gordy," she whined as she pushed him away weakly. "You're getting water everywhere."

He pulled back and acted like he was embarrassed.

"Oh shoot, sorry, babe…" he said as he stood and stripped off the rest of his layers. "I picked up some milk, bread, eggs… a couple of sticks of butter. Oh, and some of those powdered doughnuts you like so much."

She smiled up at him and scooted her chair back, giving him room to carry the bags into the kitchen.

Gordon carried the grocery bags to the counter and started unpacking the things that he'd bought. He dutifully put the jug of milk and two yellow bars of butter into the fridge. The loaf of bread and bag of doughnuts, he left on the counter. He stuck his hand back into the bag like a magician who was about to pull a rabbit out of a silk hat.

"I also found this…" he said with a smile.

He pulled a flat, cellophane wrapped tray from the bag and his presentation implied a silent 'ta-dah!' A thin slab of meat lay on a Styrofoam tray that had been wrapped in clear cling film.

Paula smiled and wheeled herself closer.

"Is that *Italian* Sausage?" she asked and her voice had almost a sense of wonder to it. "Gordy… you shouldn't have. We can't affor… It's so expensive."

Gordon held the wrapped cut of meat up for her to see. He smiled brightly at her and he pointed with one finger at the large, red '70% off' sticker. His eyebrows danced in appreciation of his own frugalness.

Paula smiled and rolled her chair back to her spot in front of the television. She turned up the sound and voices began pouring like syrup from the speakers. On the screen, a man in a green hood stood on a rooftop aiming a bow and arrow at a villain.

"Is that last week's episode or this week's?" Gordon asked as he went about washing his hands before cooking. After toweling them dry, he started pulling pots and pans from the cabinets and set about cooking their dinner. "Hey, I hope you're not watching ahead."

Paula laughed and shook her head. "You remember… I fell asleep because of my medication last week. I missed the end of the episode, so… I just wanted to get caught up before we watch the new one when it comes on later."

Gordon nodded while he filled a large pot with water. When it was full, he set it on the stove and threw in a handful of spaghetti from the cupboard. Picking up another pot, he poured a jar of Ragu he also had in the cupboard into it and put it on a burner to heat. Finally, he retrieved a skillet in order to heat up the sausages.

Paula sat watching her show for a minute, but then, she reached over for the remote and turned the sound down. She moved her chair so that she could see Gordon as he worked in the kitchen.

"You know," she said in a tone that was designed to sound congenial, "I was about to start calling to the police... or the hospitals to see if you were dead. I was so worried."

The loud clatter of Gordon putting the stainless steel lid on the pot of boiling water was heard from the kitchen. Gordon poked his head around the corner a moment later.

"What's that, honey?" he asked with his usual empathetic grin.

A look of being annoyed passed over Paula's face and she moved herself closer to the kitchen door, so she didn't have to yell to be heard by him.

"I said that I was about to start calling the police... or the hospitals. I was so worried when you took so long at the store."

Gordon set the dishrag in his hand down and went back over to kneel near the love of his life. He smiled broadly at her as he rested one hand on her forearm.

"I know, honey... and I'm super sorry," he said as his eyebrows lifted in sympathy. "The traffic was so bad... and the snow... I wanted to get home to you safe, so I took a little extra time, went a different way because I thought it would be quicker. I was wrong and I'm sorry that it took so long..."

She halfheartedly waved his excuses away even as she was sure to make the effort look grueling. Rationally, she trusted the veracity of his story, knew he would never—*could* never— do anything to jeopardize their relationship; much less do something like cheat on her. She just wanted him near her, to help her, to care for her, should she need something. In her condition, she told herself many times, it was bad for her to ever be alone and uncared for.

"Look," he finally said as he kissed her on the forehead. "I should have planned better... I should have taken a more direct route home... I just wanted to make it back to my baby safely."

She nodded and suddenly felt a little foolish. She was well aware of everything he'd said, but... She loved him and couldn't bear the idea of anything ever happening to him. How would she ever deal with something like that? Who would take care of her?

She looked up in time to see that her episode was ending. A sudden sense of sadness embraced her as she realized she missed how the show ended once again.

She shrugged and decided it was okay... Gordon was home now, thank the Lord, and he would make sure to explain it all to her before tonight's episode. She often fell asleep as a result of her medication. Bringing her up to speed on her programs was just one more thing he did to make her difficult life that much more livable.

She settled into the seat of her chair and waited for him to finish making them their spaghetti.

Gordon pulled the thin blanket and sheet back from the hospital bed that was set in the middle of the bedroom. His bed, a small, child's twin, was set in one corner next to a wooden dresser and a bookcase. The rest of the room was dominated by Paula's things and by her ever present bed.

Paula wheeled herself into the room and rolled over to the side of her bed. There she sat, arranging and rearranging the numerous pill bottles on her nightstand, and patiently waited for Gordon to finish getting himself ready for bed.

Gordon stood at the sink as he started brushing his teeth and washing his face. The warm water felt good as it splashed over his face, its heat urging a reddish bloom from his cheeks.

"Thank you for going to the store, Gordon," Paula called from the other room. "And I'm sorry I worried... You're such a good man, Gordy... you take such good care of me."

Gordon came out of the bathroom, water still dripping from his chin, and he walked over to her. Drying off his forehead and eyes, he bent over and kissed her ardently.

"I love you, Paula..." he said warmly. "You know I'd do anything for you."

Paula nodded and smiled up at him.

He kissed her again gently on the lips.

"I love you too, honey," she said and her face took on a familiar coquettish nature. She grinned up at him demurely.

"I'm so lucky to have you here to take care of me."

He smiled broadly at her as he walked back toward the bathroom.

"I'll be right back, okay..." he said in his little boy's voice. "I need to tinkle before bed."

Gordon partially closed the bathroom door and opened his underwear so that he could pee. Taking himself out, he sighed in relief as a stream of urine splashed into the toilet water and against the porcelain.

Standing there contentedly, he let his mind reel back to when he had first met Paula. In reality, it had been his first relationship after a lifetime of celibacy. When they met, he found Paula to be smart, nice, and into the same things he was: media, genre, and board games. He'd tried *so hard* to impress her. The fact that she was unable to walk never really entered his mind.

And beggars couldn't exactly be choosers, he remembered thinking at the time.

The stream of urine slowed, and soon, it was just drops left. He sighed and the sound was hollow in the small tiled room. As he was putting himself away, he looked up at the mirror and noticed how it gave a clear view of the side of Paula's bed. And as he washed his hands before leaving the bathroom, he watched as Paula set the brake on her chair. She fussed with the front foot pads for a second, and then she stood up. Drying his hands, he watched her as she walked from the chair to the bed. Once she was lying down in the bed, she bent over, and pulled the bedding up and over her legs.

Gordon returned from the bathroom and went over to the side of Paula's bed. He pulled the covers up to her chin and kissed her gently on the cheek. Smiling at her, he brushed a few strands of hair away from her forehead.

"All snug as a bug in a rug?" he said and his eyes looked watery in the low light.

Paula sank even deeper into her pillow and she too smiled, her heart brimming with love for this man who'd dedicated his time and energies to caring for her. She couldn't imagine the state of her life if she had not found him. He was, quite literally, someone who had saved her life.

"I love you, Gordon," she said warmly.

Gordon stood up and went over to shut the overhead light off. He looked over at her, the one person he loved more than anything, and wanted to remember how beautiful she was in that moment for the rest of his life.

Smiling broadly, he blew her a kiss and shut off the light.

"I love you, too…" he said to the darkness.

STANDING TALL

This was originally a piece I did for submission, but I failed to find the right market for it. I wanted to play with subtlety and with telekinesis and this tale is what I came up with. I like the gentle repartee between the two main characters. I hope I got Jeff's mindset right. If not, then again... mea culpa.

A warm wind blows through the towering alder trees of the small community park, spinning the few kites that circle in the air like vultures scanning the savanna for carrion. Groups of families gather around chained and padlocked picnic tables and noisily discuss the latest happenings in the oftentimes soap operatic events that make up their lives. The excited screams of children erupt like flowers from the picnic sites and playgrounds.

On the worn field at the far end of the park, a pickup soccer game is being pulled together; various kids and a few adults all vie for a spot on either team. On the benches behind the dugout, the player's spouses, parents, and siblings sit and chit-chat with one another as they covertly drink from the tops of brown paper-covered cans.

Beneath a sprawling willow tree nearby is a tan-bark covered play area where a dozen toddlers run around playing the games that only the truly innocent can understand. On a stretch of grass nearby, several barely school-aged children kick a soccer ball around, miniature imitations of the older kids playing nearby.

Across the playing field, under some thinly-leaved trees, the small, withered form of a boy sits in a large motorized wheelchair, quietly observing the tableau going on around him. The boy watches as the agile players run and shout, kicking the ball back and forth between them. He idly wonders what that rush of physical competition must feel like; the thrill of the exertion, the pounding of his blood through muscles that were strong and confident. He'd been placed into his chair long before he could offer an opinion about it, a victim of a well-known (and annually popularized) muscular disorder, and knew, as well as he knew his own name, that he would remain there until he kept his all-too premature appointment with Death.

The wind stirs and reaches out to gently tousle his hair, as if it too thinks of him as something too fragile to touch and does not wish to harm him. The boy breathes in the cool air and catches a hint of acrid wood smoke wafting in from the barbecues on the south side of the park. His mouth waters as the pungent smell of cooking meat and barbecue sauce coats his tongue and nostrils like morning dew.

A shout erupts from the playing field, punctuating an errant kick that sends the game ball sailing over the goal. The sphere bounces toward the disabled boy sitting under his tree, rolling to a stop just a few feet from one of the large rear wheels on his chair. A player breaks away from the group on the field and runs over to where the ball lies. He stoops to pick the weathered, black-and-white checkered ball up. And as he gets back to his feet, he notices the small figure in the chair sitting quietly in the shade.

"Hey," the athlete says and does everything he can *not* to look at the gleaming metal and chrome of the wheelchair.

"Hey," the boy in the chair replies, his voice cracking from its lack of use.

"I've seen you here before," the soccer player says. Then, he asks, "Haven't I?"

"Yeah, I come here pretty much every day," the thin child in the chair replies and does what he can to adjust himself on the leather pad on which he sits so that he might appear taller. "My mom says the fresh air will do me good," and he gives a small eye roll to puncture the sentiment.

"Yeah..." is all the standing boy can think of to say; his

nervousness being all too apparent.

"Yeah…" and the invalid boy watches as the young Pele squirms in his sneakers as he formulates his next question.

"So…what happened?" A pause, then a nod in the chair's direction.

The boy in the chair stares up at him blankly. No one had ever just asked him so plainly, so innocently, so without malice, about it before. Usually, it was the boy's habit to watch them as they searched for comfortable answers, all while being crushed under the weight of their euphemisms, drowned by their own self-imposed sympathies. The frail boy hated it when they came to him with those pasted-on smiles and that empty-headed 'wokeness.' To him, it was all so infuriating. The boy looks at the other child and smiles, "You ever hear of Jerry's kids?"

The boy with the ball thinks about it for a second. He dimly remembers his grandmother talking about some show full of old people that was on TV for sick kids every year just before school started. Somewhere… there was the name 'Jerry' attached to that memory.

"Yeah…"

"Well, I'm one of them."

The soccer player looks at the atrophied legs and spindly arms of the other and, just for a moment, tries to imagine what being in such a thing might be like. He opens his eyes and shakes his head. "Wow… that's messed up."

"Yeah… it is."

A nod. "I'm Mark."

A smile. "Jeff. So, you like soccer, eh?"

The young athlete looks down at the ball in his hands and nods.

The two of them stand awkwardly together for a moment, as they both searched for another—*different*—topic of discussion. They are interrupted by a shout that comes from the playing field behind them.

"Hey Mark! You gonna keep playin' or what?" an older kid in a Metallica shirt calls. "If not, kick the ball back over here, okay?"

Mark turns back to Jeff and, looking suddenly embarrassed,

says, "Uh, I have to go."

"Yeah," Jeff says. "I sorta figured."

Mark stands for a second and searches for the words that he wants to say next. "But hey… if you're around here later, I'll come back and we can talk."

"Cool," Jeff replies softly.

"Cool!" and a broad, genuine smile spreads across Mark's face. He turns and runs back toward his game. Along the way, he expertly kicks the ball back and forth between his feet before passing it off to one of the other kids on his team.

Jeff watches Mark as he runs back to his game and remembers other days when the children who approached him were far less kind than this boy had just been. Their questions often had more of an edge; their comments cutting him like ragged glass.

"Are you a cripple?" they'd say.

"Wow, you look we-e-eird!"

He'd cried himself to sleep on more lonely nights than he could remember, wishing he had someone he could talk to about it all; someone he could trust. Just one person to show him that there were indeed good people out there in the world. And, in the end, all he ever really wanted was to have someone to talk *with* rather than someone to be pitied *by*. Someone to care, y'know? Mom cared. But, that was different. Dad didn't; he'd left soon after Jeff had been born. Mom told him that the divorce wasn't his fault, but Jeff knew different.

He continues to sit under his tree and watch as Mark goes on with his soccer game. Mark is a good player who always seems to be where the ball is going rather than chasing after where it had already been. Even Jeff was able to see that much…

After a minute, Jeff looks down at the ground in front of him and notices a rock about the size of his fist resting on the ground. He slowly looks back to the game in time to see his new friend kick the ball through the goal and score a point. Jeff smiles when he sees Mark nod his head at him while his teammates slap him on the back.

Looking back toward the ground, Jeff focuses his attention back on the rock. Once more, he carefully checks around him to see if anyone is watching, and, once secure that the coast is clear, he focuses his attention back on the center of the stone.

As he had done so many times in the past, Jeff calms all of his thoughts and concentrates on nothing... nothing but the rock. Silently, he contemplates its size, its weight, its density, even the look and imagined feel of its surface. When he finally has a crystal clear vision of it, he pauses, then he pushes, just a little, with his mind. Almost imperceptibly the rock wiggles on the ground, not much, only barely. Seeing this, Jeff knows that the necessary connection has been made. Then, he pushes again, harder this time, and the rock moves more dramatically this time; so much so that Jeff is compelled to look around to make sure no one has noticed. Convinced he is in the clear, he returns his attention back to the stone that is still rocking on the ground.

He nudges it again to verify that he still has the connection, and then, he pours his focus beneath it, like water. Slowly, he lets a little of what his mother has called 'his gift' off its leash and the stone leaps several feet into the air. The orb hangs there and spins around slowly in the air. And just as he is about to push harder...

"Hey," a sudden shout from his left, "What happened to *you*?" A young girl, about the same age as his younger sister, comes into view from under the trees by the playground. "Man, it must *suck* to be you!" she cackles before running off.

Jeff watches her as she crosses the field to rejoin her friends. When she is gone, he looks back to the rock and frowns. A small cloud of dust is just settling around it; the result of its falling from his 'grasp.' The boy stares intently at the stone, hearing the girl and her infuriating taunts still echoing in his mind's ear. Gently, he nudges the rock once again and watches as it rocks back and forth; almost as if it were dancing. He pushes it again, fast and hard, and, with a subdued, crunching sound, the rock fractures and is reduced to sand.

Jeff looks back to the playing field and sees that the soccer game has begun to break up. He watches Mark as he collects his things. Unbelievably, the boy begins to walk back in Jeff's direction as he raises his hand in greeting. A bright smile lights up his face.

Maybe this kid really *does* want to be a friend, Jeff thought as he tried to temper his excitement with his usual splash of pessimism.

Jeff's gaze travels from Mark's approach to where the girl was just laughing with her friends. He watches for a second as the girl proceeds to boss the other kids in her group around, forcing them all to adhere to her idea of what they should be doing. He sees the way the other children look at her and can tell that she isn't well liked; not at all. He lowers his gaze and winds up focusing on the pile of rubble that had, a few minutes ago, been his rock.

Surreptitiously, he smiles to himself.

"Hey Jeff," Mark calls out, interrupting his train of thought.

As the disabled boy lifts his head to greet this new acquaintance, he pushes the button on his chair's armrest, sending his motorized chair in the direction of, what could just be, his very first friend.

FOR DUST THOU ART

Another Pre-Carpe Noctem concept... I like this one because it prompted me to think about the life of a serial killer who truly believed he was Death. I took this out for a spin for CN, but... then, things got busy and the idea languished. I finally picked it back up this past year and retooled it a bit for this collection.

"It is old age, rather than death, that is to be contrasted with life. Old age is life's parody, whereas death transforms life into a destiny: in a way it preserves it by giving it the absolute dimension. Death does away with time."

—Simone de Beauvoir

Death stood in the small, cramped bathroom of a Lower East Side tenement apartment. He stared solemnly at his reflection in the cracked mirror that was hung like a Calvary Prophet from some bent and rusting nails. The lens reflected the face of a tired traveler; one that was in search of refuge from the torrential storm of the spirit within the confines of the chipped and tarnished frame. His deep-set, blue eyes were rimmed with streaks of red that resembled shafts of crimson lightning shooting across a pale yellow-white sky. He smiled at his slivered image in the mirror, his expression a contradiction made flesh, and his too red lips crawled back to expose long white teeth filed sharp. He slowly ran his fingers through his thick, dyed-black hair as he carefully continued to appraise his bone structure in his reflection. High cheeks, which give a look of aristocracy in others, make his features appear skeletal and drawn. The spider web displacement of the glass fragments his image into a hundred pairs of eyes which all stare back at him accusingly.

Mirrors have, for as long as he could recall, held a deep fascination for him. They were like silent, all-seeing witnesses to what he considered to be 'his work.' In the past, he'd always tried to catch reflected glimpses of his magnanimity in the eyes of the people he had visited, but was always somehow denied. He found the mirrors after that... and the darkly-compelling secrets they held.

Now, staring as deeply into this one as he was, he tried to remember a time when he was not who he was; not *what* he is. He distantly recalled spending long summer days running in fields of golden wheat, the sun beating oppressively down atop his young blond head. The memory, however, could well have been stolen from one of the many lives he'd claimed. And he'd claimed many over the years. Lives like forgotten birthday candles that had been allowed to burn on past their time. He blew out his lungful of air. No. He had always been Death and would always *be* Death. And that's just how the world worked.

Looking away from the glass and all of its implications, he unzipped his pants and urinated into the sediment and soap scum-stained sink. He sighed softly to himself as he emptied his bladder. Once he was finished, he closed his trousers and turned to leave. As he stepped from the dark, neglected bathroom, he stopped and looked over his shoulder at the mirror once more. He saw his reflection standing in the doorway. His image told him everything that he needed to do next.

Death walked out of the bath into the main—and only— room of the stranger's apartment. He stopped and stood, surveying the aftermath of his inspired handiwork. The décor of the room was Early American Squalor which seemed to have suited the occupant just fine. A man in his forties—Samuel Joseph Anderson according to a driver's license discovered in a wallet—lay draped across the day bed. Heavyset and graying, Sam looked like a man who'd had a pretty rough time of it; existence-wise. It also appeared that he'd had an even tougher time of it rather recently. His eyes were visible through his sweaty hair and were closed. His arms lay outstretched as if he was in the middle of a dream in which he was an eagle soaring the warm thermals of the desert sky. The walls of the room were splashed red with heavy arterial spray; an Impressionist's attempt at conveying the trite and tawdry emotion of bloodlust. Once-white sheets are now dyed a deep maroon. The sticky fabric lays glued to the corpulent form which now lay beached and abandoned upon the shore of the bed. Silver glints from the exposed handle of an enormous Buck knife deeply embedded in the man's now-still back. The stench of mildew, sweat, urine, and—the sweetest of aromas to Death's nose—fear, permeates the room and hangs in the air like a corrupt cloud. And through it all, Death simply stood there still, smiling, and approving of all that he saw.

"The darkness of death is like the evening twilight; it makes all objects appear more lovely to the dying."

—Jean Paul

"Well, Sammy Boy...what d'ya think? Transformative, isn't it?" Death asked aloud of his silent host. He sat at the foot of the man in his bed, his hands crossed demurely across his lap. "Happier now? The trials and tribulations of existence don't seem like such a pressing concern any longer, eh?" He sighed. "Hell, even that nagging, smoker's cough you had is gone." Absentmindedly, he reached out and meticulously adjusted a corner of the bed sheet so that it lay flat. "Now, you have only to rest, Sammy...rest and dream."

A slow, peeling smile crept across Death's features and it was an abomination of the anatomy from which it was cast. Sam... did the only thing Sam could do at this point, he stared up at the forever-spinning ceiling in a wide-eyed gaze and quite rightly kept his opinion to himself.

Out of the corner of his eye, Death suddenly noticed a teardrop pooling in the corner of one of Sam's rapidly-darkening eyes and grinned. "Oh!" and he pressed his hand to his chest in a gesture of feigned modesty, "Tears shed? And for me?" He abruptly reached over and grasped the hilt of the buck knife and pulled, slowly but with obvious delight. In the silence, he relished the wet, drawing sound in the otherwise silent space. "Oh Sam…" and he rolled his eyes toward the ceiling, "Sing me your death song, and die like a hero going home."

The blade slid from the wound and came free with a lot less effort than it had taken to put it there just a few scant hours ago. A crimson blood drop was flung from the knife's sharp edge and landed on Death's pallid cheek. He lifted his hand and carefully wiped the sanguine fluid onto his index finger. Pulling his hand back to examine the liquid, he gently, almost lovingly, licked it away with his tongue.

"Well, my friend," and Death gave a sigh of resignation that drifted into the air like a balloon, "I'd love to stick around and discuss the pitfalls of your existence and continue to sample the saltiness of your tears, but, alas, I simply must be off to my next appointment. Our time here is done and, by my count, I have a pretty full itinerary this evening."

He slowly rose from the bed and was accompanied by a symphony of creaking springs. He stood, adjusted his belt, and walked toward the door. With a flourish, he threw the door open and shut off the light from the single hanging bulb with his free hand. In the other, he held the still-dripping Buck knife. Darkness fell across the room like a drape.

"I hope you enjoy Eternity, Sam." Death whispered as he stepped out into the cold hallway. With a muffled click of the lock, he deftly shut the door and checked the lock. "I know I have," he said to no one but himself and the empty corridor. His quiet chuckling could be heard as it followed him down the barren passageway.

"I don't fear death so much as I fear its prologues: loneliness, decrepitude, pain, debilitation, depression, senility. After a few years of those, I imagine death presents like a holiday at the beach."

—Mary Roach

DANCIN' DAYS

This is the first text written for NO FLESH SHALL BE SPARED 3 and I wanted to try something a little different with it. The piece is essentially about change and how our kids ultimately grow up (whether we want them to or not). I also needed to lay a little groundwork identifying Cleese as an unconventional, but still effective, parent.

"Again," the big man standing in front of her said in a voice that brooked no debate.

The young girl looked up at him and felt the familiar tingling in her limbs which signaled exhaustion. Her back was bent and her arms hung heavily at her sides.

All of the color had drained from her face and her breath was now coming in short, sharp pants. It was clear to her that her 'tank' had gone nearly empty and she was just coasting on fumes. She smiled and climbed to her full height, pulling her shoulders back defiantly and glaring at him.

The man before her wasn't huge by athletic standards, but he was thickly muscled and well-defined; not 'gym big,' but rather 'life big.' Like life had given him a workout regimen that would either make him as tough as nails… or kill him.

His shadow blocked out the overhead lights as he stood panting from the exertion of their technique flow. Black short-cropped hair hugged the crown of his skull; stars of gray speckled throughout. His broad shoulders rose and fell quickly as he drew more and more oxygen into his bloodstream; feeding his cells. Sea-blue eyes glared at her from under a heavy brow. Gone was the benevolent gaze that had saved her life a short time ago, gone too was the gentle hand that once soothed her brow.

And through it all, his eyes never left her.

"Again," Cleese insisted and his words were drenched in a palpable menace.

Kekoa climbed to her feet and grinned slyly. From the sand in between her toes to the oppressive heat on her back, it all felt vaguely familiar. She swore she could almost hear the sound of surf and gulls crying in the distance.

Cleese moved around her slowly, like how a mongoose circles a snake. They'd been technique sparring for nearly an hour now, and, if he were being honest, he was getting a little bored with it. She'd come a long way; gobbling up the information he'd been giving her like mother's milk. Even given her relatively young age, she was already a formidable opponent.

After they'd returned from the fiasco on the island and she'd fallen under his care and tutelage, he'd learned all about Father and the girl's training. The full scope of the body of knowledge he'd given her was impressive, to say the least. Cleese had seen its full application and then some back when he'd first found her alone in that house. She'd proven herself an excellent tracker and hell on wheels when it came to fighting the Dead. He may have found her abandoned back in the little village, but she'd earn her place on his team via her ability to think and act flexibly in a bad situation.

"Come on, man…" she moaned like a child negotiating a new bed time. "Can't we just free-spar?"

Cleese smiled. The play had been a favorite of hers since they got back to the Training Ground and his course of instruction began. She'd been pretty affected by everything that had happened on the island. Shit… weren't they all? But, in her case, It was especially true. Her entire village, the place where she'd been born and raised… her entire family… all lost to the machinations of Masterson and his chuckle-headed goons. It gave Cleese no small amount of pleasure to think of how he'd put an end to all of that ridiculous scheming.

"*Please…*" the girl begged and a light of hopeful amusement lit up her eyes.

Cleese recalled the girl describing her philosophy to him

thusly: if training and technique classes were the rudiments of fighting (as they were in, say, music), then what she called 'free-sparring' was just Jazz; pure innovation and improvisation. Where the application of technique met Life's inherent luck and fickle providence. He had to appreciate the ingenuity of the perspective.

Since returning to The Fold, Cleese had hesitantly returned to a training schedule that was both familiar, and yet, still heartbreaking. Ghosts walked these grounds; ghosts that knew where he lived and exactly how to hurt him... with the blunt edge of memory.

He looked forlornly at the young girl and imagined the life she *should have* had and his heart melted like an ice cube in a microwave. He grinned broadly and nodded.

"Okay... but only for a round or two."

Kekoa made a silent fist-pumping motion. "Yesss!"

She arched her back and stretched out the tightness of the drill from her shoulders. She rolled her head around on her neck and it sounded like someone was cracking their knuckles.

Abruptly, she stopped and grinned at him excitedly.

"Music?"

He chuckled and the sound was alien in a place where few came to laugh.

"Ooo-kay..." he replied indulgently.

She happily ran over to where her gym bag lay in the sand of the Training Pit. She momentarily dug into its depths, then, returned triumphantly holding her cell phone. As she walked back across the hot sand, she fiddled with some controls on the touchpad.

"What are you doing?" Cleese asked, his hands placed firmly on his hips.

"Patching into the Hall's Bluetooth," she replied with an evil grin.

Whatever it was that was playing in the Hall overhead unexpectedly stopped. Cleese always thought the idea of playing any music was a bit of a waste since everyone these days had their own headphones, but... a few of the old school guys had argued for the practice since it was a holdover from the old gym days and everyone else acquiesced. Cleese himself remembered far too many days spent lifting heavy shit while philosophers like Thin Lizzy, UFO, and The Allman Brothers serenaded him about love, loss, and the dangers of having your heart broken.

"Here we go," Kekoa said pressing the last button with a flourish. She casually tossed the phone back over her shoulder toward her bag. It landed inside the zipper; nothing but net.

The twangy sound of an electric guitar erupted in the otherwise silent training space. The instrument was seductive and sounded like a snake moving in for the kill. Fat drums and bass pounded an odd, syncopated rhythm that immediately grabbed you by the soul. It was the *perfect* choice.

Cleese ambled to the center of the wide fighting space and waited for her. Looking down, he dug the toes of his boots into the soft sand. He felt a sudden exhilaration at the idea of watching the girl spar. It endlessly fascinated him to watch the light of understanding come on in her eyes. Like a bulb that grew brighter and brighter every day; with this bulb being the brightest of all.

And now that the fundamentals she'd been taught by Father were set like concrete in her foundation, true virtuosity and innovation could bloom. He looked up and watched her as she approached and saw only an explosion of fiery, blood-colored blossoms.

Kekoa felt her heart pick up its pace, leaping up into her chest like a trapped foal. The rhythm reached out to her and touched her down to her core. She felt her body tugged by the unquenchable desire to move.

Like a viper mimicking the odd time signature, she came closer, dancing toward him like a belly dancer. He watched her as she cavorted around his periphery, spinning like a top. Then, without warning, her right hand lashed out like a whip, striking him across the flat side of his jaw.

The speed of the punch made him blink.

Then, it made him laugh.

Christ, she was fast.

He countered her follow-up and the fight was officially on.

As they moved around one another, Cleese noticed that the girl's lips were moving as her body set and reset itself in response to his movements. She moved ambidextrously from Left Lead to Right seemingly without effort. He chuckled when he realized she was singing along with the song.

"You told your mamma I'd get you home, but you didn't say I had no car..."

A quick shuffle of her feet as a distraction, she hit him with three quick jabs. As she faded past him, she unexpectedly threw a back-fist that flattened the side of his nose when it landed. She chambered a roundhouse kick and, when she caught him looking down, that's when the Mike Tyson 'right-right hook-right upper-cut' combo came out of nowhere.

Where the hell did she learn Cus D'Amato's 6-4 combination? Father?

Cleese's head rocked back and his focus momentarily went a little fuzzy. When his vision cleared, he saw her standing right in front of him, taunting him. She had one hand on her hip and the finger of the other pointed toward the ceiling.

"I saw a lion; he was standing alone, with a tadpole in a jar."

She threw a lightning-fast front teep kick that collapsed his chest and stopped his advancement cold. He brought his hands up to deflect any follow-up, but instead found her once again dancing just outside his range, wearing that same devilish smile.

"You know it's alright," she cooed at him, shaking her shoulders and chambering her fists. "I said it's alright...I guess it's all in my heart." She wiggled her body playfully in counterpoint to the song's rhythm. "You'll be my only, my one and only..." She pirouetted, kicking out with her leg in a perfect reverse-crescent kick. It missed... good thing, but had he been a foot closer it would have taken his head right off. When her body came back around, she stopped, striking a fierce pose. "Is that the way it should start?"

Another flurry of punches landed—not hard, but hard enough—and Cleese reached out to get a handle on her. She moved around so fluidly , interacted with that damn song so well, it made it hard for him to focus. He marveled at her innate understanding of the space between them as she drifted in and out of range. He knew lifelong fighters who never, *ever*, got the concepts she was casually stringing together. To see her integrate everything so seamlessly, Cleese was once again humbled by the girl's natural ability.

He didn't like to use the word "savant" when it came to things like fighting, but it seemed pretty applicable here.

"Okay, quit fuckin' around," Cleese reproached. "You get sloppy and you drop your hands when you do that shit."

She gleefully danced away from him.

"Oh, come *on*."

"No," he said emphatically. "I've told you before... You're relying on distractions and distractions have a *very* limited shelf life. They can get you out of a jam, but..." He shrugged. "You better have more up your sleeve than just wiggling your ass and prancing around like a ballerina."

Cleese knew belittling her ability would get a rise out of her, but he'd told her time and time again that a fight is not a place to fuck around. The stakes were too goddam high. Too high with him... and, given the potential of her upcoming competition, too high with Them. Not for the first time since coming back, Monks voice echoed down the corridor of his memory.

The fighting space... it's like fuckin' church, man. It's sacred and it's where you go to give thanks to whoever it is that you fuckin' pray to. Act accordingly, shithead.

Her eyes flared and her center of gravity dropped into what he'd come to know as her fighting stance. She dug her feet into the sand and particles of sand glittered on the toe of her boot. Battle tension wrapped itself around her shoulders like a shawl. He had her attention now and she was coming in hot.

The song and her dance now forgotten, Kekoa stalked forward. Her hands came up and he noticed her gaze shift from a sort of general 'take it all in' to a more focused one; one that remained locked on the body's center.

They'd talked a lot about physicality, geometry, anatomy, and physics in the past. And over the ensuing months, he'd patted those concepts like mortar into the structure Father had given her. Under his tutelage, she'd come to understand things like 'Kinetic Connections,' 'The Gate,' 'Outside vs. Inside,' 'Flow,' and what he liked to call 'String Theory.' Salient concepts for doling out pain that he'd adapted from everything *he'd* learned over his lifetime.

He'd taught people before. Some of them even lived. Now though, with her, he had a vested interest and he wasn't holding anything back. Every principle. Every tactic. He was giving it all to her after taking her on as one of his own. Ever since the day he'd found her on the roof of that house, he'd done what he could to help keep her alive.

Why? He couldn't exactly answer that. It wasn't something that he ever questioned. But, as a result, he'd come to think of her as both his student and, as weird as it sounded to him, his daughter ever since. As he watched her move about the sand, he had to laugh.

Him… a father.

She subtly moved to his right, attempting to flank him.

He quickly cut her off.

Once they'd gotten back to the Training Grounds, he'd sorted out his position with The League and made sure that the two of them were safe. Well, safe enough so that he had some breathing room in order to figure out what they were going to do next. During that time, he'd been able to quantify what Father had taught her and what he'd need to teach her himself. As it turned out, she pretty much had all the basics down… as well as a few things even he'd never seen. But she'd learned enough from Father that Cleese's teachings were like gasoline thrown on an already burning fire.

And boy… was that fire ever raging right now.

She came in hard, landing a lot of bullshit 'pitter-pat' stuff off of his arms and shoulders. He deftly batted them away as he circled her. Now that he'd gotten her attention, it was time to see what he could do with it.

He pivoted on one foot, ducked under her jab, and slid passed her. As he did so, he left his left arm lag behind his body, turning it into a sweet little hook punch at the last minute that took the girl's breath away. As she seemed to fold from the pain, her foot lashed out and caught Cleese square in the ass. Pain shot up into his intestines and twisted there like a burr. They separated from one another, each rubbing at their respective wounds.

She stood holding her ribs; he gripping his buttocks.

They both looked up at one another; wide smiles splitting both of their faces.

"Fuck!" Cleese barked as he hopped from one foot to another as he probed his butt crack with his fingers. "That *really* hurt."

Kekoa giggled, but winced as she held the lower part of her rib cage.

Cleese settled down once his pain had subsided. He grew reflective and stared at the girl with a sudden concerned look on his face.

"Hey," he asked. "You doing okay?"

She looked back at him, still grimacing and rubbing her ribs. "Yeeaah…"

"No," he said, shaking his head. "I mean, *really*."

"Really?"

"Really, really."

She knew what he was talking about, and had, in fact, been waiting for this conversation since they got here months ago. There hadn't been a lot of time between them to talk about her… and him… and this place… and the future. She instinctively knew how he felt. But neither of them was in any rush to talk about it.

Talking about it made it real.

Kekoa relaxed her stance and took a step backward.

And making it real… made it *real*.

"I'm okay. I mean, I've gotten settled. Some of the people have been nice. I'm not sure what you want me to say…"

Cleese pulled off his gloves and Kekoa reluctantly did the same. Together, they both walked over to where their bags were; it being a given that 'class' was over. He nodded his head as he continued listening to her; grateful things were going so smoothly for her in a place that was anything but smooth. As they gathered their gear—pads, focus mitts, and sticks—they continued to talk.

"That's good. That's good," he responded. "I'm sorry I

couldn't get you further away from all of ..." he looked around the hall, "this." He stared into his hands. "I did what I could."

Kekoa looked up at him, looking sad. She zipped up her gym bag with a sense of finality, then gazed up at him solemnly.

"You have *nothing* to be sorry for." She chuckled darkly to herself as she picked up the fabric bag. "You helped me when no one else would... when no one else could." She shook her head in disbelief. "Don't be silly. You saved me..."

Cleese felt his cheeks grow warm, so he looked away from her.

Who saved who? he silently asked himself.

"Well, I just want you to know," he said looking around the Training Hall, "this isn't forever. We'll leave here one day..."

Kekoa stared at him and her expression was openly confused.

"Why would we ever want to leave here? I mean, we're safe..." She looked around her, and then spoke quietly, under her breath. "Safe enough. The League wouldn't put us in danger, right?"

Cleese laughed and knew that was a topic for another time. It was too soon to tell her everything. Let her get her feet back under her before he had to pull them back out again. His plan had always been to play along with Weber up until the time that they were back on their feet, healthy, and he could figure out where his fuckin' money went.

"We have weight training next," Cleese said walking off. "Then, focus mitts."

She shouldered her bag and her gaze never left his. It felt a little like being sized up. Shaking his head, he put the thought—and any others like it—out of his head. She was a child and he wasn't about to get into an argument with her; especially over *this*. They'd leave when he said they'd leave... and not a moment later.

Still... it was clear to him that the kid was slowly growing into something other than a kid. He looked her lithe body over and realized, perhaps for the first time, how much she'd matured. Small breasts poked at the front of her shirt and her hips were definitely looking more round. Like a jolt to the heart, it dawned on him that she *was* growing up.

Kekoa jerked her head toward where the door out of the Training Pit lay.

"I need to fill my water bottle before we do, okay?" she said casually, moving her head from side to side, working out any residual muscle kinks.

Cleese nodded and they walked out of the training space.

At the door, he glanced over his shoulder and saw a couple of guys hanging out on the upper observation deck. He couldn't quite make out who they were, but they were up there, staring down at them. Cleese continued down the short gangway that led back into the hall.

As he came into the corridor outside of the Pit, he heard Kekoa's voice talking to someone. As he got closer, he could see the same two men—not much more than boys, really—who were in the upper bleachers, no doubt the ones he'd seen a second ago.

Kekoa laughed at something one of them said and the sound of her laughter was like the ringing of fine crystal. One of the guys spoke and, while Cleese couldn't hear what he said, the person's intentions were quite clear.

Cleese came up behind her and their conversation ground to an abrupt halt. He looked up at the two of them standing with their hands on the railing and he instantly knew their game. Kekoa was young, pretty, and new to the Training Ground… She should be easy pickin's. A dark smile played across his lips.

"Something funny, boys?" he asked with a wry grin.

Kekoa looked embarrassed in a way that only preteen girls can look. She shook her head as she continued walking down the corridor, heading toward the gym. "No… it's nothing. Let's go…"

"Oh, come on…" Cleese replied, his gaze zeroing in on the two men above. "I love a good joke." He wasn't sure why he was coming on so strong, but, as always, he trusted his instincts.

Cleese recognized them now: Quaid and his buddy, McCready. He saw their names appear on the roster a few weeks ago. He'd seen them working out on the mat a time or two—Brazilian Jujitsu, or some grab-ass shit… with some Kenpo and

Hapkido thrown into the mix for good measure—but he wasn't much impressed. More of that fodder The League liked to use to keep their well-oiled machine lubricated.

Cleese gave them both a month.

Surprisingly, it was McCready who spoke up.

"We just… We were just saying," he paused and looked to his pal for encouragement. Seeing only the dull look of a frightened animal, he proceeded. "…how good… how *great* Kekoa looked out there. I mean, even though you're bigger… stronger… um… older." He quickly added, "No disrespect," before continuing. "She was able to hold her own."

Cleese stared at the kid for a second and idly wondered how closely related his parents were.

"Hey…" he chided, "for your information, I *was* holding back."

Cleese heard Kekoa giggle behind him.

Their expressions fell like a soufflé.

"No… I… I mean…" the kid stammered. "It's just that it was impressive."

"Impressive as fuck!" Quaid chimed in.

Cleese scowled at him and another dark cloud passed over his eyes. "You're not helping."

Suddenly, he felt a small tug on the back of his shirt.

"Come on, please…" Kekoa said, sounding irritated, as she pulled him off balance. "This isn't getting us anywhere."

Having little other choice, Cleese began following her; his gaze remained locked on Quaid and dough-headed pal.

"They were just being nice," Kekoa admonished him and she moved her bag to her other shoulder. "I appreciate the concern, but… they're harmless."

Cleese scowled and thought back to a tent in an encampment in a forest… and the back of a beautiful little girl's head exploding like a flower. His brow furrowed as he felt the first real pangs of paternal worry grip his heart.

"They're *male*, Kekoa."

Kekoa stopped walking and looked over at him angrily. "Aaand…?"

Cleese frowned. "They're trouble."

Kekoa acted dramatically overwrought. "Oh, jeeez! Can you spare me that whole 'protective parent' thing, okay? I mean, I made it off the island… with your help. But I'm fine."

Cleese ambled after her as she strode away from him. She was talented, smart, and getting more beautiful by the day… she was quickly becoming a formidable woman. He idly watched the muscles of her back flex as she continued walking along the hallway.

He indulged himself for a moment and allowed his thoughts to go back to a time when Chikara was still alive; alive and stunningly vibrant. This child here… could well have been the product of their coupling. Christ… when the light was right, she looked enough like her to take his breath away.

And God knew… she was every bit as lethal as Chikara had been.

Maybe even more so…

Especially now with her under his watchful eye. She took everything he threw at her—every fucked up concept and twisted application—and soaked it up like a sponge. She learned… and she adapted… and had no hesitation in doling out her personal brand of considerable punishment. For her, it was all a kind of game.

Soon, she'd even be giving him a run for his money.

He often had to remind himself that she was still only a kid; barely fifteen. And the only thing that filled him with more anger than the thought of her ever being made to fight in The Pit… was that one of these mutts would try and, as Monk once called it 'pick her locks?' The idea of one of them ever putting their filthy booger-hooks on her… filled his vision with red.

"Hey," Kekoa's voice echoed from down the hallway.

He hadn't realized that he'd stopped walking. He looked around to get his bearings and saw her standing, hand on hip, a few dozen yards away.

"You coming or are you gonna daydream all day?" she called to him and her expression was one of curiosity and concern.

He shook the cobwebs from his mind, setting each of his thoughts and concerns into their own respective boxes in his brain. With a bit of effort, he blinked himself back into the moment, back to the blossoming young woman who'd somehow become the most important thing in his life and he hurried to catch up.

"Yeah… sorry, coming."

A few days later, Cleese found Kekoa sitting in the Mess Hall, alone and off to the side of the room. When Cleese entered, he noticed how she had purposefully set herself far away from everyone else, brooding over her plate. When he came up to her table, he saw her shake her head a little causing a few strands of her hair to fall over one eye.

"Hey," he said in greeting.

"Hey."

Cleese sat down and dipped his finger into her pile of mashed potatoes. As he stuffed them into his mouth, he looked at the girl earnestly.

"I need to talk to you."

Kekoa didn't look up from staring at the center of her plate.

"Okay," was all she offered in response.

"It seems there was an altercation last night in the Training Hall."

Kekoa looked up at him through her eyebrows. "Oh?"

Cleese smiled.

"Yeah, it appears that those boys from a few days ago, Quaid and McCready, had themselves a bit of an accident."

"Were they bitten?" she asked, which was good. It's what everyone here should ask if they hear the word 'accident' used in a sentence.

"No," he shook his head. "Nothing like that. But they were hurt pretty badly."

Kekoa remained quiet. "That's a shame."

"Yeah," Cleese continued, "Somebody hyper-extended McCready's elbow and busted his femur. Quaid… Well, this same someone also snapped his sternum. I'm guessing that's who you hit first."

Despite herself, Kekoa looked up at him.

"Me?"

Cleese helped himself to more of her potatoes.

"Don't bullshit me, kid. The femur break... looked like something I showed you in class last week. The sternum... that was your 'shock and awe,' right? Take out the big guy first... it's what I would have done. Tell me what happened."

Kekoa stared into her mashed potatoes and watched them bleed coagulated gravy onto her plate for a second, and then, she slowly started speaking.

"The other day, when we saw them... they were nice. They said I was pretty and that I reminded them of..."

Cleese cocked an eyebrow. "Reminded them of who?"

"Of someone they said they'd seen fight in the Library... someone named Chikara."

Cleese felt like a mule just kicked him in the balls.

"Well, that's a bit of bullshit, kid. They're too young to have ever actually seen her fight... and those tapes aren't exactly required viewing by the League."

She shrugged. "That's what they said, so..." She pulled away the strands of hair over her eye with a finger. "Anyway, I couldn't sleep, so I went to the gym to run on the treadmill."

Cleese looked down at the table and tried to get control of his rising temper. He held up his hand to stop her. In reality, he'd heard this story a lot of times before and it made him crazy every time he heard it. When he felt in control, he continued his inquiry.

"So, what happened?"

She looked up at him angrily and her eyes brimmed with tears.

"They touched me," she replied as she pulled back the hair on the left side of her head to reveal the beginnings of a shiner.

Cleese closed his eyes and prepared himself for the worst.

"So... you..." he asked almost fearing her answer. He opened his eyes and looked at her and the deepening contusion.

She smiled a devilish smile. "I touched them back."

Cleese couldn't help but chuckle. His mind immediately conjured the looks of surprise on those boys' faces when they found themselves in her laser focus. He himself had been there a time or two and it wasn't fun.

"Well, they're both done here; being sent home."

"Shit happens, is what they say, right?" she replied with a shrug.

"It *is* what they say."

She looked up at him and he could tell she had decided to say something. It was written all over her face. Her mind worked at it like it was a bit of overdone steak.

"Look, I'm not going to feel any sympathy for those two. They tried to take something from me..."

"So, you took something from them?"

"What did I take from them?" she scoffed.

Cleese leaned forward.

"Maybe you didn't hear me," he explained. "They're both going home. With injuries like those... yeah, they were done. Here's another thing they say... 'They may get better, but they'll never be well.'"

She shrugged coldly.

"Hey," he said forcefully and he waited until she looked up at him before continuing. "I fully understand that those little shits deserved everything you gave them, but... *you* also need to acknowledge—and take ownership of the fact—that you changed those boy's lives forever."

She glared up at him. "If I hadn't... they'd have done the same thing to mine."

Cleese thought about that for a second and, deep down, he knew she was right.

And that he was a bit of an asshole.

"So," she asked defiantly, "am I in trouble?"

Cleese chuckled darkly.

"No. Management doesn't give much of a shit what fighters do to one another... and the other fighters are happy as clams that the two spots opened up."

The two of them sat quietly for a minute simply looking at one another.

"I won't apologize for anything," Kekoa finally stated emphatically.

"Nor should you. I just need you to take accountability for your actions, the things that we do have consequences. And if you," he poked his finger into the flesh of her forearm, "knowing those consequences, feel justified in proceeding, then… who am I to tell you anything different?"

She thought for another minute, then, nodding her head, she looked up at him.

"Agree… and I do." She leaned forward in her chair. "Those boys need to do the same: they need to take accountability. And now, they need to deal with the consequences of their actions. Right?"

He dipped his head in acknowledgment of her point. "Okay, then… we won't talk about it again."

Kekoa stood up, bussing her plate and tray. She walked over to the trash cans and, dumping her plate's contents inside, she set the tray, plate, and utensils in the bin to be washed. When she returned, her mood was visibly lighter, like a weight had been lifted from her shoulders.

"One last thing," Cleese said as they walked from the Mess Hall, "If you ever find that you do want to talk about what happened, I'm here, okay?" He draped his arm protectively around her shoulders.

Kekoa didn't speak, but leaned into him slightly, hugging him; grateful for his understanding.

HEART OF CHRISTMAS

This was one of those ideas that don't happen to normal people. It was Christmas of 2017 and I wanted to do something that had to do with the holiday, so... I started with Rudolph and tried to come up with another property that would fit. Then, one day after working at a local dispensary, I figured it out (go fig!) and put it to paper. This one was weird... even for me.

A polar wind howled across the barren landscape and blew the snow that lay on the ground into the air like a whirling white curtain. Winter had arrived earlier than usual at The Pole this year and the world outside was held in its eternally frozen grip. Inside a small cottage set at the periphery of a compound of other—larger—buildings, a solitary elf sat huddled near a roaring fire. He sat in an overstuffed chair and had a caribou skin blanket pulled tightly around his shoulders. He looked tired, his eyes burning red beneath the strands of his dangling blond hair that hung in front of his face. The crackling of the wood fire was the only sound in the sparsely decorated room.

The elf got to his feet and walked over to the large window at the front of the house. He brushed the dew from the interior of the glass with the palm of his hand and gazed out onto the frozen landscape. Outside, he saw several Bavarian style buildings that were set in a loose circle amidst miles and miles of snow and ice. Multi-colored lights on strings illuminated the way from building to building and acted as a guide during the snowstorms that happened here almost daily. A large barn dominated the compound and was set at its center. Warm light and heat emanated from inside the storybook building. The elf stepped away from the window, letting the drape fall forgotten from his grasp.

"The North Pole. Shit." He let his head hang despondently. "I'm still only at The North Pole."

Slowly, he walked back to his spot by the fire. Lack of movement over the last few weeks had made his muscles sore and his joints feel stiff. It was in times such as these that he really felt his ever-increasing age. Simply put, he wasn't as young of an elf as he once was and if he didn't keep himself active, he stiffened up. 'Move lest ye rust,' was the expression, he remembered his old Aunt Bertie using. Once he was nearer to the hearth, he sat back down in his chair and drew his furry blanket back around his shoulders to help fend off the cold.

He sat looking deep into the fire, contemplating his situation... and his foreseeable future. He'd been cooling his heels in this cottage for weeks now. Waiting. Waiting to be summoned. Waiting for The Fat Man to call for him. Waiting for Santa. Waiting for him to decide to bring him back into the Workshop after all these years to talk about some special project he had up his sleeve. Some kind of mission.

The elf had worked for The Big Guy before, but it was *years* ago. He'd grown up in Santa's employ and had toiled in the Workshop ever since he'd been able to hold a hammer. Time passed and he eventually grew to maturity. All too soon though, he found himself falling out of love with the art of making toys. His heart pulled him in other directions, drew him toward different things. Things like papillas and stellate reticulums. Conditions such as Pappillon-Lefevre Syndrome and the ever-present danger of Periodontal Disease and Gingivitus. It had taken him helping a friend on a wild and woolly adventure to help him to decide that he too could question his role in elven society, to go out into The World and live out his dreams. That he too could dare to be happy. And so, the decision was made for him to leave The Workshop and travel across the snow and ice so that he could go to school to study the time-honored discipline of Dentistry.

Thing was... there wasn't much call out in the world for a three-foot dentist.

And so, after many years of him banging on doors and

trying to develop a practice, he had little else to do but return to The Workshop to do his best to try to fit back in with the other workers. The other elves though… they never understood. Nor did they forgive him.

'High and mighty,' they'd said of him. 'Being an elf not good enough' comments were made and their derision stung him. This was supposed to be his family… if they didn't understand an elf's desire to follow his dreams, who in the world would? No matter what he said though, no manner of explanation would assuage their contempt.

And so, little by little, the dentist elf was pushed to the side: ostracized and isolated. He had no family, and now, even his friends (even the one he'd once helped) had let their relationships fall into an apathetic stalemate. But Santa had said he'd find a place for him. And one thing that could be said of the old guy, he never lied. So far though, that promise had equated to The Dentist being given bed and board, but being left to rot in this little room in this little house while the snow blew in blinding flurries outside.

Waiting.

Waiting for Santa's mission.

After a while, he dozed and his thoughts were filled with dreams of crossing a great sandy desert amidst nomads who spoke to him in a strange, yet musical, tongue.

There was a sudden knock on the door and the sound of it startled him awake. Dragging the animal skin blanket along with him like a ceremonial robe, The Dentist went to the door and opened it a crack. In the hall outside, there stood two elves.

One was short and fat with a bulbous nose and a dark goatee. The other was tall with a long face and wore a pair of black-rimmed glasses. And while their faces were smiling, their demeanor was anything but friendly.

"Hello, Dentist," said the short elf with a noticeable sneer on the last word.

The Dentist didn't say anything. Instead, he walked back to where he was sitting before the fire, leaving the door behind him open for the elves. The taller elf with the glasses nudged the heavy wooden door open with his foot and the two of them both stepped inside.

"You with me?" the shorter elf asked.

"Yeah?" replied The Dentist wearily as he sat back in his chair.

"The Big Man wants to see you."

The Dentist shook his head. "Finally."

"Hey, you ok?" the elf with the dark glasses asked.

The blonde elf nodded, but didn't move.

The tall elf clucked his tongue and nudged his shorter companion. He pointed to the small table near where the dentist was sitting. On it, there was a nearly empty pitcher of thick, creamy Egg Nog. A half-filled glass of the stuff sat nearby.

"Having yourself a bit of a party, eh?" said the elf with the goatee. "We have a minute... Why don't we get you cleaned up?" He reached out and led The Dentist to the shower by the hand. "C'mon, man... Santa's waiting."

The tall elf shook his head in disgusted amusement as he walked back to close the door.

"Misfit."

Santa and Mrs. Claus were just sitting down to their dinner when the two elves arrived and escorted The Dentist into the room. Cooks had just brought in a repast of sliced beef, shrimp, and peas when they ushered the young elf in. It broke Santa's heart to see the condition he was in. Gone was the bright-eyed youth he'd once known. This was an elf that had clearly lost his Spirit, abandoned his very purpose. It wasn't that he looked sick, but more that he had the look of a plant that had been too long out of the sun. Withered. Withered and completely out of sorts.

They sat him at the far end of the table. The elf with the glasses stood guard by the door so that they might not be disturbed. The short one with the dark goatee joined them at their meal. It took a minute for everyone to settle in, but once they did, all eyes seemed to gravitate to The Dentist.

"I hope you've been satisfied with your lodgings," Santa said as he unwrapped his serviette. Setting his utensils aside, he tucked his napkin under his wide chin, the majority of the linen being hidden beneath his long white beard.

The Dentist smiled. "It's been a bit dull."

Santa smiled as he stabbed a slab of beef with his fork and brought it, still dribbling juice, to his plate. The action was taken as a signal by Mrs. Claus and the others to begin grabbing bowls and dishing out their portions. The Dentist sat unmoving, ignoring the food and staring intensely at Santa.

"Yes, well," Santa said with a hearty chuckle. "We do what we can with what we're given, eh?" He thought silently for a moment as he cut his piece of meat into bite-sized pieces. He watched his knife intently as it slid effortlessly through the tender flesh. Lifting the morsel to his mouth, he nodded to the goateed elf, who then got up and went over to a nearby desk.

The elf picked up a file from the stacks of papers and manila folders that lay strewn across the desk. He brought the folder back to the table, tabs of multi-colored paper sticking out like dried leaves being pressed in a book. Opening the folder, the short elf sat back down. He retrieved a stapled-together group of documents from it and handed them across the table to The Dentist.

The Dentist looked the papers over and it was pretty clear that it was a collection of transcripts from various recorded conversations and meetings; reconnaissance mostly, anecdotal reportage concerning a series of abductions and disappearances that were happening on and around The Island of Misfit Toys. The Dentist knew the area well. He'd been there before.

Even met the king once upon a long time ago.

"This all sounds messy," The Dentist said. "But I don't see how any of it concerns me."

Santa looked over at Mrs. Claus. She smiled at him and nodded slightly, silently begging him for his patience. Santa wiped his mouth with his napkin and gave their guest his full attention.

"Hermey, do you remember Moonracer?"

Of course The Dentist immediately remembered the winged lion monarch. They'd met him back when he and his friends once ventured to his island. He remembered the king as having helped them, after they'd found their way to his realm. In return, they'd talked Santa into finding homes for all of the island's lost residents.

"Yes," The Dentist replied. "The Manticore King. I remember him."

Mrs. Claus took an audible sip of her tea. "For years, Moonracer was considered a kind and benevolent leader," she said, taking over the narrative. "His subjects—the toys—loved him. His hand rested lightly on the rudder of his kingdom. And as a result, his realm flourished. Then, one day, his bride bore him a child, a *son*, and Moonracer loved that child more than he loved Life itself. It was just prior to this that, I believe, you met him."

The Dentist sat quietly in his chair and waited patiently for the rest of the story. He looked at the piles of food in the bowls in front of him and never felt less hungry.

"A few years passed," Santa continued. "The boy grew, but… he was frail and pekid. One day, he fell suddenly ill and was taken by a great fever." Santa looked into the depths of his dinner plate and his eyes became fixed. Absentmindedly, he batted his peas around his plate with his fork like he was playing hockey. He finally set his fork down with a sense of finality. "The boy died soon after."

"Moonracer turned cruel after that," interjected the bearded elf. "Many were abruptly enslaved and thrown into his dark dungeons without as much as a trial."

The Dentist noticed Santa staring at him intently.

"It cannot continue," Santa said, removing his napkin from under his chin. He wiped his mouth with one corner. He stood, unceremoniously dropping the table linen onto his plate. The linen soaked up the meat's liquid like a sponge. The fat man ambled over to the window and looked out over his domain. Snow continued blowing over his village in a whirling, chaotic flurry.

The Dentist allowed his gaze to wander around the table. "Again…" he asked. "What does any of this have to do with me?"

Santa looked back from the window and a dark shadow passed over his face.

"Simply put…" Mrs. Claus said quietly. "We want you to go

up Silver Mountain." She stared straight ahead, her lips moving slowly. "Travel by sleigh to Moonracer's castle and convince The King to abdicate his reign."

"Abdicate?" The Dentist asked.

"To give up his throne," said the bearded elf.

The Dentist looked around the room incredulously. He knew what the word meant. It meant that, should the king not do as he was asked, The Dentist was to assassinate the winged monarch... with extreme prejudice, if necessary.

He couldn't believe what he was hearing; especially being spoken out loud, but then again... it wouldn't be the first time the fat man got his hands dirty. "And if he refuses?"

Santa picked up his pipe from a small table near the window and loaded it with a practiced hand. He then walked over to the fireplace and stared into the fire for a moment, watching the flames dance and the smoke spiral up the chimney. Plucking a length of straw from a broom that had been set in the corner, he lit its end by holding it to the fire. Once it was alight, he held the flaming twig to the mouth of his pipe. He puffed heartily and smoke circled his head like a halo. When the tobacco was burning brightly, he blew the impromptu match out with a plume of smoke. He then returned his attention to The Dentist.

"I want you to convince him otherwise."

"*Convince* him?"

Santa sat down in his broad leather chair and took another long pull on his pipe. He let the smoke out slowly before finally responding. "Yes... *Convince* him."

The Dentist stepped out of Santa's house and pulled his jacket tighter against the biting cold. The wind had kicked up and there was a palpable chill in the air. Cold... even for The North Pole. Immense drifts of alabaster fluff stretched across the horizon for as far as the eye could see. Snow was piled high on the roofs and ice frosted the windows of all the buildings.

The Workshop dominated the compound, brooding over the village like a protective hen. The largest of the structures was shaped like an old barn. The building was like a hearth around which all the other buildings were gathered. To its left were the elves' quarters: small, squat bunkhouses set in regimental rows. And at the far side of the compound lay the stable for the reindeer and the sleighs.

The bearded elf followed him out of the house and stepped up alongside him.

"Cold today," he said, trying to sound conversational.

When The Dentist failed to respond, the elf silently led the way across the snow toward the stables. They crossed the open center of the compound, going around the huge decorated pine tree that was perpetually in the square without any further conversation, trudging their way through the deep drifts.

The smell of hay grew stronger with every step they took, followed by the musky smell of the reindeer. As they approached, The Dentist saw a familiar face in the small group of elves and reindeer gathered around one of Santa's sleighs. With that glowing red nose, he was kind of hard to miss.

"Hello, Rudy," The Dentist said once he got close enough to be heard over the howling wind.

"No way," the reindeer said, his nose pulsing brighter in the dim light. "I heard Santa had brought you here, but..." He pawed at the ground with his hoof. "Well, heck, man... how are you?"

The Dentist grinned and shrugged resignedly. "Meh... I'm here."

Rudy walked over and rubbed his head against The Dentist's upper arm.

"Well, it'll be good to travel with you again, man."

The Dentist nodded, but looked a little surprised.

"Are you leading this sleigh?"

Rudy smiled and his nose burned a bright crimson.

"Are you kidding? When I heard it was for you, I insisted on being a part of your team."

The Dentist scratched the back of the reindeer's head, just behind the ear, where he knew he liked it.

"Have they briefed you on the mission?" the elf asked.

Rudy shook his head and the bells on his harness jingled brightly.

"Not yet," he said and shook his antlers. Minute flakes of white fell like dandelion florets. "They said you'd fill us all in."

Before The Dentist could say anything in response, the goateed elf approached and pulled Rudy aside to discuss some of the last minute details. As they talked, The Dentist looked around the stables. It made him a little sad when he failed to recognize anyone.

"Sleigh's fully loaded," the goateed elf informed him once he was done talking to Rudy. "We've put in water, some of Mrs. Claus' biscuits, and there's hot cocoa in two thermoses under the seat. It should be enough to last you for the trip up the mountain."

"The mountain?" Rudy asked innocently.

The Dentist nodded as he climbed up the runner and got into the sleigh. He made himself comfortable beneath the furs while they harnessed Rudy to the front of the team. "We've business on Silver Mountain."

Rudy nodded and was already beginning to calculate their route in his head. "We'll head up Hollyberry Ridge and over The Great Gingerbread Plateau," Rudy called back over his shoulder. "Once we're through The Candylands, we'll use the ice like last time to cross the water to the island. Then, it's straight up the mountain and on to Moonracer's castle."

The Dentist nodded as he burrowed deeper into his seat beneath the caribou blankets. He pulled the furs about him and gazed up into the slate-gray sky. He imagined Rudy's route in his head; like a lifeline that led like a river straight to the king. He drew the furs even tighter, drawing his arms and legs into their warmth. He knew it would be cold out, especially now with the sun starting to go down, but the chill in the air felt like it somehow cut deeper. Like the cold he was feeling on the outside was being matched by the iciness he felt in his soul.

He took a quick look back at Santa's compound. There, in one of the wide windows, he saw a fat silhouette watching them as they headed off into the cold white wilderness.

Soon, even The Pole was out of sight.

Hours passed and The Dentist was left to his own thoughts as the miles of blinding white tundra slid by. He dozed for a bit, but sleep proved erratic and elusive. While fumbling about in the sleigh, he discovered a leather satchel mixed in amongst the furs and foodstuffs. Inside, there was a dossier and photographs all focused around King Leonid Moonracer. He read the dossier over while Rudy led the way, his nose shining like a beacon in the diminishing light ahead of them.

From what he could see in the file, Moonracer had lived a pretty privileged life. Born into royalty, his youth had been spent being molded for the throne by his parent's most trusted inner circle. Educated and pampered, he was driven to be a good and righteous king. The Dentist remembered when they'd met him while they had been on their adventure. He found Moonracer to be a noble and honorable king in their brief interactions. He couldn't imagine what might have driven him to start enslaving the very folks he'd been so dedicated to protecting, but, The Dentist supposed, grief could oftentimes do terrible things to people.

He continued to leaf through the documents as the sun started slipping behind the mountains.

He soon grew frustrated with trying to read in the waning light, so he moved on to the photographs. The majority of them were of Moonracer through the years. Some were from his youth, his tail held high and proud. Others were more recent. In all of them though, his long mane swirled about his head majestically and a righteous certainty burned in his eyes. A few of them featured Moonracer and a woman; the queen, presumably. They sat on their high thrones amidst an adoring public. Toward the back of the pile was a photo of Moonracer and the woman holding a small child. Their faces beamed with the pride and joy of new parenthood.

He turned to the next image.

It was alarming how similar it was to the last photo, but the image was clearly different. While it was the same Moonracer and his Queen, there was an overwhelming sadness to the image. Clearly, something had happened that affected them profoundly. Then, The Dentist noticed the absence of the child.

From then on, that same sense of loss pervaded every photo. You could almost see the couple's hearts breaking as the photos progressed. Then, that loss slowly began to sour into anger. The Dentist shook his head as he gathered the papers and put them back into the satchel. What he'd seen had disturbed him. The loss. The sadness. It was too much. He stuffed the satchel back beneath the furs where he found it and stared into the gathering darkness.

None of it made sense. Not the sudden change in the King's demeanor. Not the subjugation of an already persecuted population. How were they to blame for the things that he'd lost? And what was up with Santa hard-lining it like that? He knew what they'd meant when they'd said 'convince him.' That was the fat man's way of sanctioning the rough stuff; of going in heavy.

Of saying, comply... or else.

And as the gray sky gave way to the fullness of night, he never even noticed when he slipped off to sleep within the warm embrace of Santa's sleigh.

The Dentist roused several hours later when the sleigh bumped over a small log as it raced across the unbroken landscape of The Great Gingerbread Plateau. He stretched his back and looked out over the sleigh's rail at a terrain of all-encompassing white. The sound of the reindeer's bells on the air was crisp and the bright tones seemed to echo for miles. Looking forward, he saw Rudy's incandescent light as it continued to lead the way.

The Dentist called forward for Rudy to stop the sleigh. Nature was calling and he wanted to stretch his legs after having spent far too many hours cooped up in the carriage. Rudy picked a spot near the low-lying foothills that led around Candy Cane Flats. He slowed the team and the sleigh finally came to a stop.

The bitterly cold wind bit into his cheeks as The Dentist walked a short distance away from the sleigh to do his business. After some initial 'stage fright,' he stood urinating into the snow, one hand on his hip, staring out over the desolate white landscape. As he was finishing up and redressing himself, he spied a small clump of foliage just ahead of him poking its head out of the snow. On closer examination, he saw that they had bright green leaves with small purple berries tucked underneath.

He smiled.

Jollyberries.

He looked over his shoulder at the sleigh and saw the

reindeer team quietly nibbling snow and resting in their harnesses. He looked back at the plant just ahead and he licked his lips in anticipation of their rich, sweet taste.

He loved the small purple berries. His mother had made Jollyberry Pie when he was a kid and the memory was a fine one. He remembered smelling her pies and tarts as they sat cooling on the windowsill of the house where he'd grown up. He glanced back and saw that the reindeer were still occupied with their refreshment. On a whim, he decided that he had a bit of time. Time enough, anyway.

He trudged over to the plant through the snow and plucked a few of its small, round fruits. He rolled the tiny orbs around in his hand and purple juice stained the skin of his palm a deep purple. He threw the handful into his mouth and their skins burst with rich flavor. A nostalgic wave washed over him as the fruity juice splashed over his tongue. Looking ahead, he saw another, larger plant with a lot more berries and quickly walked over to it.

When he got close, he looked back toward the sleigh and saw that he was now several hundred yards away from it. He looked out over the polar landscape and saw nothing but a lone grove of trees a short distance away. The trees grew like stubble along the horizon. He couldn't imagine that him being so far away from the sleigh would ever be a problem, so he returned his attention to the Jollyberry bush.

He bent over and looked more closely at the plant. There were a lot more of the berries on this one. Rather than spend a lot of time plucking them off one by one, he drew a small knife from his belt and cut through the plant's thick stalk just above the ground. The bush came away in his hand like a bouquet.

As he turned to go back, a great roar erupted from the grove of trees and the sound of it echoed across the valley. He looked up and saw the tops of the tree line suddenly shake, snow falling from the boughs in heavy clumps. Suddenly, the trees crashed apart and he saw a gigantic ape-like creature coming through the curtain of trees.

The Dentist was running before he realized it. His feet sank into the snow and it seemed like a dream, like no matter how hard he ran, it would never be fast enough. He pushed himself harder, and finally, he started gaining ground. As he came sliding in, he slammed into the side of the sleigh, rocking it on its skids. Quickly scrambling to his feet, he climbed inside.

"Never get out of the sleigh, man," he whispered to himself as he fought for breath. "Never get out of the sleigh."

He raised his head to call to Rudy to go—and to go *fast*—but his voice was cut off by the sound of someone shouting in the distance.

"Ya-hoooo!"

The voice, clearly human, echoed across the valley.

"Go!" The Dentist shouted to Rudy. "Go, go now!"

The team took up the slack in their harnesses and the sleigh leapt forward, slamming him into his seat. The ape creature kept coming in their direction, bent over and loping across the fields very quickly. The Dentist was finally able to get a good look at the creature now that it was closer and it seemed vaguely familiar. Like he'd seen it before… or had caught a glimpse of it once in a dream.

The beast was covered in long, white hair with long arms and short, squat legs. It had a wide mouth, but, oddly, no visible teeth. The creature raised its head as it ran and roared mightily, its call echoing across the glade.

As the creature came even closer, The Dentist saw that a man wearing a parka and a knit cap was perched on the back of the thing's neck, riding the creature like a rodeo cowboy.

"Ya-ha-hoooey!" the man cried again.

Suddenly, The Dentist felt the sleigh slow and finally begin to stop. He frantically looked around, yelling out to question why they weren't still racing to escape. He looked back desperately and finally got a good, clear look at the rider's bearded face. Bit by bit, he started to put it together, to remember… remember who these two were and from where he knew them.

He remembered back to their trip so long ago, when they traveled across some of these very same stretches of ice. This was very near to where he and Rudy had been. It was that experience that had helped him to finally decide to buckle down and actually become a dentist. Slowly, the memory of their boisterous companion on that trip and of how he'd once saved the day played across the screen of his memory.

The Dentist saw the man grab hold of Bumble's ears and pull them back like reins. The beast slowed to a stop and knelt down onto one knee to let him off. The man climbed down from his back gingerly and, once he was back on solid ground, he approached the sleigh with a swagger.

"Hellooo!" he shouted and his voice rolled melodically across the silent ice.

"You," Rudy called out even as he struggled against the restraints of the sleigh harness. "Hey, I remember you. You... you're..." His nose lit up brightly as the name suddenly came to him.

The man pulled a woolen scarf away from his face and laughed heartily.

"You got that right, Sonny Jim. I am! I am indeed!" he cackled and his voice was deep and resonant. He nodded toward the giant ape. "Me and my bumblin' friend here are still out here scouring these mountains, looking to sell or trade all manner of commodities: furs, blubber, even precious metals like gold and silver..." He slapped his thigh and laughed excitedly. "Silver and gold!"

The man deftly pulled an ice ax from his belt and threw it high into the air. The ax spun and glittered brightly in the early morning's light. It struck the ice in front of them, the tip of its blade sinking deep into the downy fluff. The man pulled it out of the snow by its handle and licked the crystals of ice that were left clinging to the metal. He tasted the substance and appraised its content.

"Hmmm..." he said, sounding disappointed. "Nuttin'."

A frigid wind came up and blew across the icy plain, the cold itself interrupting them.

"Storm's brewin'," The Prospector said, looking up into the rapidly darkening sky.

The Dentist climbed out of the sleigh and did his best to recover his dignity.

"We're on our way up Silver Mountain," he tried to explain.

"I know you know these parts," he said hopefully. "We could use a guide…"

The Prospector laughed uproariously.

"But, of course! I do indeed know these lands. And I know them well!" he chuckled. "I've worked throughout these parts the whole of my life." He held up a finger. "One moment…"

Without another word, he stepped away from the group and walked over to where the large ape stood waiting patiently. The thing stood nearly as tall as the trees and had a ferocious—albeit toothless—countenance, but it stood by and waited on the man passively. By its look and attentiveness, it clearly held a deep loyalty toward the man. The animal's demeanor was more like that of a large dog than the ravaging beast it appeared to be. The creature bent down and listened intently as The Prospector spoke softly into its immense ear. When he was done talking to it, the beast nodded its understanding and turned its back to them, running off and disappearing into the snowy hills.

"I sent him back to my basecamp. He's too big for where we're goin'," The Prospector explained as he walked back to the sleigh.

He looked down and noticed that there were small clumps of snow sticking to his pants leg and boots. After kicking the powdery white stuff off of his boots on the runners, he climbed in to the sleigh next to The Dentist and they gave Rudy the 'all-clear.' The sleigh lurched forward and both occupants were pushed back into the furs on the seat. Once underway, they both settled in for the long ride ahead.

The group soon came to the edge of a large, frozen plate of ice which had spread over the majority of the surface of the sea. The frozen glacier extended out well passed the shore and the group soon found themselves with no choice but to take the sleigh across the large sheet of ice. Rudy carefully led the team onto the frozen sea.

The Prospector got out and walked a good distance back toward the shore. Taking out his ice ax, he started chopping ferociously at the ground. The piece of ice on which they were sitting suddenly broke away and the ocean's current began gently carrying them away.

"This current should take us across the ocean to The Island," The Prospector shouted so that all could hear. "Once we make land, we can follow the path up Silver Mountain to the castle. I'm assuming that's who you want to see... Moonracer?" he asked and a sly look passed over his face.

The Dentist nodded, but revealed nothing. He didn't particularly feel the need to explain anymore of his mission to him or anyone else. From here on, that information was simply beyond anyone's 'need to know.'

More time passed and the group drifted along on the ice with the sky moving slowly overhead. The Dentist and The Prospector talked for a while, reminiscing and catching up, but they soon all fell into a relaxed silence and just waited. After a while, everyone but the dentist dozed.

Standing watch, The Dentist retrieved the leather satchel from under the seat where he'd set it. Opening it, he picked up Moonracer's story where he'd left off. Toward the back of the file, he found a separate envelope with an official-looking letter inside. The note had come from Santa and was written on his personal stationary. Accompanying the letter was a report of Santa having sent someone else—someone *before* The Dentist—to try and talk to Moonracer. Perhaps it was for the same reasons. Perhaps not. There was really no way to be sure since the report didn't say.

The Dentist looked at a photo that was paper-clipped to the main piece of paper. The picture was that of a reindeer who was standing in front of The Workshop with Santa. His expression was friendly, but concern still haunted his features.

"Blitzen," The Prospector interrupted, having roused and looked over.

The Dentist looked up and saw his companion looking at the photo in his hand.

"What'd you say?" he asked.

The Prospector reached over and tapped the photo with his index finger.

"That's Blitzen. One of Santa's team. One of the best. Word is... he disappeared into these very mountains a while ago. Word has it that he vanished into the ice and has never been heard from again."

The Dentist looked back at the photograph and scowled. He didn't like the sound of it. Not any of it. Santa not telling him that he'd sent a previous messenger was problematic. It spoke to what *else* he didn't think he needed to know. Worried now, he slipped the letter back into the satchel and closed it.

Why would Santa send him on this mission and *not* mention having already sent someone? Further, why would he not say anything about him 'disappearing' into these very mountains?

He pushed his thoughts aside as he returned the papers and photos to the case where they belonged. He slid the valise back where it had been under the seat. Silence returned to the confines of the sleigh, both of them returning to their own private considerations as they floated on the frigid sea.

It was several hours later when they felt their ice sheet raft run aground on the shore of Moonracer's island. It took a bit of doing on all of their parts to get the sleigh back onto solid ground, but once they had, they were soon loaded up and back on their merry way.

Rudy carefully led the sleigh and its team up the mountain. The spires of Moonracer's castle loomed forebodingly in the distance. A few more hours went by and they soon found themselves passing through the gates of King Moonracer's castle just as the sun was starting to peek over the horizon. Their progress slowed to a crawl as they cautiously made their way along the narrow streets and into the interior of the palace's courtyard. High on the walkways overhead, a rag doll and a teddy bear with wings looked down at them suspiciously; their fingers moving nervously along the shafts of their spears. They passed a cowboy riding an ostrich who stared at them balefully while a water gun stood nearby nervously dripping jelly.

Rudy finally brought the sleigh to a stop in the middle of the castle's central courtyard. The stones were wet with morning dew and they shimmered in the low light of the day. Christmas wreaths, now long past their prime, hung rotting to dust in nearby windows. In a place where Christmas was touted to be celebrated every day, it was pretty clear that the holiday hadn't been celebrated here in a long time.

The Dentist stepped down from the sleigh and was quickly

followed by The Prospector. They walked up the line and began helping to unstrap the reindeer from the harnesses. Once free of their restraints, Rudy instructed his team to stow the reins and stay near the sleigh so that they could guard it.

A loud, wooden clomping sound suddenly broke the quiet. It sounded like a gate was being slammed shut again and again by the blowing of the wind. From out of a shop's doorway hopped a clown whose head was on a spring which came out of the top of a wooden box.

"Hello! Hello! Welcome!" the clown called cordially. He gazed up into the castle's ramparts, calling, "It's ok. It's ok... All is well." He returned his attention to the castle's visitors. "Come along! Come along!"

The Dentist squinted at him.

"I remember you..." he said. "You're..."

"The Jack in the Box!" shouted The Prospector.

The clown scowled. "Charlie," he said under his breath. "My name... is Charlie."

The Prospector clapped his hands and laughed uproariously.

"That's right... Charlie," he laughed and clapped The Dentist on the back.

The clown shook his irritation off like it was rainwater.

"We're here to see The King," The Dentist proclaimed.

The clown looked surprised. "The King?" he said. "Really?"

The Dentist nodded and his expression remained stern. "Santa sent me... to come see him about a very important matter." He nodded toward the castle's highest parapet as he spoke.

The clown bowed his head at the old man's name. "S-S-Santa sent you?"

The Dentist nodded again. "I've been instructed to discuss a few things with the King." He eyed the clown suspiciously. "Some things have come to his attention and must be explained."

A deeply concerned look passed over the clown's face. "Yes... very good. Very good. But, of course. Well... seeing as it was Santa that sent you... I guess it's ok. Yes... yes. Absolutely!" He turned and hopped away. "Follow me, please," he called over his shoulder. "I'll take you to see the King."

The Dentist and The Prospector left Rudy and the reindeer to watch over the sleigh while they went to see Moonracer. They followed Charlie into the castle, taking the grand staircase to the upper floors where the throne room lay.

Along the way, they saw more small toys gathered in groups along the hallways. The Dentist noticed a train with square wheels on its caboose, a plane that couldn't fly, as well as a scooter with two wheels in front and one in back.

Further along, a teddy bear was riding a bike while a small Russian nesting doll was involved in a heated debate with itself. From what he could hear, their argument was over the validity of someone named 'von Clausewitz.' The Dentist wasn't sure who that was, but the debaters were ardently arguing their chosen sides. A small mechanical mouse stood next to them. He eyed the duo with an exasperated acceptance; like this was an argument that had been going on for a long time.

Presently, the three of them arrived at a large door where two Nutcracker guards stood watch. To the left of one of them, The Dentist saw a reindeer that lay drowsing on the floor, near a low stone table. The Dentist didn't recognize him, so, he didn't let his gaze linger. But as the clown knocked on the door with his forehead, The Dentist glanced back at the dozing buck. Realization washed over him like a cold rain as he slowly recognized the face from the photos he'd just been looking at earlier.

"Blitzen?"

The reindeer looked lazily up at him and meeting his gaze was like staring into an empty well. His eyes were uninhabited windows that no one had looked out of for a very long time. The door in front of them suddenly opened and a large, spotted elephant poked its trunk out.

"Hallooooo!" the pachyderm called, his voice sounding congested. "Who ith it that dareth to bother The King?"

The Dentist stepped forward. "I do," he said. He paused, and then he looked into the elephant's eyes defiantly, "Santa sent me."

The elephant stared back darkly. "Santa, eh?" He squinted at him and gave him an assessing up-and-down. "Well…"

The Dentist put his hand on the door and pushed it open.

"Stand aside, Nelly… I'm here on *official* business."

The elephant stumbled back, cursing. He walked off toward the gallery, grumbling under his breath. "Well, that'th all you had to thay…" then, under his breath, "didn't have to puth me like that."

The Dentist and The Prospector strode to the center of the immense throne room. More cathedral than ballroom, the place opened into a massive, cavernous space. Slate grey rock walls rose into space, arching high overhead like a basilica. At the head of the room, a tall golden chair sat upon a raised dais.

Suddenly, a winged lion flew into the room through a high overhead window. He was large even for a lion with wide, feathered wings that cupped the air that held him aloft. He circled the room and landed lightly on the dais at a trot. He circled the chair several times, eyeing the intruders suspiciously, before finally settling onto the throne's seat.

"And, what do we have here, eh?" the lion said and his voice dripped with open contempt. "Messengers? Sent by the Fat Man, I presume?"

The Dentist stepped forward, frowning. He may not have much liked Claus, but… at the end of the day, he *was* Santa and that deserved a certain amount of respect.

"I beg Your Majesty's indulgence," he began, speaking slowly, "Yes, I have been sent by Sa—"

"Yes," Moonracer interrupted. "Santa, that corpulent megalomaniac. Sent to assess my stability, I understand… and to judge my ability to Rule."

The Dentist looked at him blankly. He thought it best not to lie. "Yes."

The lion roared with laughter as he shook his mane.

"As if he… as if *you*… could ever possess the moral authority to judge *me*. Him on his candy-striped throne. And you… with your failed dental aspirations."

The Dentist took another step closer. He now stood at the foot of the carpeted stairs that led up to the throne. He stared unwaveringly at the monarch, ignoring the personal jab, as he quietly assessed the king's mental state. Since he'd gotten closer, he could see that there were dark circles under Moonracer's eyes and his mane looked matted and unkempt. There was a kind of desperation to his countenance, like someone barely managing to maintain control of his emotions. His grief had clearly broken him, crushed any sense of right and wrong and sent him down a dark path of hate and retribution. But it was clear, even after a cursory examination such as this... he was unfit to rule.

"My instructions were to come here and implore you to lighten the weight of your royal hand on the residents of this island. They look to you for leadership, to shepherd them toward a better life. Like a parent mi—"

"Hold your tongue, *Dentist*!" the lion roared and his tone soured with derision on the last word. "You come into *my* home and speak to *me* of parenthood, of my being unable to rule my people adequately."

The Dentist looked around with an expression that bordered on disgust.

"Well, you must admit... Your kingdom is not what it once was, Sire."

Moonracer smiled and, very much against his will, a chill ran down The Dentist's spine.

"Please inform Santa that I will take his words... under consideration."

The Dentist bowed, knowing that the king's words were all a lie. "Thank you, Sire. I will inform Santa that an understanding has been reached."

The lion scowled derisively and got up from his seat. He stalked across the platform slowly.

"But please..." he glared down from his throne at the small group gathered at the foot of the stairs. "Stay the night. You are no doubt tired from your journey. You are welcome to enjoy the hospitality of my humble home." He looked up toward the open window he'd flown through. "A storm is brewing, but it should pass quickly. You will be able to get back down the mountain in the morning."

The Dentist bowed lower and thanked him once again. He knew he'd need to consider his next actions carefully. His mission had been specific. 'Convince him,' Santa had said and they both knew what he meant.

With all he had seen, The Dentist quietly decided in that moment that the king had to die.

Night fell and The Prospector, Rudy, and the rest of the team were all gathered around the sleigh drinking toddies with some of the toys they'd met around the castle since arriving. As the others partook in their revelry, The Dentist excused himself and, excused himself to use the lavatory. Silently, he made his way through the shadows to the back of the sleigh. Once he was sure that the coast was clear, he carefully removed The Prospector's ice axe from where it had been left on the floor of the sleigh. He hid the tool beneath his coat and quickly (and quietly) made his way back through the castle to Moonracer's throne room.

When he arrived at the large door of the throne room, he found it locked. He pushed against it with all of his weight, but its locks remained steadfast. At first, he was crestfallen, thinking his mission was compromised at its most critical point. But after searching some of the nearby vestibules, he found access through one of the vents that fed the throne room's fireplaces. Sensing no heat, he wriggled his way inside through the flue and angled his body down into the cold hearth.

He crossed the throne room stealthily, keeping himself to the shadows. Far up on the raised platform, he saw Moonracer's form lounging on his shadow-enshrouded throne. As he crept closer, he saw the lion bent over and writing in a large book with a plumed instrument. His pen moved quickly across the book's pages and he spoke aloud the words he was inscribing.

"I once saw a polar bear... leading an army of penguins. And their eyes... were filled with a bloodlust that burned over their angry grins. And the Fat Man... The Fat Man continues to sit on his throne... his throne of lies."

The Dentist edged closer. The more he heard him say, the more he was convinced that his decision to kill him was correct. The King had clearly gone mad and he had become a liability. Not just to Santa or his people, but to the world. Clearly, he must be made to give up the throne. The Dentist thought back to what Santa had said back at the compound at that dinner, 'Convince him.'

He hefted the ice ax in his hand as he edged closer. Better to replace him with someone new, than let his madness spread and infect others.

"He holds those elves imprisoned in his 'village,' and then, he has the nerve to call me jailer?" Moonracer continued speaking. "What do you call it when the jailers accuse the jailers anyway?"

Deciding that he'd heard enough, The Dentist stepped up behind the king, raising the ice ax over his head. Without any word or warning, he brought the weapon down with all of his strength.

The blade dug deep into the back of the lion's neck, just at the base of the skull. The king whirled, roaring out in pain and anger. After tugging the weapon free, The Dentist struck again. The ax sliced deeply into the other side of his thick neck. The King's legs went stiff and he pitched forward onto his face, landing with a grunt. The Dentist raised the ax once again. Moonracer looked up toward the ceiling, his eyes focusing on the glittering surface of the stone wall of the throne room.

"The tinsel…" he whispered softly. "The tinsel."

And The Dentist brought the ax down for the final time.

The small crowd gathered out in the courtyard of the castle was slowly starting to disperse. The Prospector, Rudy, a few of the other reindeer, and some of the toys remained, huddled over a small fire. A few of the reindeer dozed at the far side of the fire. Most of the castle's citizens had returned to their homes and their beds. It was late and the Jollyberry wine had run out a short time ago.

The small group that remained had found their way past most of the small talk and had settled into a quiet reflection. The fire was warm and the company was pleasant, so they were all content to sit back, enjoy the chill of the night and the warmth of the fire, and contribute to any further conversation as the mood struck them.

The Charlie-in-the-Box yawned and looked up toward the castle's tall spires. It had been a long day for him and sleep beckoned him to bed. The arrival of these strangers had only made an already hectic day all the more tiring.

He suddenly saw something moving up on one of the castle's lowest balustrades. He gasped and silently pointed up toward the entryway to the castle. He motioned with his hands for the others to look as well. As the group turned to see what he was pointing at, Charlie drew a breath and screamed aloud.

On the stairway that led up to the castle's front door, The Dentist stood in the moonlight with the blood-covered ice ax in one hand and the severed head of King Moonracer in the other. The Prospector leapt to his feet and rushed forward before anyone else could move.

"Leapin' Lizards, kid... what have you done?!?"

He might have protested further, but the grave look on The Dentist's face stopped him in his tracks. The toys all looked up at him horrified, parting as he walked through them.

Others, who were asleep in their beds, roused upon hearing Charlie's anguished scream. They all came running out of their houses and gathered excitedly in the streets. The Dentist stood gazing out over the crowd menacingly. He dropped Moonracer's head and they all morbidly watched as the head bounced like a blood-soaked ball down the stairs.

Charlie hopped to the front of the group, spreading his arms in an attempt to calm the crowd. His eyes met The Dentist's and he slowly bowed his head, the sound of his spring twanging in the silence was unmistakable.

"Sire..." He turned and raised his hand toward the rapidly massing crowd. "The King is dead. Long live the King!"

The crowd cheered enthusiastically, even though none were exactly sure what had transpired.

The Dentist walked down the stairs and passed Charlie-in-the-Box.

"No," he hissed as he walked by. His eyes were hard and without emotion as he stared out over the crowd. "Govern yourselves."

The Dentist found Rudy and told him that they were leaving. Rudy and The Prospector immediately set to hooking up the team. Charlie chased impotently after them.

"Please… please," he pled, his face a frightened, twisted thing. "You can't leave! Who will *lead* us? What will we do?"

The Dentist said nothing. He only silently packed up the sleigh and got inside. Soon, all around him was in readiness and he gave the signal for them to head out. And in that final moment, The Dentist looked down from the sleigh at Charlie and his encouraging gaze somehow made Charlie feel as if everything was going to be all right. And as the sun rose up over the horizon, the sleigh slid off into the night, Rudy's bright, red nose leading the way.

TERIMA KASIH!

This book is dedicated to some very important people:

All of my love and gratitude goes to my wife, Cat. You've been there for, well… ever, and I love you more, if that's even possible, every single day. *that thing*

To my kids (Jhustin / Alesia / Ripley / Connor / Taylor), you all make me so very proud. Thank you for allowing me to watch you grow into such talented and honorable people. It's been a privilege and my distinct honor.

I couldn't have completed this book without the help of my good friend, Heather Strbiak. Without her, these stories might never have left my hard drive. Thank you… you're the best.

Also, much love to David Niall Wilson and the supportive folks at Crossroad Press. You guys have stuck with me through all the madness and I appreciate it more than mere coffee could say.

This book, like all my books, was written and edited while listening to some podcasts; specifically those done by Dana Gould, Doug Benson, Kevin Smith, Ralph Garman, Marc Bernardin, Gilbert Gottfried, Frank Santopadre, Paul Scheer, June Diane Raphael, Jason Mantzoukas, Tony Hinchcliffe, Redban, Jeremiah Watkins, Joel Jimenez, Chroma Chris, Jessie "Jetski" Johnson, Jeff Ross, Ryan Sickler … and the Mommies (Tom Segura and Christina Pazsitzky). Huge thanks go out to all of them for keeping me company during those long, "what am I going to do next?" nights.

Thanks also to my dog, Rocko, who sat by my side and helped me eat my Peanut Butter and Jelly sandwiches while I worked on this book.

All three of these short story collections were written with one person very much in mind. I miss you, Mom. These three books have been for you...

Until next time...

ABOUT THE AUTHOR

Thom Carnell. As a journalist, his interviews and profiles can be found in Carpe Noctem Magazine (for which he served as Head Writer and Creative Consultant), Fangoria Magazine, Dread Central.com and Twitchfilm.com. Carnell's fiction has been featured in Carpe Noctem 20, the Pill Hill Press anthology Bloody Carnival, Swank Magazine, in his novel No Flesh Shall Be Spared, No Flesh Shall Be Spared: Don't Look Back, and in his short story collections Moonlight Serenades and A String of Pearls.

www.thomcarnell.com

Curious about other Crossroad Press books?
Stop by our site:
http://store.crossroadpress.com
We offer quality writing
in digital, audio, and print formats.

Lightning Source UK Ltd.
Milton Keynes UK
UKHW011857161220
375343UK00001B/74